THE SLAVE AUCTION

He laughed into her deepening frown and said, 'I want your submission, Frankie. You want the slave, then you can have her. All that I ask in return is an afternoon's submission from you.'

Frankie glared at him, appalled at the suggestion. 'You can't be serious.'

'I'm deadly serious.' The mirth was gone from his expression and his firm gaze told her he wasn't joking. 'Think about it, Frankie, because I'm sure you'll agree that it's a tempting offer. Think about it and let me know when you've made up your mind.'

Turning his gaze away from her he took the whip and then flung it at number three's exposed backside.

THE SLAVE AUCTION

Lisette Ashton

This book is a work of fiction.
In real life, make sure you practise safe sex.

First published in 2000 by
Nexus
Thames Wharf Studios
Rainville Road
London W6 9HA

Typeset by TW Typesetting, Plymouth, Devon

Printed and bound by
Cox & Wyman Ltd, Reading, Berks

ISBN 0 352 33481 9

One

'You'll get your comeuppance one day,' Jane growled. Tears of shame stung her eyes and her breathing had deepened to a guttural pant. The flaring line across her backside burned like a filament. 'You'll get your comeuppance,' she hissed. 'And when it happens, I hope I'm there to watch it.'

McGivern's cruel laughter trailed over the lapping waves. 'One day, I hope that happens,' he replied earnestly. 'People have been threatening me with it for so long, I'm dying to know what it will feel like.'

Jane tried to glare at him but he towered above her. The sunlight was behind him, obscuring his face as it would the underbelly of a thundercloud. Unable to fathom out if his mood was playful or threatening, she turned her gaze to the polished deck. Past experience had taught her that it was best not to antagonise McGivern unless she was one hundred per cent sure of his mood. The ache on her buttock was a reminder that she should have remembered that. She pulled herself up from the deck, brushing at the hem of her skirt as she tried to regain her sea legs. Smoothing the fabric over her backside, Jane felt a sparkle of discomfort where his crop had struck. It took an effort of willpower, but she managed to ignore its shameful thrill.

Her uniform, identical to those worn by the rest of the crew, had been styled by McGivern's depraved imagination. Wearing it was a sign of her servility to him. The outfit was more modest than anything else he had designed

1

for his submissives but its style was tainted with his penchant for the torrid. The navy-blue skirt was barely long enough to cover the tops of her thighs, yet it was compulsory to be knickerless underneath. Her white waistcoat fitted snugly, revealing an ample swell, a deep cleavage and a sun-bronzed midriff. Those parts that the uniform did cover were sculpted by its clinging silk. The waistcoat made the curves of her femininity as visible as if she had been naked. The circles of her areolae darkened the flimsy fabric at her chest and the thrust of her nipples was more prominent than the three white buttons that ran down the front.

She had already decided that the costume was another of McGivern's exercises in humiliation and, as with every other weapon in his armoury, he used it to good effect. Aboard the ship they should have been safe from the prying eyes of the normal world and, in that environment, Jane could have tolerated dressing like a slattern for him. But McGivern insisted that all his crew perform their deck duties in full uniform, regardless of where they were docked. Memories of the last port they had visited still made Jane cringe with shame. If she closed her eyes and concentrated, she could relive the lewd wolfwhistles and vulgar appraisals that had assailed her and the rest of the crew. Swarthy sailors had shouted what they would like to do to her if she came ashore. Dockers and deck-hands had catcalled her as though she was nothing more than a cheap whore who was there to be used and abused. Although Jane hadn't understood all their words, their graphic gestures had been disturbingly clear. And, if the humiliation hadn't sparked a wet longing between her legs, Jane would have contemplated insurrection far more seriously.

She reached for her straw hat from where it had fallen, checking that its decorative band was positioned correctly, before jamming it over her platinum curls. McGivern was adamant that the crew's uniforms should remain meticulous and, considering his current mood, Jane had no doubt that he would pounce on the slightest reason to punish her again. When she turned to face him, she knew he would be able to read the words MCGIVERN'S SLAVE SHIP from the brim above her eyes.

'I only asked where we're headed.' Trying not to make her tone too truculent, she added, 'Since you told me to navigate, I didn't think the question was that unreasonable.'

'You've got the co-ordinates.' His voice was sullen and he had already lost interest in the topic. 'You don't need to know any more than that.'

'But I –'

'You're my slave now,' he broke in, not allowing her to continue the argument. 'You willingly agreed to that title and you've signed the deeds of indenture. You're my slave, I have your deeds, and you're in no position to question my authority.' He paused and smiled slyly at her. 'That is, unless you want to endure another punishment?'

Jane's cheeks flushed crimson and she glared down at the deck. His threat filled her with a hateful excitement but she knew better than to exploit it. She had already discovered that he was being particularly vicious with the crop today and, whilst that didn't make her unwilling to submit, it did make her hesitant. 'I wasn't questioning your authority,' she told him meekly.

He sniffed and settled himself back in his deck-chair, all but dismissing her. The crop was placed by his side, hooked between the seat's wooden legs so that it didn't roll away as they sped through the waves. Surreptitiously, Jane tried to study his face and see if she could read his mood now that the sunlight wasn't behind him. The brim of his cap cast an unfathomable shadow across his eyes and she cursed the gods for making his temperament so difficult to gauge.

'Before you resume your duties back in the pilothouse, I'd like an iced Scotch.' His head was tilted away from her, as though he was trying to discern something beyond the endless blue horizon where they were headed. The straight line of his lips revealed nothing about his mood.

'An iced Scotch, master,' Jane muttered. She paused before attempting to leave, wondering if she dared to broach the other subject that weighed on her mind. Their destination had been only one of her intended questions and her arse still burned for that impertinence. She decided against voicing her other query when she saw his deepening frown.

'I'd like an iced Scotch now.'

His measured tone was a warning and Jane didn't need another reminder about the repercussions beneath it. The burning line on her arse was begging her not to antagonise him. Hating herself and her servility, Jane turned and stormed towards the stern.

She saw that two slaves were oiling one another on the roof of the pilothouse. Their uniforms had been discarded and, as the morning heat kissed their bodies, they worked protective lotion into each other's skin. With slippery hands, they caressed one another, lubricating hips, chests and thighs. Jane glimpsed feminine fingers massaging an oiled breast and she glanced away. The burning line on her buttock was already igniting her arousal and Jane didn't want to fuel it any further. Much more sexual excitement and she could picture herself returning to the bow and begging McGivern for chastisement.

The couple's giggles were little louder than a murmur and Jane knew that the sound of their growing pleasure was being muted for fear of McGivern hearing. She suspected the pair were managing to conceal their interlude beneath the drone of the racing engines and the sound of the lapping waves. She grudgingly conceded that they were more daring than she was. Although she was brave enough to stand up to McGivern and argue her point, she could never find the will to disobey him directly. Liaisons between his slaves were strictly forbidden and she wondered how this pair had managed to conceal their relationship for so long.

As she walked through their shadows, the blonde slave hissed for her attention. She leaned over the roof, gesturing for Jane to step closer. Her redheaded companion looked down and her features turned serious.

Jane stopped and dared to glance at them. Their bared

4

breasts swayed provocatively above her and she could see a teardrop of sun lotion preparing to drip from one nipple. With a determined effort, she forced herself to look at the slaves' faces.

'Did you find out?' asked the blonde.

'Did he tell you?' asked the redhead.

'He told me to get him a drink.' Jane kept her voice to the same husky whisper they were using, casting her gaze warily in the direction of McGivern's back. They all knew his hearing could be annoyingly acute when he wanted it to be. Even though his attention seemed focused on the horizon, he was close enough to eavesdrop on their conversation. 'He wants an iced Scotch,' Jane told the slaves.

'Is there going to be an auction?' the blonde pressed. 'Did he tell you that? Or did he tell you where we're headed?'

'He didn't tell me anything. He just used the crop on me and said he wanted a Scotch. If you're that curious, why don't you ask him yourself?' It was a challenge that she knew neither of the slaves would accept. McGivern had made no secret about his volatile mood since they started on this journey. From their position on top of the pilothouse, Jane knew the two slaves would have seen what happened when she questioned him.

The redhead put an arm around the blonde's shoulders and gave her a reassuring squeeze. 'It's only a rumour,' she whispered, pulling her lover back to the roof of the pilothouse. 'It's probably unfounded. These things usually are.'

Jane could hear the emptiness in the redhead's comforting words and she empathised with her unease. The rumours were the only topic of conversation below deck and their omnipresent threat had touched a chord of fear in every submissive. The torment of not knowing was like a maddening itch and Jane wished she had found the courage to demand an answer from McGivern before he chastised her.

Seeing the pair of slaves embrace more intimately, Jane

started back to the chore McGivern had given her. She didn't try to excuse herself from the naked couple: they also both knew that McGivern didn't like to be kept waiting. If there was any truth behind the current rumour, it would be wise for the pair to relish whatever moments of shared happiness were still left to them.

'If you do learn something, you will tell us, won't you?'

Jane nodded at the blonde and promised that she would. She stepped into the pilothouse and blinked her eyes until they were used to the shaded surroundings. After the searing heat of the sunlit deck, the pilothouse was the cool balm that her body needed.

'Did you find out? Did he tell you?'

Jane tried to smile at the slave called number three but it was difficult to put any conviction into her expression. The woman was the most beautiful of McGivern's charges and Jane suspected she was also the most servile. This dark-haired slave had given up her name and taken a number for identification. The shape of the number three tattooed on her right breast was clearly visible through the gauzelike silk of her waistcoat. Its garish red and gold colours turned the fabric pink and yellow over the swell of the orb. The lower curl of the number circled her areola, the intimate branding symbolic of her submissive status. More than any other slave in McGivern's entourage, number three was petrified by the rumour. Jane knew that her own smile lacked conviction because she still had no words of comfort or consolation to offer. 'Everyone is so on edge about this, aren't they?'

'Of course we're on edge,' number three snapped. 'There's the rumour of a slave auction and, in case you hadn't noticed, any one of us could suddenly become a lot number.'

'You're already halfway there.'

Number three frowned and Jane could see that her levity had been misplaced.

'Did he tell you anything?' number three asked.

Jane shook her head. 'He didn't say a word. He caned my arse just for the impertinence of asking where we're

6

headed. See?' She half turned and lifted the hem of her skirt to show where she had been marked. Looking down at herself, she saw the raised line glowing painfully against her buttock.

Hesitantly, number three reached forward and brushed her fingers over the weal. 'Does it hurt?'

Jane sucked a pained reply through her teeth. 'What do you think?'

'I think you're very lucky,' number three whispered. Her fingers moved over the red line, following the course from Jane's hip to the cleft of her arse. Rather than stopping at the end of the mark, her fingertips trailed further, brushing through the curls that covered Jane's sex.

'Why do you think I'm lucky?'

'I think you're lucky because the master marked you.' Without qualifying this answer, she placed a finger on the centre of Jane's sex and pushed it forward.

Jane bit her lower lip and toyed with the idea of asking the slave to stop. McGivern had awoken her arousal and the sight of the two slaves on the pilothouse roof had added fuel to that need. She was torn between submitting to the relief that number three offered, and abiding by the master's rules. This was a liaison between slaves, she remembered. It was the sort of forbidden encounter that could render her backside properly striped before the end of the day. The finger at her pussy promised to satisfy her growing appetite but Jane knew there would be repercussions if McGivern discovered them.

And none of those thoughts made Jane shift herself away from the slave's caress.

'You're very wet,' number three murmured.

The slave's observation nudged Jane from her reverie. She knew she had to make some token effort to extricate herself from the situation, in spite of her longing to stay there. Swallowing thickly, she said, 'You shouldn't be doing that.'

'I'm just trying to make you feel better.'

The slave pushed deeper and Jane allowed a wave of excitement to ripple through her body. Glancing at the

7

hand between her legs, Jane watched number three slide her finger free. Its manicured length was sodden with the viscous smear of her arousal.

'Consider this a soothing balm,' number three said, smearing pussy juice over the raised line on Jane's arse. 'The wetness might cool its sting.'

Jane studied the slave carefully. 'Is that all you're going to do to make it feel better?' She had tried to keep the lecherous timbre from her voice but it was a futile attempt. The words came out as a husky pout, tainted with disappointment.

Number three wore a sly smile. 'Would you want me to kiss it better?'

Jane closed her eyes and stifled a groan. 'That doesn't sound so intolerable.'

The slave kneeled on the pilothouse floor and stroked Jane's arse lovingly. She moved her face close to Jane's buttocks and her lips blew a soothing kiss against the searing flesh. As she began to draw her tongue against the crimson line, Jane stiffened. She leaned forward, steadying herself by holding on to the navigational console. The rekindled sting was inspiring the delicious conflict of pain and pleasure that McGivern had taught her to relish. Knowing that the slave's mouth was moving closer to her cleft, Jane briefly contemplated the idea of stopping this interlude. Once the weight of the slave's tongue was against her, she realised the decision was out of her hands. Her appetite was going to keep her there until number three decided they were finished.

'The caning excited you, didn't it?' Number three's words were muffled against her sex but Jane could hear her clearly enough.

'Am I that transparent?' Jane laughed.

By way of reply number three pushed her tongue deeper. 'You taste excited.'

Jane could feel the squirming muscle probe inside and she savoured another ripple of pleasure. Her clitoris ached with a need to be touched and she bucked her hips back, hoping the slave would take the hint of her obvious

8

posture. As though she was reading Jane's thoughts, number three allowed her tongue to caress the pulsing nub. An electric thrill sparkled from Jane's sex and she pressed her fingers more tightly against the console.

'Iced Scotch shortage. There's an iced Scotch shortage on the bow of the boat. Could someone please deal with the iced Scotch shortage?'

Jane coughed back a cry of despair as she heard McGivern's booming voice. She glanced down to her backside and saw number three was already moving her mouth away. They treated one another to disappointed frowns, both seeming certain of where the moment could have led.

'The master's drink,' number three whispered. 'I'll do it.' She climbed up from her knees and stepped towards the pilothouse's optic to prepare his Scotch.

Jane adjusted the hem of her skirt and wished an awkward silence hadn't fallen between them. 'You said I was lucky to have been caned,' she remembered. Her tone was slightly flustered and she tried to make her words sound even for when she next spoke to McGivern. 'Are you missing the master's crop that much?'

When number three turned to face her there was a frown twisting the slave's lips. Her eyes were shining with the threat of tears which still remained even after she tried to blink them away. 'If the rumours about a slave auction are true, then you're lucky that he's still caning you,' number three explained.

Jane shook her head, not understanding. She took the glass from the slave's hand and said, 'They're only rumours. And even if there was to be an auction, I can't see McGivern getting rid of you.'

Number three wouldn't meet her gaze. She stepped back to the console and made a handful of unnecessary adjustments to the controls. When she spoke, she allowed the words to carry over her shoulder. 'I think there is going to be an auction,' she whispered. 'And once, maybe it was true that McGivern wouldn't get rid of me. But now ...' Her voice trailed off to a miserable sniffle.

'But now?' Jane said encouragingly. She put her hand on the slave's shoulder and turned the woman around. Their mouths were close and she could picture herself enjoying the sultry pout of the slave's lips against hers. The knowledge that she would be able to taste her own pussy honey made the idea even more appealing, but she resisted the impulse. It was enough to smell the sweet scent of arousal on the submissive's breath. 'If McGivern was going to sell any of his slaves, don't you think he'd be selling me? Aren't I the one who tells him he's a bastard? Aren't I the one who argues with him at every opportunity? Aren't I the one who slapped his face the other day?'

Number three smiled tearfully as she revisited that moment. Her snort of laughter was muted and Jane saw that the memory had done nothing to raise her spirits. 'Yes,' number three agreed. 'You're the one who does all those things. But I think the master has grown to like that.'

Jane shook her head, determined to deny the accusation. McGivern was a disciplinarian who abhorred all forms of insubordination. Jane knew that he hated insolent slaves and she considered herself living proof of the punishment he delivered to the impudent.

'Iced Scotch! There's an iced Scotch shortage at the bow of the boat! The iced Scotch drought is growing more severe.' McGivern's voice grated between them, his harsh tone threatening all manner of consequences.

Jane turned to the pilothouse door and drew lungfuls of air before bawling her response. 'I'll be there in a fucking minute!' she yelled. She turned to face number three and then saw that she had just proved the slave right. Any protest or denial she had intended making would now sound more hollow than ever. She was McGivern's submissive but there was a twist to their relationship that none of the other slaves enjoyed. 'So, why do you say I'm lucky that he marked me?' she asked. 'I don't understand that.'

'He's hardly going to sell marked goods at an auction, is he?' Number three's voice was sullen and almost aggressive. 'He can stripe your arse from now until

10

doomsday and it won't matter to anyone because he's not selling you. But if you've noticed, since we started out on this little mystery tour, the master hasn't raised a finger to the rest of us.'

Jane tightened her grip on McGivern's Scotch. Her hand trembled with the effort and she heard the tinkle of the ice cubes bouncing merrily in her hand. Now that the facts had been explained to her she could see more than a glimmer of possibility to the rumour. Her own secure status was immaterial as she contemplated the misery of number three's predicament. 'I'm going to find out what he's playing at,' she declared.

'You can't,' number three told her.

She opened her mouth and Jane could see that the slave had a hundred and one reasons as to why McGivern couldn't be confronted. Not wanting to hear any of them, Jane said, 'Just you bloody watch me and we'll see if I can't.' Before the slave could protest, Jane had turned her back and stormed out of the pilothouse. She thundered past the blonde and the redhead, not surprised that the pair both jumped as she approached them.

'You look livid, Jane,' the blonde whispered. There was a warning in her voice as she hissed, 'Don't try winding him up. He'll make you suffer for it.'

Jane ignored her. She stormed to McGivern's deck chair and stared angrily down at him. She had wanted to cast a shadow and intimidate him with her body language but the sun was in the wrong position for that.

He glanced from beneath the brim of his hat and graced her with a sardonic grin. 'You took your bloody time with that,' he complained. 'It's meant to be aged eight years but that's not supposed to include my asking for it and your delivering it.'

Jane could picture herself hurling the Scotch in his face. She was holding the glass at the perfect angle to commit the crime. She could see the orange liquid splashing against his forehead, dripping over his cheeks, then soaking his T-shirt. It took no effort of her imagination to see him jumping out of his chair, his features dumbstruck with

11

shock and outrage. These images passed through her mind's eye in a blink and then they were gone. They were replaced by the saner picture of how she would really behave.

'Your drink, master,' Jane said, offering the glass to him.

He took it from her and sniffed its surface before taking the first sip. 'You're excused now,' he said. 'Go away and perform your duties.'

Jane swallowed nervously and remained where she was.

He pushed the brim of his cap back and fixed her with a scowl. 'I said you were excused. You don't have to wait for the glass. I intend throwing it over the side of the boat once I've finished with it.'

'I have a couple of questions,' Jane told him. 'Do I have permission to ask them?'

'Ask them later,' he said. 'You're blocking my view.'

She glanced behind herself and saw that the view was as barren in that direction as it was everywhere else. The empty waters of the ocean stretched out towards every point on the horizon without a single landmark to break the view. Turning back to face him, she said, 'I'd appreciate some answers to these questions now.'

'Would you also appreciate another stripe from the crop?'

Jane considered moving out of his vision and walking away. The realisation that she would have to go back to the pilothouse and suffer number three's melancholy made her bolder than normal. 'If that's the price I have to pay for your answers, then I'll happily pay it.'

His smile lilted and he shifted position in his deck-chair. 'An answer for a stripe? That's an interesting proposition, Jane. It's no wonder that I enjoy having you around so much.'

She wanted to tell him that that wasn't what she meant. She opened her mouth to retract the suggestion. How had she managed to talk herself into such an arrangement? Instead of saying anything, she nodded and met his gaze. 'An answer for a stripe.'

He grinned at her, snatching the crop from beneath his

12

deck-chair. 'You're a game little bitch,' he laughed. 'I think that's what I like best about you. Put yourself over the bow and let me listen to your questions.' He eased himself out of the chair and Jane felt an anticipatory thrill lurch in the pit of her stomach.

'I want to know where we're going,' she told him. 'And I want to know if there's going to be a slave auction.'

The sunlight was behind him again and Jane squinted into the shadows masking his face. She was trying to read some response from his expression but it was a futile task. This was the first time any of the crew had dared to broach the rumour of an auction with the master and she hoped she hadn't overstepped the bounds of her position by revealing this knowledge. But the set of his jaw remained unmoved and his lips were an inscrutable line that told her nothing.

'Bend over the bow and prepare yourself,' he said. 'An answer for a stripe was the deal. You can ask your questions once you're in the proper position.'

Jane glared at him but she could see he was determined to go through with this game now the idea was fixed in his mind. Setting her shoulders defiantly, she stepped towards the bow and gripped the handrails at either side of the pulpit. On the horizon, barely discernible between the melded blues of the sky and the ocean, Jane could see a swelling, black dot. It was too far away for her to bother trying to name it and, even though it was the first sign of land since they had left the foreign port that morning, she dismissed it as unimportant. She glanced back over her shoulder and saw that McGivern was finishing his Scotch. After draining the glass, he studied the tumbler thoughtfully before tossing it overboard.

Behind him, on the roof of the pilothouse, the two slaves had forgotten their frolics. The redhead held her companion tightly while the blonde chewed at a fingernail. Their worried gazes were focused intently on Jane. Beneath them, peering through the window of the pilothouse, Jane could see number three shaking her head.

Jane wiped them all from her mind and turned to the

13

bow of the boat. She gripped the metal rails even tighter and stared down at the prow as it broke through the waves. White crests were carved from the azure surface as they hurried towards their unknown destiny. She supposed that if she was going to get some answers from McGivern, then this indignity would probably be a price worth paying. It wasn't a convincing thought but it was the only one she could cling to as she heard his footsteps approaching.

'An answer for a stripe,' he reminded her. 'That was our deal, wasn't it?' He brushed the hem of her skirt away with a flick of his crop. Jane could feel its cruel tip grazing her flesh as her buttocks were revealed. The flimsy garment had hardly been covering her but once it was removed, she felt the chill of the ocean's breeze caressing her exposed flesh. It took a powerful effort, but she resisted the urge to flinch.

'Yes, master. An answer for a stripe,' she repeated. Her cheeks were burning crimson and the sound of the waves was lost beneath the pounding of adrenaline in her temples. 'But it has to be an honest answer,' she added quickly. She had played games with McGivern before and knew that he always had his own interpretation of the rules. 'It has to be an honest answer, OK?'

'Dear God,' he frowned. 'I should beat you just for the implication behind those words, you impudent little bitch. Are you calling me a liar?'

Jane glanced back over her shoulder and saw he was raising the crop. She snatched her gaze away, braced herself, and stared down at the breaking waters.

'What's your first question?'

'Where are we headed?'

The stripe stung her arse like a razor. A shriek of pain erupted in her right buttock and Jane groaned. She closed her eyes, then realised that the darkness was making the sensation more intense. When she opened her eyes, she was left dizzy by the blinding sparkle of sunlight on the waters ahead. Her breathing deepened as she tried to contain her response to the crop's cruel bite.

'We're headed forward,' McGivern told her cheerfully. 'Next question.'

'You bastard,' she muttered.

'Say that again.'

There was something in his voice that made Jane sure he was raising the crop in case she dared to voice her insolence for a second time. Resisting the urge to argue with him, she tried to compose her thoughts for the game they were playing. She had to phrase her questions so that he couldn't give ambiguous answers. It was difficult to concentrate above the flames that burned her arse, but with a determined effort, she managed it. 'What's the name of our destination?' she asked.

The crop landed against her left buttock and the explosion left her giddy. Jane released an inarticulate growl and pressed her chest against the handrails. Her arse cheeks stung with burning lines. She drew gulps of air as she tried to bring her body to terms with the indignity of McGivern's punishment.

'Do you want to hear the English name?' McGivern asked.

'Yes,' she hissed.

He brought the crop down with a smart blow to her left cheek. There was the hint of laughter in his voice as he said, 'There is no English name.'

Jane pushed her hand to her backside and clutched the aching orb with defensive fingers. She hadn't asked a question and, under the rules of McGivern's game, she felt sure that meant he wasn't entitled to stripe her. 'What the hell was that for?' She turned back to face him, not caring that he would see the loathing on her face. 'We agreed an answer for a stripe,' she reminded him. 'That was our deal and I didn't give you a question.'

His eyes were concealed by shadows but his mouth was visible and his grin was broad. 'I haven't reneged on our deal,' he assured her. 'I've just given you an answer and a stripe.'

Mentally backtracking over their conversation, Jane realised he was right, even if he was working to his own

15

bastardised version of fair play. She lowered her gaze, trying to block out the three slaves behind him. Their interest was still tinged with expressions of sympathy and Jane despised the pity that she could see on their faces.

'Do you want to stop playing this game?' McGivern asked innocently. 'Or do you have other questions for me?' His grin was infuriating as he whispered, 'I have a tip. Perhaps you might want to give your questions some more thought before you ask them.'

Jane dared to glare at him for a final time, then turned her face away before he took offence at her expression. She circled her aching fingers again around the handrails and drew a deep breath to steady herself. Holding her backside out for him, she decided to ask her other question. Their destination could have been anywhere and, even if he had told her the name, Jane doubted it would have meant anything. She took a second breath before speaking, not sure that she wanted to hear an honest answer in the unlikely event that McGivern could find one. With a determined effort, she asked, 'Is there going to be a slave auction?'

The crop landed across both buttocks. A flare of pain erupted across her arse-cheeks and she willed her pulse to stop hammering so loudly for fear that she might miss his response.

'I would imagine there's bound to be a slave auction somewhere.' He sounded as though he was struggling to contain his own good humour as he delivered another evasive answer. 'Terrible inhumanities like that go on all the time, don't you know?'

Jane bit back a defeated sob, wondering if she was going to get any answers to her questions. McGivern dealt with the truth like a miser using gold sovereigns. 'Are you taking us to a slave auction?' she growled.

This time, the stripe landed against her right buttock. Her arse-cheeks were burning even more and she could feel the heat warming the lips of her sex. Bent over, she knew that the pout of her pussy would be visible to him and she doubted he could miss the sight of her arousal. It was a

16

shameful position, humiliating and degrading, but that realisation only acted like a spur to her libido. Inside her waistcoat, her nipples were rigid pellets that needed to be caressed.

'I just might be taking you to a slave auction,' he said. 'But I don't imagine that answer will satisfy your curiosity. I expect that now you'll be wondering if I'm going as a buyer or a seller.'

The question hadn't entered her head but now that McGivern had voiced it, Jane saw that it was the key to those answers she really wanted. 'Are you going as a buyer?' she asked quickly.

The crop sang through the air before branding her left buttock.

'If something at the auction catches my eye, then I might make a purchase.'

Cringing against the blistering euphoria, Jane gripped the handrails tighter. 'Will you be selling a slave at the auction?'

Both cheeks were kissed by the crop's stinging blow.

'It's not called selling at an auction. At an auction, one "enters a lot". If you want a proper answer you should ask your question properly.'

The sunlight was unbearably hot and Jane could feel her body running with rivulets of sweat. She didn't know if it was the day's heat that had warmed her, or the effort of enduring McGivern's crop. Whatever the source, she realised it was strong enough to fuel trickles of perspiration between her legs. She could feel their icy tickle as they travelled down her inner thighs. From between gritted teeth, she asked, 'Will you be "entering a lot" at the slave auction?'

He struck her left cheek. 'No. I won't be entering a lot. Not in the singular sense of that phrase, anyway.'

Jane tried to focus her thoughts on this revelation, not sure she understood his meaning. She turned to face him and saw that he was holding the crop high, preparing to strike her arse yet again. The image was threatening but that only excited her spreading arousal. 'You're planning to sell more than one of us?' she whispered.

17

Too late, she realised it was a question. His malicious grin widened and his eyes focused on her exposed orbs. She watched the cane descend, its black length turning grey as it sped towards her backside. In turning, she had pushed her right cheek further forward and she felt the blaze burn into her buttock with more force than he had used previously. She gulped air and tried to ignore her racing pulse. Her body wanted to revel in the thrill of his punishment but she willed her thoughts to focus on his latest revelation.

'I'm planning to sell a couple of lots at the auction,' he explained. 'As I'm going to be the auctioneer, I could have been pedantic and tried to mislead you but I think it would be underhand to behave like that, wouldn't you agree?'

Jane could have accused him of misleading her with any one of his evasive answers but the discomfort in her backside was sufficient to keep her quiet. Staring defiantly at him, she asked, 'Which of us will be entered at the auction?'

'That's one hell of a direct question,' he laughed. 'And it deserves one hell of a direct answer. I'm not telling you.'

'But –' Jane began.

'However, I will answer one of your earlier questions, if you turn around and assume your position once again.'

'Which question?' Jane asked.

'Turn around.' He was holding the crop but he wasn't brandishing it. She watched him throw it towards his deck-chair and then reach for the belt at his waist. For an instant, Jane wondered if he was going to use the strap on her. He was adept at making the leather tip sting her flesh and he could land each blow with pinpoint accuracy. When he threw the belt to join his crop, she realised he had other appetites that needed satisfying. Her inner muscles clenched, responding eagerly.

He pushed his trousers down and stepped out of them, revealing himself hard and ready for her. 'Turn around,' he repeated. 'I still owe you that answer.'

Hating herself for responding so meekly, Jane turned to

face the bow and stared down into the churning waters beneath the prow. McGivern gripped her waist with both hands and she felt the heat of his erection pressing at her cleft. Jane made no attempt to stifle her roar of pleasure as he bucked his hips forward.

He pushed into her with a ferocious lunge, filling the length of her sex. The dark curls of his pubic hairs pressed against her buttocks and scoured her bruised arse cheeks like wire wool. He leaned over her, moving his hands to the swell of her breasts. With rough fingers he plucked at her nipples through her waistcoat.

Jane gasped, overwhelmed by a rush of excitement. This was what servility was all about, she thought happily. She had been humiliated by this man and he had treated her to the most degrading of punishments, yet still she responded to him as though she had been born to hold his cock between her legs.

'You asked me where we're heading,' he reminded Jane. His mouth was pressed below her ear as he chewed roughly on the lower lobe. Turning her head to one side, Jane could smell the stark scent of Scotch on his breath, bitter but no less exciting because of that. Her responsive groans deepened and she squeezed herself around his shaft.

McGivern drew a shivering breath. He continued to ride in and out of her, thrusting between her legs with the force of a pile-driver. 'You asked me where we're heading. Do you still want me to tell you?'

She grunted her response, managing the word 'yes' between cries of pleasure.

He snatched at her hair and pulled her head backwards. The muscles in her neck protested and it felt like her hair-roots were being torn from their follicles. Muting her screams, Jane tried to turn and face him.

He was still pushing into her, his pace quickening as excitement began to erode his self-control. Jane could feel that his orgasm was close. The inner walls of her pussy were being treated to the electric tingle that his cock always exuded in the moments before climax.

McGivern jostled her head away, forcing her to look

forward. 'That's where we're headed,' he said, pointing to the horizon.

She glanced in that direction and wondered how she could have been so blind as to not see it before. Quite how it had loomed out of the waters so quickly was a mystery. The dot that had been swelling on the horizon was now a visible island. In the centre of the island, sitting on top of some natural hill and rising above the lush foliage, was a castle. Bleached by the sun, the crenellated embattlements and sheer, stone walls were a vision of splendour. She recognised it instantly: the castle where they had first met, the place where McGivern had introduced Jane to the dubious pleasures of submission.

'That's where we're headed,' McGivern growled.

He was close to orgasm and Jane could feel herself nearing the point as well. She stared at the majestic building, ignoring the thousand questions that cascaded through her mind. It didn't matter why they were going to the castle, or what business McGivern thought he had there. Her curiosity was meaningless and it was only the urgent need between her legs that demanded satisfaction.

McGivern squeezed hard on her nipples. His breathing had deepened to ragged bursts. Pushing his mouth close to her ear again, he whispered, 'If you can keep a secret, I'll tell you something else about our destination. Do you think you can keep a secret?'

His words were slurred and Jane knew it was excitement that rendered him inarticulate. The thrust of his cock was a frantic blur inside her and she was being driven beyond the brink of elation. In a breathless voice she said, 'I can keep a secret.'

His grunts were tinged with mounting pleasure. 'Of course you can,' he agreed. 'But it has to stay between you and I. Do you promise?'

'I promise.'

Seemingly satisfied, he said, 'We're headed back to the castle.' He continued to thrust in and out, the point of his climax nearing with each frantic movement. 'We're headed back to the castle, and once we've arrived there, I'm going to enjoy the sweetest conquest I've ever known.' He released a bitter chuckle and said, 'I am so looking forward to it.'

With those words, McGivern's eruption shot deep inside her.

Two

Not for the first time, Frankie caught herself thinking of McGivern.

She raised her whip and hurled it downwards as though she was trying to exorcise the image. The creaking of the rickety plough drowned out the noise of the impact and, fearful of her wrath, the team ran faster. Her cart lurched across the field and the scratch plough carved a satisfying furrow in the soil. The team's animal grunts made a pleasant background music to the island's tranquillity.

McGivern had featured prominently in Frankie's thoughts since she became part-owner of the castle. It wasn't just because he possessed the most pliant submissive that Frankie had ever known, although she supposed that was a part of it. The submissive called number three was destined to live in Frankie's memory as the embodiment of servility and she still judged each new slave by the standard that number three had set. But, whilst his slave had been truly memorable, it was the fact that McGivern had brought her to the point of ruination that made Frankie think of him so often.

McGivern was a regular topic of conversation on those evenings when she and Simon dined together. Over several glasses of wine, they had plotted the outrageous humiliations they would pile upon McGivern if they ever saw the bastard again. Their plans were graphic and invariably sadistic and, while she suspected Simon was joking with some of his suggestions, every one of Frankie's scenarios was based on the dreams that one day she would happily make real.

Yet this time she wasn't plotting McGivern's suffering. As she drove her plough forward, she was thinking of those improvements that she and Simon had managed to make in spite of him. McGivern had fleeced them with the asking price for the castle and its island. To make that situation worse, he had left them with a property that needed expensive renovation and, in spite of the castle's remote location, there were still some historical societies trying to prevent the necessary improvements. Frankie and Simon had found that their hands were tied by a combination of inescapable red tape and crippling penury. Those two factors had been potentially ruinous but with a determined effort, and a lot of good fortune, they had managed to pull themselves back from the brink of a precipice.

'Faster, you worthless curs, faster!' Frankie called. She raised the whip again and snapped it in the air. The retort sounded like a pistol shot and she saw a flock of startled birds take flight from the cornfields. They fled towards the towering walls of the castle, then turned in unison before scattering across the endless blue sky. Aiming the whip at the flank of one straggler, Frankie pictured herself striking McGivern's arse. It was a childish exercise but she couldn't resist the excitement it gave her when she heard the tip smacking its target. The plough hurtled faster through the field, churning up lines of earth ready for the afternoon's crop-spreading. Frankie was almost unbalanced by the lilt and roll of the cart and she gripped the sides to steady herself.

Simon was proving remarkably easy to live with, Frankie thought, unaware that a fond smile had crept across her lips. They had become brief lovers on one drunken night after the castle became theirs. Her memories of that evening were wine-fogged but those parts she did recall evoked a wealth of pleasurable shivers. She supposed it would have been nice to enjoy a repeat performance of that incident but, because they were both sexual dominators, and because she was unsure of the appropriate etiquette for such situations, Frankie had never taken that

23

idea beyond her fantasies. A part of her feared Simon's rejection and while she knew that was a stupid and cowardly way to behave, there were enough sensible reasons to reinforce her hesitancy. That night, they had both been pissed out of their brains but even more than that, they still had to share the castle and its island. It would be foolish to unsettle the delicate balance of their friendship. And in her heart, she knew that they were too much alike to be truly compatible. All of those thoughts had the hollow ring of convenient excuses but even now, almost six months after that night, Frankie found herself hiding behind them.

'Work harder, you bastards,' she screamed. This time she snapped the whip twice, catching the flanks of those on the left and the right of the team. The plough charged ever faster and she laughed as the cart was almost toppled by their renewed burst of speed.

Simon had called in favours from old friends who were able to manage the physical side of the castle's maintenance. Unlike her, Simon still had some financial resources available and, although he had said nothing, Frankie knew that he had invested more than just favours into the castle's repair. He also had an ability to charm those organisations who deemed it improper to make the castle habitable. As far as Frankie knew, Simon was still working his charm on a member of the International Historical Society, as he had been throughout the night.

For her own contribution, Frankie had managed the workforce.

She had offered to use her own charm against the threat of the historical societies but she didn't have the same way with strangers that Simon exuded. Contemplating her appearance, she supposed there were other reasons that made it better for Simon to be responsible for the island's ambassadorial duties. She dressed to look intimidating and both she and Simon knew that this would have presented an unfavourable image to the visiting representatives. Even today, as she drove her team through the fields, she wore a short, leather skirt and a biker's jacket. It was an

24

ensemble that was identical to everything else in her wardrobe. Her long, dark hair was up this morning but, because she had been unable to find a band or clip to hold it in place, it was tied back with a slave's garter. If she had rolled her sleeves up she would have exposed the skull and crossbones tattoo on her upper bicep. While she was proud of the artwork, she knew it would have been frowned on by visitors from the International Historical Society.

'Left, you useless fuckers, left!' she screeched. She snapped the whip like a circus ringmaster, cracking the air mercilessly.

The plough was an ancient device that she had salvaged from a forgotten corner of the south keep. Between the effects of rust and woodworm, it had barely been serviceable, but now it made for a useful tool to make the island productive. Her only complaint, aside from its lack of shock-absorbers, was the piss-poor steering it was blessed with. She pulled on the reigns, hurling the whip to the right of the team. They had started turning when she first shouted, but years of domination had taught Frankie that there was nothing like overkill to see a command properly obeyed. 'Left,' she bellowed, easing her weight from the reins. 'Left and stop.'

She was halfway through the field's ploughing and, as the cart was brought into position, she saw the morning's work laid out in front of her. Parallel channels of broken earth lay to her left, looking so neat and even that they could have been drawn with a ruler and set square.

'Not bad,' Frankie muttered. The team had come to a halt and she supposed it was only fair to reward them with a break after all their efforts. She knew that some of her actions could be thought of as austere but she had never considered herself inhumane. Dropping her whip to the floor of the cart, she surveyed the freshly ploughed field for a final time before giving orders. 'Lose your harnesses and take five. You all know where the orange trees are if you're thirsty. Try not to take the ripe ones because I can sell those.' She reached into her jacket pocket and produced a cigar as the submissives uncoupled themselves.

The harnesses had been her idea and Frankie was pleased with the way they worked. Strips of leather went around the submissives' naked bodies and they were then secured to the central chassis of the plough. Further strips were added for reins and these circled the submissives' breasts before cutting chafing lines between their legs.

When Simon had first seen Frankie's team he had laughed and said she was dressing her slaves in the same way that McGivern had clothed his.

Frankie had balked at the idea and angrily disagreed. She told him that she despised the way McGivern had treated his submissives, reminding Simon that McGivern was a heartless bastard who identified his slaves with numbers and not names. Using all the indignation she could manage, Frankie had pointed out that she was too competent a dominatrix to label her charges with a dehumanising numerical system.

'Jay, Kay, Elle!' she called. She drew a match against the side of the cart before lighting her cigar. 'Come here. I want you.'

The three responded quickly, stepping out of their harnesses before stumbling over the broken earth to Frankie's side.

'Mistress?'

Frankie grinned around her Havana cigar, pleased that they had managed to address her in unison. 'What's that?' Frankie asked, nodding towards the sea.

The three slaves squinted into the sunlight.

'It looks like a boat, mistress.' Elle was always the first to speak. When Frankie first arrived on the island, the auburn-haired French girl had been one of a group of students working on a dig in the castle's bailey. Her dress sense had been appealing, in a trashy and vulgar kind of way, but Frankie had discovered that she looked better naked. Elle had olive skin that turned brown beneath the sun's rays. Her pert breasts were tipped with chocolate areolae and her firm, brown nipples showed her near-constant arousal. Frankie found her gaze settling on this sight as she contemplated the slave's answer.

'I can see it's a boat,' Frankie said tersely. 'Are we expecting a delivery today?'

All three of the slaves shrugged.

'Supplies do not arrive on a Sunday, mistress,' Elle said. 'Not ever.'

Frankie blinked, surprised to hear that it was Sunday. Days on the island had a way of happening without names and she was just as happy not knowing if it was Thursday, Friday or Michaelmas Tuesday. Frankie had grown used to life without a calendar. 'If it's not supplies, then who do we think it is?'

The three slaves shrugged again.

'Is Simon expecting anyone?' Frankie asked, drawing on her cigar.

'He did not say he was, mistress,' Elle replied.

Thinking aloud, Frankie said, 'Most likely it's another of these historical turds. They'll be here to tell us how wrong we are to have Jacuzzis fitted in the garderobes.' She snapped her fingers, coming to a sudden decision. 'Kay, go and warn Simon that we have visitors. Jay, find some decent clothes and go and greet our esteemed guests.'

Nodding their obedience, the pair turned and began to run back to the castle.

'What do you want me to do, mistress?' Elle asked quietly.

The French girl's accent had a delicious lilt and Frankie always found the sound excited her. She grinned into the slave's enquiring face and stroked a hand against her cheek. 'We can't really carry on working until Jay and Kay return,' Frankie explained. 'You and the other two won't be able to manage the plough without them. And I didn't bring any seeds this morning, so crop-spreading is out of the question.' Her fingers moved lower, following the line of the slave's clavicle and trailing between her breasts. The effort of pulling the plough had left the slave's chest rising and falling dramatically. Her skin was slick with the fresh sweat of exertion and, as Frankie caressed her, she saw the French girl's nipples stiffen. 'What do you suggest we do, Elle?'

27

Elle's eyes were shining with excitement and her smile was a promise of anticipation. 'We can do whatever you want to do, mistress.'

'Of course we can,' Frankie grinned. 'That's one of the rules of the island, isn't it?' Stepping out of the cart, she glanced at the two remaining slaves as they staggered towards the orange trees. Mentally dismissing them, Frankie slipped her arm around Elle and held her tightly. Her hand cupped the natural groove of the slave's cinched waist. 'Let's inspect the corn, shall we?' Frankie suggested. 'I always find those tall rows of stalks offer much more discretion.'

'You want us to be discreet today, mistress?'

'I'm a dominatrix, not an exhibitionist, so don't think I'll be exercising leniency this morning. Just discretion.'

Elle's grin widened and she pressed herself into Frankie's embrace.

The rows of corn had flourished in the island's temperate climate. They stood in dense lines that were more than ten feet high in some places. Frankie had to elbow her way through a wall of waxy stems to break into the secluded corridor of stalks. She saw the leaves' silky tendrils caress Elle's body but the slave seemed unmindful of their featherlike touch against her naked skin. She eased herself through the line and turned to Frankie, her dark-brown eyes wide and smiling.

In the shade of the plants, Frankie took the slave in her arms. She lowered her mouth to the French girl's and they kissed. Unable to stop herself, Frankie placed her hands on the slave's buttocks and kneaded her backside. She moved her mouth from Elle's and placed her lips around one brown nipple.

Elle trembled in her embrace. 'What are you wanting from me, mistress?' A huskiness in her voice charged Frankie's arousal.

Frankie sucked harder, teasing the nub of flesh between her teeth. When the slave's sigh turned to a bitter wince, Frankie relented and moved her mouth to the other breast. The tip stiffened between her lips and she sucked more furiously.

Panting, Elle hissed, 'Mistress, please tell me. What are you wanting?'

Frankie moved her lips from the slave's breast and kissed her mouth again. 'Do you really need to ask?' She kept her tone as low as the slave's and breathed the words into the cup of her ear. 'Isn't it obvious what I want?'

Nodding eagerly, Elle began to slide to her knees. Frankie caught a breath in the back of her throat and held herself rigid as the slave's hands moved down her body. Elle worked her mouth down Frankie's neck, between her breasts and towards the newly pierced flesh of Frankie's belly-button. The piercing had been a spur-of-the-moment decision but she was inordinately proud of the silver ring now penetrating her flat stomach. The skin wasn't particularly sensitive and the adornment didn't add anything to sexual stimulation, but it somehow made her feel outrageous and daring.

Elle placed a gentle kiss against the silver ring and teased it with the tip of her tongue. Then her mouth moved lower and Frankie felt the familiar thrill of arousal steal over her. The excitement of cunnilingus was a pleasure that she always savoured and, after a hard morning with the plough, Frankie considered herself ready for this reward. Aside from her thoughts about McGivern, this moment was the one she had been thinking about as she worked. Hours of watching the slave's naked backsides had inspired her with a ravenous appetite. Seeing their nubile forms as they exerted themselves beneath her whip had charged Frankie's body with a need that demanded satisfaction. Now that the moment was here, she was determined to extract every grain of pleasure from the submissive's skilled tongue.

Elle's kisses teased at her inner thighs. Her lips caressed the warm skin, moving towards the heat where they were most needed.

Frankie reached for the hem of her skirt and tugged it upwards. As always, she was naked beneath it and she combed her fingers through the dense curls above her sex. The tip of one finger brushed at the nub of her clitoris and

29

Frankie steeled herself against a rush of pleasure. Contenting herself with stroking Elle's head, Frankie pushed her hips forward, hoping the slave would take the hint and start tonguing her.

With a typically intuitive response, Elle lapped at the exposed clitoris.

'No!'

The shriek was followed by a guffaw and a voice that hissed, 'Hush!'

The cries cut through Frankie's mood like a scythe. She glanced down at the slave between her legs, wondering if Elle had any explanation for the noise they had just heard. Elle stared back at her, looking equally puzzled.

Ignoring her arousal, Frankie brushed her skirt down and held a silencing finger to her lips. She strained her ears to catch a repeat of the cries and stepped towards the wall of corn stalks on her left. Through the veil of stems, cobs and leaves, she could hear the distant sound of laboured breathing. Annoyed that her morning's entertainment had been spoilt, Frankie pushed quietly through to the next corridor. The row was empty but she caught sight of a movement through the facing wall. With catlike stealth, she moved closer.

'. . . shouldn't be doing this here.'

The tail end of the whispered words reached her ears but she couldn't put a face to the voice. Intrigued, Frankie stepped closer. The movement she had seen was low down, almost at floor level, and if it hadn't been for the murmuring voices, Frankie would have suspected rodents.

'We won't get caught if we're quiet.'

Frankie supposed the hissed words would have been true but the reminder had come too late. She pushed herself between two stalks, hearing their stems break as she climbed into the next channel. Before she had surveyed the scene, she used her most authoritative voice and bellowed, 'Who the fuck are you? And what the hell are you doing in my cornfields?'

Two naked women lay on the soil. One was squatting over the other, preparing to nuzzle between her partner's legs while she had her sex licked. Behind them lay a discarded pile of clothes. Both women glanced up at Frankie, their eyes surprised and fearful.

As soon as she had spoken, Frankie realised the second question was redundant. The pair were doing exactly the same thing she had intended doing with Elle. 'I asked a question,' Frankie barked, throwing her shoulders back and making her stance more formidable. 'Who the fuck are you?' She heard Elle climbing through the stalks beside her and turned to the slave for enlightenment. 'Do you know either of these two?'

'She is Simon's maid, mistress,' Elle replied, pointing to the brunette woman. 'I do not know the other.'

Frankie turned her ferocious gaze on the pair. 'This is unforgivable behaviour,' she growled. 'Who the hell are you?' She was glaring at the unknown woman on the floor and, for the first time, Frankie noticed her cheeks were crimson with embarrassment. It always struck her as amusing that a submissive could happily tolerate degradation of any kind but blushed at being seen by a third party. She turned her scowl into a menacing expression. 'I'm beginning to lose my patience, and it might surprise both of you to discover that beneath this feminine exterior, I have an unpleasant side.'

'It was my idea to come out here,' the maid babbled. She was pushing herself up from the floor and looked as though she was preparing to beg for forgiveness. In her attempt to hurry, she fell on her knees, and so tried walking in that position rather than getting back to her feet. 'Punish me, mistress. Let her go.'

Frankie pushed the maid to one side and climbed over the prone girl. She didn't look to be much beyond her twenty-first birthday and, lying helpless on the ground, her face had a certain vulnerability which made Frankie's pussy lips tremble.

Her naked form was smeared with remnants of soil, as though she and the maid had been rolling on the ground before they had been discovered. Her large breasts were circled with crescents of earth, one nipple covered with

31

mud and the other a startling pink in comparison. Not testing her imagination too greatly, Frankie guessed that it had recently been sucked clean. Her shock of red hair was awry but Frankie could tell from its expensive cut that this was simply the disarray of passion. Glancing at the pile of clothes, Frankie saw that those items which were not the maid's uniform looked like high-priced designer wear. Frankie focused her attention on the girl's pretty face.

'Who are you? What's your name?'

The girl shook her head. 'I don't want to say. If anyone found out what I was doing here, it would cause a scandal.'

Frankie forced herself not to smile. She was touched by a prickle of intrigue and a familiar rush of excitement sparkled between her legs. 'You're here on my island, making yourself free with my best friend's staff, in the sanctity of my cornfields, and yet you still want to remain anonymous. Do I look like the sort of person who would allow that?'

'Please, mistress,' the maid begged. She had pulled herself from the floor and was reaching for Frankie's sleeve. With the strength of desperation, she tried tugging Frankie away. 'Please, don't punish her. Let her go, and punish me.'

Frankie shook the maid away and turned her predatory smile back to the girl. 'Did you hear her mention punishment?'

The redhead nodded.

'Do I look like the sort of person who would punish?'

She could see the girl was torn between answers, clearly fearful of the repercussions of replying honestly. Pointing at the maid, Frankie said, 'She knows that this is a punishable offence and you've guessed that much, too. Tell me who you are, and I'll consider being lenient.'

'I can't.'

'Are you a friend of Simon?'

'No. I've only met him briefly and I don't think he even noticed me.'

Frankie hid her smile as she considered this remark. She knew all about Simon's voracious appetites and thought it unlikely that he could overlook any girl, especially one with a chest as full as the redhead's. But she didn't voice the observation. Simon affected an effeminacy that often worked to his advantage because it made him seem less threatening. If he had intentions for this girl, Frankie didn't want to spoil his plans by revealing his secrets.

'Are you one of Simon's staff?'

'Of course not!' The reply had all the indignation of someone young enough and wealthy enough to be repulsed by the idea of working for a living.

'Then what the fuck are you doing here?' Frankie asked.

'I can't tell you.'

'What's your name?'

'I can't tell you,' she cried. Her voice was rising to a shriek and Frankie could see a flicker of desperation in her eyes. 'There'd be a scandal and it would destroy my ...' She stopped abruptly and Frankie saw that she had been on the point of giving something away.

'You can tell me,' Frankie assured her. Lowering herself to her knees, she grinned and said, 'You can tell me, and you will tell me, but you'll tell me in your own good time.' She had her knees on either side of the girl's head, pressing her sex against the line of her jaw. With a snap of her fingers, Frankie summoned Elle and the maid so that they were standing in front of her. Staring at the maid, Frankie said, 'I'm going to be lenient with you, because you've been honest. My slave has been sweating after her morning's work in the field. Lick her clean.'

'Mistress?'

'You heard me,' Frankie growled. 'You might be Simon's maid, but you know enough about the way things work around here not to disobey me.'

'Yes, mistress,' the maid whispered.

Elle stood rigid as the naked maid lowered her mouth to one shoulder. Frankie watched a tongue stroke the smooth skin beneath Elle's neck. The sight was warming and the wetness between her legs grew more intense. She glanced downwards and saw the girl beneath her studying the scene with wide, terrified eyes.

'Her tits,' Frankie called. 'Lick her tits clean, especially the nipples. She likes that.'

The maid frowned unhappily but she did Frankie's bidding. Her tongue traced around Elle's orbs and then she moved her mouth over one nipple. Elle released a shuddering sigh but tolerated the unnecessary cleansing without moving.

'And lick her cunt,' Frankie said, grinning. 'I'll bet her cunt is dripping with sweat. Lick it good and clean.'

Between Frankie's legs, the redhead moaned. Frankie glanced down and saw she was watching the two slaves with an avid expression. She wondered if the girl was excited or frightened and then realised it was a probably a combination of the two. Against her buttocks, she could feel the stiffening buttons of the redhead's nipples. Frankie didn't think it had been inspired by fear.

Elle murmured words of surprise and Frankie saw a grin twisting her lips. She was touched by a pang of jealousy, knowing that she should have been enjoying those pleasures, but she dismissed the thought. The chance to dominate the unknown redhead held more appeal than having a slave's tongue lap at her sex; that pleasure she could enjoy whenever she wanted. Glancing down, Frankie said, 'Now, look at that. I'm being lenient with her and she's having to lick the sweat from my slave. I don't feel as though you've earned any leniency, so what do you think I'll do to you?'

The redhead switched her gaze from Elle and the maid to Frankie. 'I don't know what you intend doing to me and I don't care. I can't tell you my name.'

'Of course you can tell me,' Frankie insisted. 'All you have to do is open your mouth and use your tongue to shape the words. Do you need some practice with your tongue? Let's see, shall we?' Before the redhead could stop her, Frankie shifted position and rested her sex over the girl's lips.

A squirming tongue penetrated her pussy. Ripples of pleasure cascaded through her body and Frankie arched her back, surprised by the unexpected thrill. Through a

34

hazy mist of excitement she watched the maid use her tongue against Elle and found the vision intoxicating. If the identity of the girl beneath her hadn't been so intriguing, Frankie could have given herself over to the moment and wallowed in pleasure. She allowed the tongue to plunge even deeper, grinding her pelvis against the undulating jaw. Her clitoris was tongued and in the same moment, her anus was teased by a wet chin.

'Who are you?' Frankie whispered. She moved away from the girl's face and repeated the question as she stared down. 'Tell me. Who are you?'

'I can't tell you. The scandal would be ruinous.'

Frankie sniffed. 'Whatever you think will happen, I doubt it will be as bad as the plans I have in store.'

'What are you going to do with me?'

'Lick me some more,' Frankie told her, shifting her pussy back to the redhead's mouth. 'I have to think about that.' She was trying to give herself more time by intimidating the redhead and hoped her plan would work. When the tongue entered her cleft again, Frankie knew that she couldn't concentrate on anything while such immense pleasure was being played in her sex. The idea of planning a punishment as her labia were nibbled and sucked by the girl's deft mouth seemed impossible.

Elle started making the soft cries that Frankie knew signalled the slave's nearing climax. Glancing up, she saw that the maid was hungrily tonguing Elle's sex. With one hand on each of her legs, the maid strained her neck to press her mouth over Elle's hole.

Frankie resisted jealousy and snapped her fingers for Elle's attention. 'What do you think I should do with this one?'

Elle shrugged and the gesture disintegrated into a shiver of arousal. 'They were only trespassing, mistress,' she pointed out. Her words were husky with excitement but she looked as though she was considering the situation seriously. 'It is not as though they were stealing the corn, is it?'

Frankie latched on to the idea. 'Stealing corn!' she exclaimed. 'Of course. That's what they were doing.'

'No, mistress,' the maid began. She looked appalled by the suggestion and Frankie could see she was going to list a million reasons why she would never participate in such a theft. Frankie glared at her and the slave meekly moved her mouth back to Elle's sex.

The girl between Frankie's legs was frantically shaking her head in denial. 'I'm not a thief,' she insisted. 'I'll admit that I shouldn't have been here, but I'm not a thief, and I wasn't trying to steal your corn.'

Frankie shook her head and climbed off her. She reached for a cob from the wall behind her and brandished it in front of the girl. The crop was proving well for its first year and the cob she held was too thick for her fingers to circle fully. Slowly, Frankie peeled the silky leaves away to reveal the golden kernels inside. 'This is why you're here, isn't it?' she said, grinning. 'You were trying to steal my corn.'

'Of course I wasn't,' the redhead protested. 'Why the hell would I want to steal your blasted corn? What use would it be to me?' She levered herself from the floor and exercised a conciliatory smile as she squatted on the earth. 'Please believe me. I'm being honest when I say that I'm not a thief.'

'You haven't told me anything else about yourself,' Frankie reminded her. 'Am I really supposed to believe you when you won't even tell me who you are?'

'I can't tell you.'

'But I think you could cope with a scandal,' Frankie decided. 'I'm sure you'd be happier with a scandal than what I'm thinking about.'

The redhead frowned. 'What are you thinking of?'

'Tell me who you are and you won't have to find out.'

'How many more times? I can't tell you.'

Frankie hid her anger behind a rapacious grin. 'In a way, I was hoping that you'd say that.' She lurched towards the girl and pushed her back to the floor. The redhead gasped and raised her hand as if to protect herself. Frankie brushed the hand away and grabbed a fistful of hair. She twisted the auburn locks until the girl turned over, then she climbed on top of her and sat down.

36

With her backside pointing upwards, and her face buried in the soil, the redhead couldn't even speak, let alone fight back. Frankie chuckled wickedly to herself and moved her hand to the girl's arse-cheeks. She pressed the head of the cob against the redhead's slit.

'Jesus! No! Not that!'

Frankie's laughter deepened. 'Oh, yes. I don't take this sort of crap from my slaves and I don't take it from the likes of you either. You came here to steal my corn and this is where you were going to hide it.' She pushed the corn harder at the girl's hole.

The redhead screamed trying to turn and ease herself away from the ground, but Frankie held her in position. Pushing the cob more firmly, Frankie was pleased to feel it start its slow entry. The redhead shrieked. Her fists thrashed wildly in the earth, throwing up clumps of soil in a manic flurry as she tried to resist the intrusive pressure of the cob, but Frankie doubted that the girl's determination was as strong as her own.

'Please, no. Not that!'

'Tell me your name and I might consider stopping.'

There was a moment's silence. Elle and the maid were watching with horrified expressions. Ignoring them, Frankie pressed her face close to the redhead's ear and whispered, 'Tell me who you are and I might just stop with this one cob.'

The redhead groaned. She shook her head from side to side, spluttering words of refusal into the soil. Her fists beat the ground again and she half turned to grace Frankie with a pitiful expression. 'Please, don't,' she whispered.

'Don't, mistress,' the maid began. 'I don't think that Simon would –'

'Did I ask for your opinion?'

The maid's frown cut deep into her brow. She stared helplessly from Frankie to the captive girl and her lower lip trembled. 'But she's –'

'Don't you dare tell her who I am,' the redhead broke in. Through a mouthful of soil, her voice was almost austere enough to match Frankie's. 'Don't you dare tell her.'

Frankie glared down at the girl's back and then turned to the maid. The thought that these two were keeping a secret to themselves stirred a bitter resentment in the pit of her stomach.

'But –' the maid started again.

'Don't!' The redhead warned abruptly.

The maid shook her head. She cast a defeated look in Frankie's direction then pushed her tongue back to Elle's sex.

Frankie moved her mouth down to the redhead's ear. 'You're determined to remain an enigma, aren't you?'

'I have to. Can't you just accept that?'

Shaking her head, Frankie said, 'No. I can't accept that. But then again, I doubt you'll be able to accept this.' She pushed the corn deeper into the girl's hole, smiling when she heard the loud groan of discomfort. The cob slid inside and Frankie wondered how much of the ease of entry was caused by arousal. It had been clear that the redhead was excited when she was caught with the maid and, judging by the way she had used her tongue, Frankie guessed that the girl had more than a few submissive tendencies. The combination of those two factors left Frankie with no qualms about trying to bend the redhead to her will.

She flexed her wrist and pushed as deep as she could. The redhead's protests were ragged with excitement and Frankie felt the cob shuddering in her fingers. She could visualise the knobbly kernels as they titillated the redhead's inner walls. Picturing the cob's vast girth stretching the girl's tight muscles, Frankie felt her arousal begin to mount.

'Are you ready to tell me who you are?'

'No.' The word was gasped between breathless shudders.

Frankie twisted the cob as though it was a motorbike throttle. The redhead bucked her hips into the soil. Her cries startled another flock of birds and left a ringing peal in Frankie's inner ear.

'Hold that there,' Frankie told her. 'I have a surprise for you.'

'You shouldn't be doing that, mistress,' the maid implored.

Frankie snatched a fallen cob from the broken stem and brandished it at the maid. 'Do you want me to punish you instead?' She glared at the maid, daring her to behave defiantly.

The maid looked away.

For the first time it occurred to Frankie that perhaps she was being too impulsive with this punishment. The maid seemed adamant that Frankie should stop and, even though she was familiar with the island's rules, had pressed her point more than most submissives would have dared. But knowing that she would lose face if she backed down now, Frankie peeled the silky leaves from the second cob and resumed her position on top of the redhead.

From the corner of her eye, Frankie caught a warning look on Elle's face. She refused to acknowledge it and poised the cob over the rim of the girl's anus. 'This is your last chance to tell me who you are. After this I won't be listening.' She pressed the corn firmly against the girl's arsehole as she spoke, as though driving home her threat.

'Do what you will,' the redhead mumbled. Her voice sounded broken and defeated. The only colour in her tone was a distant growl of excitement.

Frankie laughed darkly. 'If you insist.' She moved one hand down to the cob that penetrated the girl's sex and held it firmly in place. With her other hand, she pushed the second cob hard against the redhead's anus.

Her scream was deafening in the confines of the cornfields. The cob began to make its slow entry and Frankie widened her smile with bitter pleasure. The girl beneath her was rigid and her sighs had deepened to a breathless pant.

With a callous disregard for her feelings, Frankie pushed deeper. She could feel that the cob inside the redhead's sex was threatening to push out and she held it firmly in place as she pushed the second one into her. 'Do you still think you can keep secrets from me?'

'You're an evil bitch.'

'Brave words for someone in your position,' Frankie noted. 'And I trust they won't be repeated. The punishment I have lined up for you is going to be cruel enough. Any more name-calling and I'll thrash your arse with that broken corn stalk.' She fixed the redhead with a scowl, silencing any more defiance.

The girl turned her face back to the soil and released a shivering sob.

Frankie pushed the corn as deep as she could. The redhead's back arched and her fingers clawed at the earth. Dark euphoria had driven the last screams from her body and she accepted the final thrust of penetration with wanton inevitability.

Although her pussy lips were trembling, Frankie felt disappointed. She had wanted to fit the whole cob into the tight confines of the girl's arsehole, but she knew that to press deeper would make the redhead more aware of the pain, rather than the pleasure. As long as the sensation still gave her some enjoyment, the girl would tolerate her humiliation.

'I want you to stand up now,' Frankie growled. 'If you're not going to give me your name, you can spend the afternoon working for me.'

'Working?'

Frankie eased herself to a standing position and started towards the broken cornstalks. 'Working,' she repeated. 'I want you working with my plough.'

'Mistress Frankie!' The words were a distant cry but Frankie recognised Jay's voice. She frowned, unhappy at the note of urgency in the tone, and took a step towards the broken wall of cornstalks to investigate.

'You want me to work with your plough?' The redhead sounded disgusted by the suggestion and her haughty tone stopped Frankie in her tracks. The girl turned herself over, revealing a dirty, tear-streaked face. Between her legs the two corn cobs still penetrated and, as Frankie watched, they were slowly expelled. Their steady egress inspired tremors that cut short her outrage.

'You brutalise me,' the girl said. 'You violate me with corn cobs and now you expect me to work your plough?'

'And I expect you to do it without protest, unless you want to tell me your name,' Frankie warned her.

'Mistress Frankie! Where are you?'

The cry sounded closer this time and Frankie cursed the interruption. She had pictured the day developing well. The redhead would have worked with the plough before being taken back to the castle where she could have reclined on the rack. There, Frankie knew she would have broken that spirit of defiance that shone in the girl's eyes. She had even scheduled another handful of sessions with the redhead's tongue lapping at her cleft. But now, sensing that Jay was bringing bad news, Frankie realised her plans weren't going to come to fruition.

'We're in here, Jay,' she called. 'Third corridor of cornstalks.'

As a reply, she could hear the sound of creaking stems. Jay's laboured breathing began to get closer and Frankie wondered what had made the slave exert herself so vigorously.

'Mistress!' Jay broke through the wall of cornstalks and stepped into the corridor. She didn't bother glancing at the other submissives, her eyes focusing sharply on her mistress. 'I had to tell you,' she gasped.

'What is it?'

'The boat,' Jay began, panting. Frankie could see the slave had been running and there was an urgency in her features that quelled Frankie's bad mood. When the submissive spoke, her words came in breathless gasps. 'The boat. The visitor. I had to tell you, even though he just wanted to see Simon. I had to tell you.'

'You haven't told me anything,' Frankie snapped. She took hold of Jay's arms and glared at her. 'What's happening? What's put you in this state?'

'It's the man you've talked about,' Jay explained. 'The one you said you hated.'

Frankie blinked, not sure she was following this conversation. 'Who is it?'

Jay drew breath and stared unhappily at her. 'The man who just arrived. His name is McGivern.'

Three

Her arse had the reddened glow that came only from a truly thorough paddling. Both cheeks were slightly swollen and coloured crimson by the promise of a minor bruise. As Simon watched, Grace explored the new landscape of her backside. A wince wrinkled her brow as she drew her fingernails over the skin. Despite her hurt tone, there was a smile in her voice when she said, 'You really know how to chastise a woman.'

He could see his reflection in the mirror behind her and he grinned at the figure standing there. His long, blond hair was tied back into a pony-tail and his cheeks were darkened by a shadow of stubble. He still wore his shirt but now it was unfastened and hanging loosely over his athletic frame. On his little finger was a blue and green azurite ring, the oval stone sitting heavily in its gold mount. Stroking the stiff bulge inside his black, leather pants, Simon tried not to succumb to another wave of arousal as he contemplated himself. He turned his smile on Grace as she looked up from her spanked bottom. 'The licence, Grace,' he reminded her. 'It's time for you to sign and stamp the licence.'

Grace nodded. 'In a moment.' Her words were distant and her attention was miles away as she turned back to study her punished backside. He saw her fingers steal between the cheeks and watched as she touched the folds of skin at her labia. She snatched her hand away, obviously fearful of rekindling her pleasure's intensity. After the climactic release of her last orgasm, this didn't surprise him. His ears were still ringing from the scream that had torn through her body.

'We don't have much time left today,' he said quietly. 'The International Historical Society has chartered a boat and it's scheduled to collect you shortly. I also have a pressing appointment which demands my attention. Settling this business with the licence would help us both to manage the day more effectively.'

'And so the world moves on.' She released a bitter laugh and stared at him levelly. 'Last night you promised me a wealth of pleasure in return for my seal of approval on the castle's renovations.' She held up a silencing hand, and said, 'Don't worry. I'm not trying to say that you didn't fulfil your part of that arrangement. On the contrary, you've introduced me to a world of delight that I had never anticipated discovering. But there is one final thing that you can do for me before I sign your precious licence.'

His smile was patient and he nodded his encouragement for her to continue. Last night had almost certainly been a revelation for the woman before him. She had entered his bedroom meekly, hesitancy rounding her shoulders and making her edgy in his embrace. As he had removed the prim and proper clothes from her body she had grown more tense before finally relaxing. He had felt her grow truly comfortable in the moment he had felt her nipple swell beneath his tongue. The shivers that cascaded through her body erased her last, doubtful frown. When she had eventually relented to him, the explosion of her orgasm had completely shattered her last inhibitions.

'I've worked for the International Historical Society for more years than I care to remember,' Grace told Simon. 'There's something I've always wanted to do concerning my work and I think you're just the man to help me do it.'

'If I can help,' he said, reaching out to caress her hip.

She brushed his hand away and fixed him with a smile. 'I need to get myself ready first. The paperwork is all laid out on your bureau so why don't you check that everything is in order while I slip into my clothes?'

Accepting her instruction, Simon settled himself in a

chair between the desk and a window. He glanced at the documentation on the bureau, not doubting that every detail was meticulous and appropriate. He had already learned that Grace was a first-class administrator; everything she had done would be correct. Not troubling himself with the paperwork, Simon watched her from his corner of the room, enjoying the thrill of seeing a beautiful woman climb into her clothes.

Grace wasn't one of the guileless, young slaves like those he and Frankie retained to populate the castle. She was a mature woman with a lithe body that she had carefully maintained through the years. Her mane of silver hair looked premature above her elegant face but it didn't look out of place. Last night, when he had first stripped the clothes from her body, he had thought she looked frail and vulnerable. His concerns had evaporated as soon as she began to wallow in their shared passion. Grace had finally thrown herself into their love-making with wild abandon and begged him to teach her everything he knew about pleasures of the flesh.

Happily, Simon had assumed the role of her tutor.

He was an accomplished dominatrix and knew how to excite submissives. Admittedly Grace wasn't truly servile, but she had been willing and compliant and throughout the night Simon had taught her how to enjoy her body's unimagined needs. He had used his mouth and a plastic phallus to arouse her. Once her passion was stirred, he had caressed her buttocks and breasts with a multi-thonged whip. His teasing had left her writhing on the bed where she had begged him to chastise her properly. Because he considered himself a gentleman, Simon had been unable to resist the lady's request.

Her maturity and naivety was a complex blend and Simon had found the challenge of tutoring her invigorating. Even though he was drained, he now shared some of her disappointment that the evening had ended. Glancing at his wrist-watch, he saw that the evening hadn't just ended, but that it was close to noon. 'I can't believe it's so late,' he whispered. 'What were you doing to make me lose track of so much time?'

She flushed demurely and reached for her panties from the floor. He watched as she stepped into them and pulled them over her hips. The satin clung to her reddened buttocks like a jealous lover. When she turned to face him, he could see the shadow of her pubic curls darkening the gusset of the pink fabric. She eased herself into a bra then sealed the front-fastening clasp with a snap of her wrist. 'In my briefcase there's that package you asked me to collect.'

Simon glanced at the open case and saw the box she was referring to. His heart skipped a beat as he realised that this vital detail had almost slipped his mind. The black box was trimmed with gold and had the name of a jeweller emblazoned across its leather-look top. He plucked it from the briefcase and broke the box open impatiently.

Grace climbed into her shoes and stepped towards him. She moved with an elegant beauty, made more exciting because she was only wearing bra, pants and heels. Simon barely acknowledged her, his attention riveted on the contents of the box. She leaned over his shoulder to look at what she had brought for him and he could smell her fading perfume. It was a subtle fragrance beneath the scent of their previous night's passion, but it was enough to cause a stirring between his thighs.

'It's beautiful, Simon,' Grace whispered.

He nodded, studying the jewel before daring to tease it from its place on the velvet card. 'It's not bad, is it?'

'What are we looking at there?' Grace asked, peering closer. Her cheek brushed against his and he could feel the swell of her scantily clad breast caressing his shoulder. 'Is it three or four carats?' she asked.

'It was over five when I sent it away but it's probably a little less now.' His gaze was fixed on the sparkling facets, as he teased the gem this way and that so it sparkled.

'It's a very unusual cut,' Grace said.

He nodded. 'I had the sides drilled. My intention was to replace the ball in one of these ball closure rings with it.' He pulled his shirt open to look at the circle of steel that pierced his left nipple. 'I thought it would make a perfect present for a friend of mine but things have changed a little since then.'

45

She placed a kiss against his cheek and touched his pierced nipple lovingly. 'There's a hopeless romantic somewhere inside you, isn't there?'

He laughed, eager to brush over such a shrewd accusation. 'There has been in the past,' he joked. 'But I don't like to talk about him.'

Grace frowned, saw she was being teased, then smiled again. 'It's a gorgeous diamond. What a shame that it's flawed.'

He shrugged. 'It's flawed, but I can't think of anything of beauty that doesn't have some small imperfection. Even I had a mole once. The flaw in this one makes it kind of special anyway. It's earned itself a name because of it.'

She pressed even closer to study it. Through the satin of her bra he could still feel the stiffening jut of her nipple. The hardness between his legs grew.

'It just looks like a squiggle.'

'Hold it up to the light,' he suggested, offering her the diamond. 'Hold it by the sides where it's been drilled and you'll be able to see exactly what it is.'

Grace balanced the diamond between her finger and thumb and took it to the window. 'Dear heaven. It's a number three, isn't it?'

'It's the number three,' he corrected. 'The number three diamond. Highest quality, optimum clarity and containing that one, single impurity. Have you seen the way the colours shine when you shift it from side to side?' He could tell that she had from the way she was smiling as she twisted the diamond in the late-morning light. 'That was one of the features that made it so expensive.'

'It goes red and gold,' Grace whispered. 'Dear God, Simon, this is really beautiful.' She turned to look at him, her face suddenly serious. There was a shrewd sparkle in her eyes as she said, 'You really must love her.'

He started at the remark. Holding his hand out, he accepted the diamond from Grace and stuffed it unceremoniously back in the box before snapping it shut. 'Time's against us, Grace. What was this last thing that you wanted me to help you with?'

She laughed. 'You're close to blushing, Simon. I would never have believed it. You, of all men, falling in love and being too bashful to do anything about it. Do I know the lucky girl?'

He kept his tone flat. 'You're misreading the situation.'

Grace shook her head. 'I've seen enough of the world to know that a man only buys quality diamonds for one reason. Who is she?'

He didn't meet the excited shine of her eyes. Keeping his gaze fixed on the closed box, he said, 'I'm giving it to a man, and before you read anything into that, it's a man whom I despise. I'm selling it to him.'

Grace studied him warily. 'You look like a man who's trying to hurt himself in his attempts to do the right thing. Are you sure that's wise?'

'Perhaps martyrdom appeals to me?' Simon suggested dryly.

Grace sniffed and shook her head. 'No one ever painted a picture of a smiling martyr. She hasn't seen this, has she? You should show it to her before you sell it. I'm sure she'd love you for it.'

He laughed and placed the box on the desk. 'Perhaps I should force you into exile after we've finished today? You have a way of reading me that is distinctly unsettling. I'm not sure that someone with your perceptive abilities should be allowed to visit this island as and when they want. You could be a threat to my position here as master of the castle.'

Grace stepped away from him and began to slip her blouse over head. She fastened the buttons before pinning the prim brooch at her collar. Once she had wriggled her hips back into her skirt she looked like the model of respectability that he had first greeted at the island's harbour. Her beige suit, white blouse and frail build projected an image that was simultaneously stately and demure. However, the resemblance to her former self was only superficial, he thought critically. Overnight, the discoveries she had made had changed her. Now, she held herself as though she was conscious of her femininity and, even when she had shrugged her shoulders into her jacket, there was nothing rigid and formal about the way she glided around the bedroom.

'I'm not trying to intrude on something that's obviously personal to you,' she told him. 'I was just trying to offer a woman's perspective on the situation.'

He blinked away his reverie and tried to exercise a smile as he watched her comb her hair into a bun.

'You don't want to grow old and look back on a life of regrets and wasted chances, Simon. That was the main lesson you taught me last night and I think I've learned it well.' She stepped over to him and stood between his legs as he sat at the bureau. It was a more intimate position than she would have adopted the previous day. Her bare knee was brushing against him through his leather pants. Her breasts, contained inside the prim blouse and jacket of her business suit, heaved imperceptibly. This morning her closeness felt natural and Simon swallowed dry-throated anticipation of what she was planning.

'Are these all in order?' she asked, reaching for the papers.

He nodded. 'Everything seems OK. The society's approval will allow Frankie and I to maintain our residence here at the castle without being penalised for making those all-important improvements.'

She glanced at the licence, her smile momentarily cynical. 'I have colleagues who would say you've desecrated this building.'

'Would you agree with them?'

She shrugged. 'The Jacuzzis and electrical wiring – and the double glazing and the modernised plumbing – don't trouble me. I should still have reservations about the satellite dish but I no longer care. As of today, I'm going to start living a different life and it won't be contained by the boring rules and regulations of the International Historical Society.' She placed the licence on the floor then reached for a pad and stamp. Winking indulgently at him, she positioned those beside the licence, slightly to the left of Simon's feet.

Speaking thickly, aware of the mounting electricity that charged the air between them, he asked, 'Will your young colleague be replacing you?'

She glanced at him quizzically and then allowed a smile of understanding to crease her features. 'My young, red-headed colleague?'

Simon nodded.

Grace shook her head. 'She's not my colleague. She's my daughter. And before you start getting any licentious thoughts about her, I'd thank you to stop. Mothers and daughters only share their lovers in the most repugnant of soap operas and I have no desire to entertain such a base notion right now.'

'You must be very proud of her,' Simon said, remembering the curvaceous girl with the sparkling smile. 'She's very striking.'

'And I like to think that she has inherited my naivety,' Grace said firmly. 'Push her out of your thoughts, Simon, or I won't sign this blasted licence.'

He grinned. Glancing out of the window, he saw a movement in the faraway cornfields and squinted to make sense of what he could see. Talk of redheads had set his mind into that vein and he realised he was able to see the vibrant titian locks on one of Frankie's slaves. The girl was working at the front of Frankie's plough but too far away for Simon to discern her features. He wondered why he hadn't noticed a redhead slave amongst Frankie's entourage before. But Simon knew that when Frankie was around, he seldom noticed anything but her.

'This is what I've always wanted to do,' Grace told him. She had a fountain pen in her hand and she removed its cap as she kneeled in front of him. She placed the pen on the floor, beside the rest of the stationery. Moving her face over the crotch of his pants, she traced her tongue against the bulging leather.

'Grace,' he whispered, trying to mask his excitement with a pretence of innocence. 'What do you intend doing to me?'

'It's what I've always wanted to do since I started this

ridiculous job. I'm going to suck you while I sign this licence, and when you ejaculate, I'm going to stamp the word "approved" in its appropriate box.'

She sounded breathless with the thought of her own daring and Simon felt himself responding to the same tug of arousal. His erection pressed hard against his trousers and his balls felt uncomfortable as their confines were tightened.

'Does that sound acceptable to you?' Grace asked, smiling slyly up at him.

'You've always wanted to do this?'

She nodded. 'Always. The idea has often kept me sane and made me giggle when I thought my mind would shrivel up and die with the crushing ennui of the work. Occasionally, when I've been stuck with some fat, sweaty dignitary, it has repulsed me. But most often, it's left me thrilled by my own lechery.' She flexed a tight smile at him, as though daring him to ridicule her fantasy. 'I get to keep a copy of the licence and, as this will be the last one I write, I intend to treasure it. I might even frame it as a reminder of my dream come true.'

He reached out and stroked her cheek as she rubbed his concealed erection. Using his thumb to turn the ring on his little finger, he brushed the blue and green azurite against her face, enjoying the way she shivered beneath its cool touch.

The sparkle in her eyes seemed to shine brighter. 'Every time I look at this licence from now on, I'll think about this moment. Every time I look at the signature, I'll remember that I wrote it while I had your penis in my mouth. Every time I look at the stamp, I'll think about the taste of your climax on my tongue.'

She reached a finger to the button at his waistband and teased it open. His hardness strained against the zip. When he stared down at himself, Simon could see the twitching of his pulse tightening the leather. Grace began to draw the zip downwards and Simon could feel each tooth separating above his rigid flesh. He gripped the arms of his chair tightly, surprised by the anticipation she was inspiring.

'I've never done this for a man before,' she breathed.

'Or a woman?' he quipped.

She frowned. 'Don't tease me, Simon.' She continued to draw the zip downwards, exposing a glimpse of his length before it sprang through the fly of his trousers. 'I've never done this before but so often I've fantasised about it. The last time I pictured myself doing this, I was almost sick with the excitement it generated. Last night, you taught me how to focus and release that excitement.'

'Then I apologise if you thought I was being flippant,' he told her. He reached down to stroke her hair, hoping the gesture would reassure her.

Hesitantly, her tongue touched the head of his length. More daringly, she curled delicate fingers around his shaft and stroked him up and down. She rolled her tongue around the swollen dome before pursing her lips to kiss it.

He wanted to ask her why she had never done this before. There was a wedding ring on the hand she stroked his cock with and the daughter she had brought with her proved that Grace hadn't lived a sexless existence. The thought nagged at him but he knew it was bad form to discuss previous lovers and relationships during bouts of intimacy.

She placed her lips around his shaft and sucked on the end. Her eyes smiled up at him as she did this and he grinned down at her, savouring the sensations. As she lowered her mouth, Simon pressed back into the chair and gripped its arms tighter.

A knock on the door threatened to break the moment but Simon acted quickly. 'I can't be disturbed right now,' he called. Although his body was alive with sexual tension, he managed to keep his tone even and his excitement concealed. 'Wait in the banquet hall and I'll see you when I've finished.'

'When you're finished,' Grace released a throaty chuckle. She shaped the words around his cock and the pressure of her shifting tongue sent shivers trembling through his body. 'You almost made that sound respectable.'

51

He placed a silencing finger to his lips and winked at her before stroking her face. He wanted to release her hair and toy with it as she sucked him but he had already guessed that she wouldn't allow that. On some purely psychic level, he sensed that she needed to perform this act while being dressed and groomed like an ambassador for the International Historical Society.

The knock sounded again and Simon glared at the door. He could see the handle twisting and before he could raise another word of objection, the door swung open.

'I'm sorry, master Simon, but I have to tell you.' Kay stood in the doorway, naked save for the reddening stripes where her harness had been. Long, blonde hair fell over her shoulders, framing her pert breasts and giving her features an air of delicacy. She glanced at the scene she was interrupting and her cheeks flushed crimson.

Grace moved her mouth from Simon's shaft and glanced uneasily at the intruder.

Carefully, Simon pushed her face back to his rigid length. He waited until she was sucking him again before he spoke to the slave. 'Whatever it is, it will wait until I've finished.' There was a steel in his voice that rang from the walls. 'Go to the banquet hall and I'll be along shortly.'

'But down at the harbour, there's a man who –'

'Down at the harbour there's a man who will wait,' Simon broke in firmly. 'Go to the banquet hall.'

She nodded and took a step backwards, closing the door behind her.

Simon turned his concerned frown to Grace. 'That didn't spoil your enjoyment, did it?'

She shook her head, not bothering to take her lips from his cock as she reassured him. 'It was quite exciting to be caught,' she said. 'And, considering your reputation, I'm surprised you didn't invite her in here to join us.'

His laughter subsided as she sucked more furiously on him. She had taken his entire length into her mouth and he could feel the head pressing against the ridges at the roof of her mouth. The sensation could have been uncomfortable but, with the pressure of her tongue and the warmth

52

of her lips, Simon found it added to his enjoyment. 'Would that have appealed to you?'

Grace shrugged. 'She and I could have done this together. She had a very nice body and I could have explored a few other fantasies I've always harboured.'

'Why Grace!' he gasped. 'You say the most outrageous things.'

'And I'm sure that the next time we meet, I will have done them.'

She pushed her mouth back over his cock and worked her tongue against his hardness again. At the same moment, she reached for her pen and Simon watched her claw blindly for the licence she had left on the floor. As she sucked, she lifted the pen and glanced awkwardly down. Her hands were trembling and he guessed that she was concealing an excitement that matched his own. With a shaking hand, she scratched her name in the appropriate box on the licence. As soon as she had finished, she dropped the pen and released a groan of satisfaction. Her shoulders began to heave as though the exertion of pleasure was taking its toll.

Simon heard himself echo the sound. There was something infectious about her pleasure and it went beyond the normal joy of fellatio. He glanced out of the window again, trying to distract himself so that Grace could take a moment longer to enjoy her fantasy. Although she had never done this for a man before, she was blessed with an innate ability that left him close to the point of explosion.

Through the window, beyond the rows of corn, the ploughed fields and the orange grove, he could see the harbour. There were already three boats there, bobbing lazily on the sparkling water. He could see a handful of figures moving on the boats and more on the surrounding land, but each was too far away for him to identify. With the blissful sensations between his legs, he couldn't be bothered to think about them. Beyond the boats, he saw other vessels approaching, splitting lines of white through the ocean, and he tried not to let that spoil his mood.

Harbouring three boats made the dock busier than he had ever anticipated but the other vessels were unexpected. Simon found himself frowning as he tried to work out who could be coming to the island and why.

Grace teased a finger between his balls, forcing him to turn his attention back to her. She worked her mouth up and down his shaft, coating him with the polish of her saliva. The sight of her grey-haired head nodding ponderously over him reinforced the strength of his erection. When she twirled her tongue around his dome, it brushed all other distractions from his mind.

'You feel close to coming,' she told him.

'You sound surprised.'

'I'll remember this taste every time I look at this licence.'

He watched her squeeze her thighs together, then shiver, as a wave of pleasure coursed through her body. Whatever motivated her to do this, Simon was grateful that she was fulfilling the fantasy with him. The thrill she got from simultaneously signing and sucking had infected him. She used one hand to knead his balls as the other slowly wanked him.

His explosion was beginning and he braced himself for its impact. His pulse was beating hard and its relentless tempo should have been deafening. But there was another sound nagging for his attention and, as that noise grew louder, he felt his focus on Grace beginning to falter. Annoyed that this encounter was losing the smooth finesse of the previous evening, he struggled against the temptation of a bad temper.

Glancing through the window, he saw a helicopter preparing to descend on to one of the island's freshly ploughed fields. Beyond that, he could see a second helicopter approaching, with its nose tilted down and its rotor blades whirling in a blur. The sight shocked him and the reflex made him try and raise himself from his seat.

Grace pushed him firmly back into the chair. 'I don't care what's happening out there,' she whispered. 'I'm going to taste you when you climax and you're going to sit there and enjoy it.'

There wasn't much of an argument in her voice but Simon listened to it anyway. After all, the pleasure of having his cock sucked was more intense than his curiosity. His rational mind needed to know what was happening outside the castle but his libido had a more pressing agenda. Assuring himself that the helicopters and the arriving boats would still be there once she had finished, Simon settled back in the chair.

'You were almost on the point of coming,' she told him. 'Now it's gone and I'm going to have to suck you harder just to get you back there.'

'I suppose I can allow that,' he grinned, shifting position so that she had more access to his shaft.

The whirl of the rotor blades was getting closer and he realised that the second chopper was trying to land in the castle's bailey. The threat of calamity was unsettling as he pictured an explosion like those in Frankie's favourite action films. He didn't know a lot about helicopters but he felt sure that they required a landing space larger than the confines of the stone bailey. A small error from the pilot could result in a catastrophe. If Grace hadn't been so skilled with her tongue, this thought might have spoiled his appetite for pleasure.

He dismissed the unnerving images of disaster as Grace drew her tongue against his shaft. When her lips blew a warm draft against his length, Simon found he didn't care about anything happening outside the room. All that mattered right now was his impending climax.

'If I was to touch myself now, I know that I'd come,' she whispered.

He nodded understanding, feeling close to the same orgasmic point.

'I've never been this excited in my life,' she whispered. 'Even last night, when you were initiating me with all those dark pleasures of yours, none of them were as thrilling as this.' Her words were full of a guttural rasp that emphasised their honesty.

'Is the reality as good as you expected?'

She shook her head, smiling around the shaft that

penetrated her mouth. 'Not as good. Better.' Her hands moved quickly against him, maintaining a steady pressure on his balls. She rolled them between her fingers as her other hand worked up and down his stiffness. Her lips, glistening with saliva and pre-come, delivered subtle kisses to the swollen head.

Simon stiffened in his chair, aware that she was about to suck the explosion from his body. She was pushing him beyond the point of excitement and it would be impossible to delay the moment much longer. Through force of habit, he resisted the urge to climax, tightening his grip on the arms of his chair and steeling himself against the onslaught of orgasm.

Grace reached for the stamp and pad from beside his foot. As she rolled the rubber surface against the ink-sodden cloth, he could feel her tongue tickling his glans. Her fingers massaged his sac with a final, almost uncomfortable squeeze and in the same moment, she sucked hard.

Simon let the eruption spurt from his body.

His shaft was a tingling ache, sore and weary from the night of passion he had already enjoyed. But despite this and all the annoying intrusions outside the castle, the release of his climax nearly doubled him as he relished the pleasure.

His shaft was still in her mouth, her lips pressing tightly around him. She stamped the word APPROVED against the licence with a heavy thud. As she did this, she sucked the come from his length and swallowed with a gourmand's greed. Euphoria held her body rigid as his cock repeatedly pulsed into her mouth.

Simon's length shivered with another delightful spasm.

Grace sighed with the joy of release and with a grimace of pleasure closed her eyes. Simon watched his cock spurt again and imagined his seed spraying against the back of her throat. The sight of his explosion daubing the roof of her mouth inspired yet another pulse to ripple through his hardness. She had barely had a chance to swallow his last eruption before a string of semen dribbled over her lips.

Grace caught the escaping fluid with her tongue, smiling as she savoured his taste. She moved herself away from his flailing shaft and wiped the back of her hand against her face. Her cheeks were flushed but she wasn't ashamed of what they had done. Her eyes sparkled with the lustre of satisfaction. 'You've given me a memory that I will enjoy forever,' she said.

He grinned down at her. 'I think I can safely say the same thing.'

Grace eased herself from the floor, snatching for the licence before she straightened herself up. She smoothed her skirt down and handed the document to him then placed a kiss on his cheek.

Simon could smell his climax on her breath but dismissed its eroticism. Now that their shared time was over, the distractions of the world outside were intruding again. Grace no longer fired his arousal as she had before this final interlude began. Even with a tear of come spattered against her cheek, she looked the epitome of respectability. That was enough to quell the return of his ardour.

'You don't need to remind me that my boat is waiting for me,' she told him. She wiped her face with a lace-trimmed handkerchief. Her voice was crisp and cool, giving no hint of the enormous satisfaction that she had just enjoyed. 'I'll find my daughter and we'll both leave you to enjoy renovating your castle. But I do have one question before I go.'

Simon was fastening his trousers as she spoke but he nodded for her to continue. He stepped past her to grab a clean shirt from his wardrobe and pushed his fists into the sleeves.

'Will I be allowed to return to this castle one day, or are you really going to exile me?'

He laughed. 'You're welcome to return whenever you want.'

'And can I give you a final piece of advice before I go?'

He grinned as he fastened the last button of his shirt then checked his reflection in the mirror. There was no time to wash or shave before greeting his uninvited guests but he knew he was handsome enough to carry off the rugged look. Glancing at Grace through the mirror, he said, 'You're going to give me your advice anyway, aren't you?'

Laughing at her own predictability, Grace nodded. 'I suppose I am.' Her features turned serious and she stepped closer to him, placing her arm over his shoulder to emphasise her seriousness. 'Show her the diamond before you sell it,' she told him. 'Whoever she is, I know that she'll adore you for it. I know that I would.'

Simon reached for the box and opened the lid. He studied the sparkling facets with a wistful expression. For an instant he found he was considering her suggestion before he saw how ridiculous that idea really was. Grace didn't know the situation, and while she had already guessed that the diamond had been bought for a woman, she didn't know that the relationship he was proposing worked on a different level to those that she might have experienced. It was difficult enough to rationalise the situation in his own mind, so he knew he would never be able to explain it to someone as proper and respectable as Grace.

He shook his head and turned to reassure her. 'Perhaps you're right,' he agreed. 'But in amongst all those people who've arrived outside, I think the buyer is already here. If the man followed my instructions, then hopefully he's brought something that she'll love even more.'

Grace frowned and kissed his cheek again. 'I'm sure that you know best,' she decided.

From her tone, Simon could tell that she didn't believe her own words, but that didn't trouble him. Pushing the jewellery into his trouser pocket, he snatched a jacket from the foot of the bed, said goodbye to Grace, and hurried out to meet the buyer.

Four

There were three boats docked in the island's small harbour but Frankie's attention was focused on only one of them. She stormed past the innocuous white craft that bore the IHS crest and ignored Simon's vessel *The Saucy Nancy*. She was glaring at the hull of the latest visitor, repeatedly reading the name *McGivern's Slave Ship* while the words darkened her mood. Her anger was like a black cloud, obscuring everything else from her thoughts. She had seen both helicopters landing, and knew that one was wreaking inestimable damage in her freshly ploughed maize field, but that was a problem that could be dealt with later. Similarly the boats on the horizon which were rapidly approaching the island would present her with all manner of niggling questions. But they would have to wait. She was still berating herself for securing the redhead to the plough, realising now that she had been wasting valuable time. Dealing with McGivern should have been a priority then; it was certainly a priority now.

'Frankie!' McGivern stood on the prow of his boat, leaning over the railings. He was waving cheerfully at her, as though she was a sorely missed friend. 'Frankie, darling! You've come to welcome me personally. How wonderfully sweet of you.'

'Get the fuck away from here,' Frankie growled. There was a forgotten cigar stub in her hand and she tossed it away with a flick of her wrist. 'Stick your boat into reverse and get away from my island, you double-dealing twat.'

His grin widened and he leaned further over the railings,

his smug face begging for her to slap him. 'I really have missed hearing both the words from your vocabulary. How are you keeping?'

'Leave now and you can take your scrotum with you,' she hissed.

He shook his head, and made the 'tut-tutting' sounds of a disappointed nanny. 'You really aren't the most welcoming of hosts, are you?' he told her. 'Why don't you act like a good little girl and fetch Simon. I do believe he's been expecting my arrival.'

The words made her hesitate but she decided to ignore them. Simon loathed McGivern as much as she did, and she knew he would never invite their shared nemesis to return to the island. McGivern was either bluffing to buy time, or simply trying to cause animosity. The possibility that he could be attempting to do both didn't seem that unlikely. 'Get away from here or I'll hurt you.' Her words were spoken quietly but she hoped they were threatening enough.

'What's the matter?' he asked, deliberately ignoring her antipathy. 'Is your barbed-wire thong a little too tight today? Be a good girl and go and find Simon. He can welcome me ashore if you don't want to.'

Frankie bristled. The black cloud of her anger was even darker and she knew that her rage was veering towards a point where she wouldn't be able to contain it. McGivern had cheated her out of a lot of money. He had left her and Simon to struggle with the castle's renovations and he had ignored their pleas for recompense. She had planned a thousand tortures for him if she ever saw him again. She would start to practice some of them if he didn't heed her advice and leave.

And it wasn't as though he was simply ignoring her, she realised. He seemed to draw immense pleasure from the contempt she showed him. His grin grew broader with each insult that she spat out and, as his gaze constantly appraised her curves, he licked his lips as though anticipating having her.

'Frankie! Hiya girl!'

Frankie glanced up from her dark reverie and saw Jane climbing out of the pilothouse. She recognised McGivern's slave in spite of her lurid, nautical uniform. The former solicitor was brushing her short skirt down and her cheeks were flushed with spots of high colour that told Frankie she had recently been branded by some form of humiliation. Despite that, Frankie saw Jane was grinning amiably as she waved.

'It's been a long time, Frankie,' Jane called cheerfully. 'How's life treating you?'

'Speak to him, Jane,' Frankie snapped. 'Tell him to leave now before I lose my temper and do something he'll regret.'

Jane rushed to McGivern's side, aware of the animosity in Frankie's voice. Her good mood evaporated as she tried to appease the situation before it could develop into violence. 'She means it, master. Let's turn around now and –'

McGivern raised a hand and Jane silently cowered away from him. She shifted a helpless gaze between her master and Frankie.

'I'll leave in my own good time,' McGivern said firmly. 'I have business here and I'm not going anywhere until it's concluded. Do I make myself clear?'

Jane took a nervous step away from him. She still studied him warily even though he had lowered his hand.

Frankie drew a deep breath and clawed her fingers into fists. She was sizing up the boat's railings, trying to decide the best part to grab so she could leap on to McGivern's vessel and start dealing with him. Admittedly he was larger than her, and strong, but she was harbouring an anger that she didn't think he could compete against.

'Don't move, Frankie.'

It was Simon's voice, laboured from running but firm and authoritative all the same. She glared at him as he approached, unhappy with the commanding tone he used and the way he appeared to have read her thoughts.

'That's a good girl, Frankie,' McGivern encouraged. 'You do as the nice man says and don't do a thing.'

With a massive effort, Frankie ignored him. She stared at Simon and said, 'It's McGivern.'

He nodded. 'I've been expecting him.'

The words hit her like the blow of a well-aimed whip. She passed her glare from Simon to McGivern, unable to mask her confusion. 'You can't be serious,' she whispered. 'McGivern?'

'Of course he's serious,' McGivern broke in cheerfully. 'What's the matter, Frankie? Don't you know everything that's going on on the island?'

'Do you want to shut up and let me deal with this?' Simon snapped at him.

'Didn't you know I was coming?' McGivern continued. He was chanting his words at Frankie as though he was trying to goad her deliberately. 'Don't you know why I'm here?'

'I asked you to shut up,' Simon warned.

McGivern ignored him. He was staring at Frankie, his lips twisted into a mocking sneer. 'You'll be telling me next that you don't know about the auction.'

The words left her stunned. For an instant she thought she saw Simon hit by the same uncertainty, but it was difficult to gauge his emotions as he glared at McGivern.

'We have things to talk about,' Simon said. His measured tone barely concealed his obvious rage. Staring at McGivern he said, 'I've got a meal prepared for you in the castle. If you'd like to –'

'He's not coming ashore and he's not entering the castle,' Frankie said firmly. 'I'm adamant.'

Simon rolled his eyes and released an exasperated sigh. 'Could we be a little less confrontational here, Frankie?' he pleaded. 'This is important to me.'

She glared at him, appalled that he could try and appeal to her better nature over this, of all issues. 'What the hell is wrong with you, Simon?' she demanded. 'Have you gone insane? Why are you dealing with this snake? And what's this shit about an auction?'

Simon reached for the azurite ring on his little finger and toyed with it absently. A frown wrinkled his brow and Frankie could see he was struggling to find the right words.

'Should I tell her about the auction, or do you want to?' McGivern asked. He beamed beneath Simon's glare and nodded as though they had just communicated an understanding. 'Perhaps I should tell her. I haven't filled you in with all the details yet, have I?'

Simon turned to Frankie. 'I need to talk to McGivern. I won't let him on the island without your permission but I'd appreciate it right now.'

'But it's McGivern,' Frankie reminded him. She could hear the petulant whine in her tone but there was no retracting it. 'It's McGivern,' she said more firmly. She knew it wasn't going to work but it was the only defence she could think of. 'You can't really want to deal with him.'

'This is important to me,' Simon told her.

'Could anything be that important?'

'I think this is.'

She released a heavy sigh and was tempted to relent but the sight of McGivern's smug face stopped her. 'How about a compromise?' she suggested. A sly smile broke over her lips.

McGivern frowned but Simon encouraged her to continue.

'Talk to him on board his boat,' Frankie said. 'That way he doesn't have to set foot on the island.'

'This is bloody ridiculous,' McGivern declared. 'Is this how you welcome all your guests?'

'Only the twats,' she spat. She was staring at Simon, hoping he could see the desperate plea in her eyes.

'That sounds reasonable to me,' Simon agreed. He turned to McGivern. 'We can conclude our business on board your boat. What do you think?'

'I think it's a bloody insult,' McGivern decided. 'I'm invited here and when I arrive, I'm as welcome as an oil spillage.'

'So, we're agreed,' Simon said firmly.

'No, we're not agreed,' McGivern insisted.

Frankie could hear a note of ire in his voice and found that it was her turn to enjoy someone's anger. The corners of her lips were teasing into a smile.

'I wanted to discuss things with you in relative privacy,' McGivern told Simon. 'I can't do that on board with my slaves listening.'

'I'll take your submissives to the castle,' Frankie told him. 'If there's been a meal prepared, the slaves can have it instead. I wouldn't want it to go to waste.'

Simon was struggling to conceal a grin when he turned to face McGivern. 'Is that all right by you?'

McGivern shook his head. 'No, it's not. Like I said, it's a bloody insult, but I shouldn't have expected anything else from the pair of you.'

'May I come aboard your boat to talk while Frankie takes your slaves to the castle?' Simon repeated carefully. He was reaching for the boat's railings as he asked the question, appearing to have guessed McGivern's answer.

'I have little choice in this matter, don't I?' McGivern growled unhappily. He snapped his fingers and called for his entourage.

Before Simon could leap on to the boat, Frankie placed a hand on his shoulder. 'What the hell is going on here, Simon?' she whispered.

He shook his head. 'I'll tell you later.'

She frowned, unhappy with the response, even though she had half-expected it. 'What's with all the boats and helicopters? One has landed in my maize field and I can't see it helping with this year's harvest.'

She could see a glimmer of uncertainty in his eyes and realised that was unusual for Simon. It was quickly gone but Frankie suspected Simon was as mystified by this turn of events as she was.

'I'll tell you all about it later,' he said firmly. 'Trust me.'

'You're not trying to play games with him, are you?' she asked. 'He doesn't play fair, Simon. We've already learned that.'

'I know what I'm doing,' Simon said patiently. 'Have a little faith in me.'

Frankie stopped herself from telling him to be careful and took a step away from the boat. 'You'll get him to leave as soon as possible, won't you?' She said the words loud enough for McGivern to hear and was warmed by his disparaging frown.

'I won't allow him to stay a minute longer than is necessary,' Simon assured her. 'You have my word on that.' Before she could assail him with any more questions or warnings, he heaved himself on to the boat and levered his body on to the deck.

As Simon boarded, the four submissives were climbing over the sides and leaping on to the shore. Frankie turned to face them, her features twisting into a scowl of contempt. It was only when she saw the last of the slaves that her mood mellowed. She caught a breath at the back of her throat and blushed as a lurid image leaped into her mind.

The entourage of slaves walked towards her, with Jane acting as their leader. 'I'm sorry we're not welcome here, Frankie,' she began.

'You're all perfectly welcome,' Frankie corrected her. She was speaking in a stiff tone and, while she knew she didn't sound welcoming, she meant the words honestly enough. 'It's only McGivern I don't want on the island. The rest of you feel free to make yourselves at home.' Instead of looking at Jane, Frankie's gaze was fixed on the final slave. She studied the dark-haired woman, wondering if any facet of her appearance had changed since they last met.

'You know the rest of the girls, don't you?' Jane went on, stumbling through a polite introduction. 'This is seven, this is eleven and picking up the rear is –'

'Number three,' Frankie whispered.

It had been a long time since she had last seen the slave but she was as beautiful as Frankie remembered and blessed with a majestic deportment that implied serenity. This was the slave that Frankie had come to regard as the ultimate in servility. She had often used her memory of number three to gauge all other submissives but not one of them had managed to meet her high standard.

Since their last meeting, Frankie had often thought about number three. She had dreamed of having the submissive kneel before her once again and it had provided her with pleasurable ends to otherwise lonely nights. Now that the slave was standing only yards away from her, Frankie wondered if that yearned-for moment was finally within her grasp. The idea was so wonderful and tempting that she was licking her lips with anticipation.

'Number three,' Frankie repeated, an unconscious smile erupting on her lips.

The slave glanced up on hearing her name and studied Frankie's face. Her features always kept her innermost thoughts a secret but just for an instant, Frankie thought she saw the flicker of a smile on the slave's lips. It could have been her imagination, or a trick of the sunlight on her tired eyes, but Frankie clung to the hope that the slave really had been smiling at her. It was a warming image and Frankie's grin broadened.

'Number three,' Jane repeated.

Sensing an uneasy silence, Frankie realised she should lead the slaves to the castle and feed them. Simon and McGivern had already disappeared into the boat's pilothouse and the approaching vessels had almost reached the island's harbour. Not trusting herself to greet the newcomers with a cordial welcome, she decided to leave that chore to Simon once he had finished negotiating with McGivern. She encouraged the slaves to walk ahead of her, remaining by Jane's side at the rear. Number three was directly in front and Frankie was able to watch the slave's backside as she walked.

Her long, coltish legs had muscles that rippled like a lover's fingers. As the slave mounted the slight incline up to the castle, Frankie could see the lower arc of her buttocks swelling beneath the hem of her skirt. If she had craned her neck – and the temptation to do that was so strong – Frankie knew that she would have been able to see the silver ball closure rings that pierced the slave's labia.

'It's been a long time, Frankie,' Jane said amicably. 'I didn't think we'd ever meet again, but I'm glad that we're back here, even if it is only a fleeting visit.'

'Is that what McGivern said?' Frankie asked, dragging her mind away from the desirable curves of number three's frame. 'Are you just here on a fleeting visit?'

Jane shrugged. 'I was navigating and he didn't even tell me this was our destination, so I can only guess. I'm assuming it's just a brief stay because you won't let the master on to your island.'

Frankie nodded, her gaze still fixed on number three's back. Long, dark locks cascaded over the shoulders of the slave's blouse. Her narrow waist looked so inviting that Frankie longed to embrace her. As they neared the steps to the ornamental drawbridge, Frankie slowed her pace down, knowing that she would be able to see more of number three if the slave was that little bit further ahead. It was a licentious thought, twisted and voyeuristic, but she was unable to resist its siren call.

She paused to snatch a cigar from inside her jacket pocket and slowly drew life into it as the slaves continued ahead. 'What are you doing here?' Frankie asked Jane once the end of her Havana was smouldering, without shifting her gaze from number three's backside.

'I don't know,' Jane replied. 'The master says we're off to an auction but since you don't know anything about it, I guess it won't be here.'

'An auction? A slave auction?'

Number three stifled a sob and her shoulders trembled slightly. The sound had been little more than a whisper and her tremor was barely discernible but Frankie couldn't have noticed it more if the slave had broken down in front of her and started to scream.

'Which of you is he selling?'

Jane shrugged. 'You think he'd tell me that? He's putting three of us up for the bidding but he wouldn't say which three.'

Frankie was glaring at number three's back, her need to touch the slave growing stronger with each moment. The slave's movements gave Frankie the glimpse of sex that she had yearned to see. Snuggled in the dark shadows of her cleft, Frankie saw the glimmer of steel that penetrated her pussy lips. It was a secretive vision, more exciting than she had imagined, it left her dizzy with need.

Between her legs a coal had nestled and its warm glow burned inside her. Silently, Frankie cursed her growing arousal. 'Is he selling you, Jane?'

'I don't know.'

She swallowed and, without trying to place too much emphasis on the question, she asked, 'Is he selling number three?'

'I've told you, he wouldn't say which of us are to be sold.'

The slaves had reached the drawbridge and started to cross the wooden entrance. Frankie glanced up in time to catch another glimpse of number three's exposed sex before the slave moved out of sight.

Frankie's heart was racing and the dull thud of desperate longing pounded at her temples. As they all moved into the cool shelter of the castle, her skin continued to burn. She was no longer able to blame the blazing sun for the flush that coloured her cheeks. She was loathe to admit the truth to herself but Frankie knew that she was sweating with the need to possess number three. Trying to hide her arousal, she turned to Jane and forced herself to appear sanguine.

'It sounds like a lot's been happening since we last spoke. Perhaps we'd better settle down and eat so you can tell me all about it.'

'Should we be eating the master's food?' Jane asked warily. 'I heard Simon say it had been prepared for him.'

Frankie shrugged. 'McGivern can have the leftovers. He doesn't deserve anything better. And if we're about to eat, can we not talk about McGivern? The man's name leaves a nasty taste in my mouth.' She led the slaves into the south keep and, in quiet procession, they entered Simon's banquet hall.

The room had been prepared for a grand meal but Frankie noted that there were only two chairs laid out so she surmised that Simon had planned to entertain his guest alone. In the centre of the table a sumptuous piece of game, dressed, trimmed and stuffed, waited beside a carving knife. Canapés, hors-d'œuvres and carefully presented segments of fruit decked the remainder of the table. The plates stood in the shadows of brimming carafes, opened bottles and crystal wine glasses. The feast was spread out on their finest tapestry tablecloth, and Frankie thought that Simon had gone to great lengths to make the meal look inviting.

For an instant, Frankie couldn't see Simon and McGivern sitting down to talk in this room. The lengthy preparations hinted at a more intimate meeting. Rather than seeing the two men discuss their business, she pictured herself dining alone with number three. It was a potent vision that rekindled the heat of her desire and she suddenly realised that she had to make that image come true. The idea of sharing a bottle of wine with the slave, and teasing morsels of fruit against her lips, left Frankie shivering.

While Frankie was still contemplating the private meal, she saw the blonde and redheaded slaves rushing towards the table. Before she could raise a word to stop them, they were snatching at the canapés, scooping up beluga and devouring it greedily.

'What the hell do you think you're doing?' Frankie bawled.

The redhead glanced at her, a trickle of caviar smearing her lower lip. Her eyes were wide and fearful.

'We're only eating,' the blonde complained. She looked as meek as her friend but she was trying to mask her fear behind bravado. 'Isn't that why we were brought up here?'

'You weren't brought here to act like scavengers,' Frankie barked. 'Spit that out.'

The pair glared at her, exchanged a glance, then in unison they spat the beluga back on to their canapés.

Frankie marched over to the two slaves, curling her hands into fists. Jane was studying her quizzically but Frankie dismissed the platinum blonde from her mind. It wasn't as easy to ignore number three but, with her outrage welling, Frankie was able to wrench her gaze away from her as well. 'If this is the way you behave, I can understand why McGivern would want to sell you two.'

'We were only –'

Frankie slapped the blonde across the face and glared at the redhead. They both fell silent. 'Don't answer me back,' she growled. 'I'm mistress of this castle and I won't tolerate that, just like I won't tolerate insubordinate submissives.'

'But –'

Frankie raised her hand again and the slave stopped talking.

'Because I have such a compassionate heart, I'm going to give you two choices.'

They were studying her warily. Frankie could see the familiar signs of submissive excitement colouring both their faces. Number eleven's nipples were clearly visible through the satin of her blouse and her areolae were dark against the flimsy fabric. The blonde, number seven, twisted her thighs together as she tried to stand still under the threat of Frankie's glowering frown.

Frankie nodded at the regurgitated canapés they were holding. 'I want you to take those down to the boat and give them to McGivern. If you want, once he's finished every crumb, you can tell him that the beluga was partially eaten. If that doesn't appeal to you, I'll tell him once this auction is over.'

The pair exchanged another glance and Frankie saw that she had struck a chord with some mutinous streak in their make up. Frankie turned to Jane and said, 'You're going to go down to the boat with them, just to make sure they do as I've instructed.'

'Can't they just apologise?'

Frankie shook her head. She reached for a canapé, took a mouthful of beluga and then spat it out in disgust. It occurred to her that there wasn't much difference between the appearance of fresh beluga and the beluga that had been in someone's mouth. She doubted that McGivern would notice there was anything amiss. Her only regret was that she wouldn't be able to watch him eating it. She knew that Simon wouldn't touch the caviar, having expressed his revulsion for the delicacy. 'Take them now,'

Frankie said, passing her own plate to Jane. 'Decide what you're going to do as you walk down to the dock. I'm beyond caring.'

Jane gave her a final, uncertain look before nodding her agreement. She summoned the blonde and the redhead to follow her and the trio of slaves walked quietly from the room.

Frankie stared at number three. Now that they were alone her stomach was filled with nervous butterflies. She dropped herself into a chair at the head of the table and struggled to find the right words for the moment. She wanted to tell the slave that she had missed her and that she had thought of her often in the past months. But that would sound weak and contrived.

'Sit down,' Frankie said, kicking the vacant chair. It was an unceremonious beginning to a conversation she had dreamed of, but it was the best she could manage.

Number three settled herself demurely on the seat and folded her hands on her lap. Her gaze was lowered and she studied her bare knees.

'Did McGivern tell you why he's brought you here?' Frankie asked, reaching for a piece of fruit and feigning nonchalance. She was studying the tops of the slave's legs as she directed the question at her. Number three's short skirt was cut so high that when she sat down, it almost disappeared. There was enough fabric to cover the cleft between her legs but only just enough. The sight of it transported Frankie to a world of carnal exploration so intense that she barely tasted the segment of tangerine as she swallowed. 'Has he said anything?' Frankie asked.

The slave shook her head. The gesture sent a tremor through her body and Frankie watched the woman's breasts shudder inside her blouse. Because the slave's nipples were pierced, they raised an unusual shadow from beneath the satin, and Frankie was mesmerised by the sight. 'He hasn't said a word, mistress,' number three whispered. 'But there's the rumour of an auction.' She gasped the final word as though it hurt her throat.

Frankie could hear the threat of tears in the slave's voice

71

and she resisted the urge to lean forward and reassure her. The idea of giving anyone a comforting embrace had never occurred to her before and she didn't want to spoil the mood of this moment with something so alien. 'I can't believe he would try and sell you,' she said, shaking her head with genuine bewilderment. She reached for another segment of tangerine and ate it without tasting. 'You're the perfect slave. I should know.'

Number three graced her with a watery smile before lowering her gaze back to her lap. 'I still think about the time we shared here before,' she whispered.

Frankie swallowed, aware of a glorious tension in the atmosphere. It felt as though the ozone had thickened when number three made her quiet declaration.

'The memory has helped me through a handful of lonely nights,' Frankie confessed. She could feel her cheeks flushing as she made this admission and she kept her gaze fixed on the slave, desperate to see her response.

Number three glanced up, her dark eyes studying Frankie's face as though she suspected mockery. She reached forward and placed a hand on Frankie's leg. It wasn't the commanding caress of a powerful lover but there was a warmth in the gesture that went beyond the platonic. 'If there is an auction, would you consider buying my deeds of indenture?'

Frankie leaned towards her, her fingers reaching for the slave's arms. Before she could respond the slave was spluttering out an apology.

'I know I shouldn't ask such a thing, and if you don't want me . . .' She swallowed, as though about to voice her greatest fear. 'If you don't want me, I could understand that and live with it but I –'

Frankie silenced her with a kiss. She felt the slave's tongue continue to move, as though she was silently concluding her speech while their mouths met. Frankie tried to stop it with her own tongue. The intimate exchange was brief but no less exciting because of that. As she relished the slave's easy acquiescence in her arms, Frankie was struck by a rush of arousal. 'If I could afford your deeds of indenture I wouldn't hesitate to say yes,' Frankie mumbled. 'But at the moment, I'm penniless.'

The slave stifled a sob. 'You don't want me,' she moaned. The threat of tears made her eyes glassy and she tried to pull herself out of Frankie's embrace.

Frankie held her tightly, squeezing her fingers into the soft flesh of the slave's arms. 'Don't pretend that you believe that,' Frankie whispered. 'Since you left the island, a day hasn't gone by without me thinking of you.'

The slave stared at her, confused by conflicting emotions.

'I wake up thinking about you. I train my slaves to be like you and, when they fail to meet the standard that you set, I punish them because they aren't you.'

Number three was trembling and Frankie wondered if her grip was too tight. She could feel the swell of the slave's breasts against her thumbs and suddenly, that pressure was electric. Having the submissive so close, feeling the tingle of her arousal, heightened Frankie's need.

'You mean that, don't you, mistress?'

Frankie nodded. Her face was close to the slave's and she contemplated kissing her again. From this position she knew she would feel the pressure of number three's nipples against her own chest and the temptation became unbearable. 'You know that if I had the money, I'd invest it in buying your deeds of indenture,' Frankie told her. 'But I've got nothing.' She paused for a moment, turning over their limited options in her mind. 'Could you become a runaway? I could grant you sanctuary here on the island.'

Number three shook her head. 'The master would have your name branded as a slave-rustler.'

Frankie shrugged. 'Like I care? I live on an island, remember?'

'But you don't live here alone, do you?'

Remembering Simon, Frankie frowned and realised it would be unfair to have his name tarnished because of his association with her. She toyed with the idea of borrowing the money from Simon, then stopped herself from thinking like that. Simon had contributed enough with the castle's

73

restoration. To ask anything more of him would spoil their friendship and, as much as she wanted number three, that was a higher price than she was willing to pay.

'There must be something we can do,' Frankie growled. She pushed the slave callously back into her chair and reached for a fresh cigar. Her mind whirled through a dozen hopeless alternatives. There was no solution. The inescapable fact left her feeling impotent and frustrated.

Number three stood up and reached for the top button of her blouse. As Frankie watched, the slave released the other two buttons and opened the garment, before shrugging it from her shoulders. The satin fell to the floor like a dying ghost. By the time it had reached the Persian rug, number three was already pulling at the waistband of her skirt.

Frankie considered the slave with widening eyes. If the air had been thick with tension before, by now it was unbearable. The hairs on the back of Frankie's arms were tingling as though she was building up static electricity.

Number three tugged her zipper down and allowed the skirt to fall to her ankles. She stepped out of it, moving gracefully on her punishingly high heels, and placed her naked body in Frankie's embrace. 'If you can't buy me, then we don't have much time left together.'

Frankie stabbed her cigar into a plate of hors-d'œuvres and wrapped her arms around the slave's body. She explored the fondly remembered contours and the sensation of number three's warm skin thrilled her fingertips.

'We shouldn't be doing this,' Frankie warned her. 'I hate McGivern but he's a fellow dominatrix and there are rules to follow.'

'Then break the rules,' number three insisted. 'Just this once, with only you and I knowing about it, break the rules and use me the way that we both want you to.'

Frankie drew a deep breath and tried not to contemplate all the images that the phrase implied. She could have banished the thoughts by closing her eyes, but that would have spoilt her enjoyment. The number three tattoo was as

74

vibrant as she remembered it on the slave's body and Frankie saw the dark edge of its lower curl had been extended so now it completely circled the slave's breast. Without thinking, she reached out and traced her fingers along the outline of embedded black ink.

Number three shivered and her pierced nipple stiffened. Frankie watched the silver ball closure ring tilt upwards as the erectile tissue grew harder. The slave's sigh was lost beneath the release of her own pent-up breath.

'We shouldn't,' Frankie whispered, licking her lips and thinking the exact opposite.

'Don't you want to, mistress?' number three asked, her gaze flickering over Frankie's features. Her voice had the coquettish charm of innocence.

Frankie thought of replying, then realised she was wasting time. She reached a hand behind the slave's head and grabbed a fistful of hair. Pulling number three closer, she pressed her mouth over the slave's and relished the submissive's cry of pleasure while they kissed. With her other hand, she reached down towards the slave's hip.

Between Frankie's savage kisses, number three told her, 'You're as brutal as I remember.'

Frankie laughed against her mouth, pressing her kisses harder. Her inquisitive fingers followed the line of the slave's pelvis and she was excited by the warmth she found there. 'Only as brutal,' Frankie whispered, pushing her fingers closer to the slave's warmth. 'I thought I'd made my style more menacing over these last months.'

Lowering her head, Frankie placed her mouth over the slave's breast and sucked at one pierced nipple. Her tongue played with the ring of steel, stimulating the breast with an almost accidental gesture. The slave stiffened in her arms and Frankie shivered as she realised she was empathising with number three's excitement.

Number three twined her fingers in Frankie's hair, tugging away the garter that kept the tresses from her face. With the dark locks released, she began to comb her fingers over Frankie's scalp, encouraging the dominatrix to play more brusquely with her breasts.

Unable to contain her passion, Frankie pushed the slave on to the table. She heard the clatter of plates and bottles as she cleared most of the prepared banquet. From the corner of her eye, she saw the game tumble to the floor and come to rest in a spreading puddle of Chianti but her attention was focused on the slave. Forcing number three to lie back, Frankie moved her kisses down the slave's body, teasing each rib before tasting the flat of her stomach, then moving lower.

'No, mistress,' number three hissed. There was a note of panic in her voice and she tried to raise herself from the table as she made her protestations. 'You shouldn't be doing that for me. It's not right.'

'It's what I want to do,' Frankie said, using a single hand to push the slave back down. She delivered another kiss to the top of the slave's pubic mound. The salty flavour of fresh sweat tainted her lips and excitement coursed through her.

'But that's the chore of a submissive,' number three insisted, trying to wriggle free from beneath the pressure of Frankie's hand. 'It's not the chore of a mistress.'

'I'm the mistress,' Frankie reminded her. 'And I decide who does which chore.' Her lascivious smile was lighting up her eyes as she glanced up at the slave and winked. 'Besides,' she assured her. 'I could never consider this a chore.' With a dart of her head, Frankie pressed her face into the musky warmth between number three's legs. Her nose was treated to the delicate fragrance of the slave's arousal and without hesitating, Frankie pressed her tongue against the glistening pussy lips.

Number three drew a sharp breath, and released the sound with a whistle of pleasure.

Frankie continued to glide her tongue against the swollen lips, indulging herself in the aromatic flavour. The slave's labia were shaved with such precision that it seemed as though the woman had never had pubic hairs. Her inner and outer lips were pierced with small, steel rings, tinier and more delicate than those through her nipples. Behind the hood of her clitoris there was another piercing. This was the one that Frankie teased with her tongue.

Number three gasped, wrenching the tablecloth in her hands as she tried to control her response. Another carafe hit the floor and Frankie heard it smash. Each time she pressed her lips to the piercing behind the clitoris, number three shivered as though she was on the verge of a climax. The slave's responsiveness mirrored Frankie's own mood and, although she was receiving no stimulation, Frankie could feel her pleasure growing.

'I want to do that for you,' number three gasped. The plea in her words begged to be heard.

Frankie ignored her. She teased her tongue further between the pierced folds of flesh and drank from the fountain of the slave's arousal. Her upper lip tickled the ball in the clitoris piercing and she felt the slave writhe maniacally on the table. A crystal wine glass shattered on the Persian rug but its sound was unheard by both of them.

'You can do this for me later,' Frankie growled. 'For now, it's my turn. I'm going to do this for as long as I can.' She pushed her tongue forward and savoured the slave's sweetness once again. 'I've dreamed about this moment and no one, not even you, is going to stop me from enjoying every second of it.'

Number three gasped again and eased herself away from the table. She stared down between her legs and Frankie was able to enjoy the unique perspective of glancing up from a submissive's point of view. But she was puzzled by the frown of concern that she saw on the slave's features.

'You've dreamed about this moment?' number three whispered.

Frankie nodded, seeing nothing unusual in the admission. 'Shouldn't I have?'

'I've dreamed of this, too,' number three confided. 'Long and often.' With a fond smile, she said, 'You did this for me once before, remember?'

'How could I forget?' Frankie grinned and placed her tongue back against the dripping hole of the slave's sex. Number three squirmed in response and her chest shivered as she released another sigh.

'I can't believe we've both dreamed of this moment,'

number three repeated wistfully. Her words were thickened by an undercurrent of arousal. 'But I always thought it would be only a dream. I never thought it could be made real, and I would never have believed it could feel this exquisite.'

Frankie ran her tongue against the slave's pussy lips, relishing the sensation of intimate flesh against her mouth. 'I've dreamed of tasting you,' Frankie whispered, snatching a segment of tangerine from the table. She drew the fruit against the glistening lips of the slave's hole and coated it with pussy honey. 'And of sharing your taste,' she told the slave. Without another word, she pushed the piece of tangerine towards number three's mouth and watched the slave accept it. Moving her head quickly back to the slave's sex, Frankie pushed out her tongue and knew that in that moment, they were both enjoying the same delicious flavour.

'More,' number three hissed. Her words were fired by the urgency of an impending climax and Frankie didn't stop helping her get there. She reached for the plate of tangerine pieces and pressed another segment against the spread lips of the slave's sex. Her pussy was like a small, suckling mouth that begged to be given another treat, and Frankie rubbed the piece of tangerine firmly between the inner lips.

Number three had started to moan on the table. Frankie stood up and dangled the piece of fruit over the slave's mouth. At the same time, she pressed her fingers against her hole and pushed them between the slippery lips. 'Do you want to taste this?' Frankie asked.

Number three parted her lips and sighed. Frankie pressed her fingers more firmly between the gaping lips of the submissive's sex and allowed her thumb to rub over the clitoris. She could feel the nub of flesh being pinched against its piercing and the slave's pelvic bone.

As she watched number three groan with ecstasy, Frankie rubbed the sodden piece of tangerine against her upper lip. Number three's tongue darted out to catch the fruit and Frankie snatched it quickly away. 'Do you want to taste this?' she repeated.

'I want to taste a lot more than that,' number three told her. She bucked her hips forward and rubbed her pelvis against Frankie's fingers. Her entire body stiffened and her leg muscles convulsed as the orgasm swept through her. Frankie watched the slave's face darken in a glorious hush before she opened her eyes. They stared at one another with matching expressions of admiration. Frankie released an unexpected burst of laughter, delighted that she had done such a good job of satisfying the slave.

'I want to do that for you,' number three told her. She was pushing herself up from the table, trying to pull the jacket from Frankie's body as she spoke. 'I want to do that for you.'

Frankie shook her head and tried to extricate herself from the slave's embrace. She wasn't fast enough and felt number three's mouth circle her breast and suck at her nipple. The sensations were debilitating, but though the temptation to relent was strong, Frankie found the willpower to push the slave away. 'Not now,' she told her. 'There isn't time.'

'We'll make time,' number three insisted. There was a desperate need in her tone and her actions. She pushed her mouth forward again and scored a direct hit on Frankie's nipple, the intimate kiss sparking a thrill that was almost irresistible.

Frankie shook her head and forced the slave away. 'McGivern would be outraged if he knew what we're doing here,' she explained.

'I no longer care about him,' number three told her. 'He's going to sell me, so why should I care?'

'And I care even less,' Frankie agreed. 'But until he actually puts you up for auction, there's always the hope that we could make him see sense.'

Number three regarded her warily. 'There's no hope of that,' she said meekly.

Frankie silenced her with a kiss. 'He hasn't had the auction yet,' she whispered. 'And that means there's still hope.'

Number three stared at her uncertainly, her defeated

expression showing that she no longer believed in such naive concepts. Lowering her gaze, she said quietly, 'There's no hope.'

Frankie shook her head. There was determination shining in her eyes and she wanted to infect the submissive with her mood. 'There's always hope,' she insisted. 'And if I have a chance to own your deeds of indenture, I'm going to take it.'

'But you said –'

Frankie didn't let her finish. 'I've already decided,' she growled. 'Whatever it takes to make you mine, I'm going to do it.'

Five

'The number three diamond.' McGivern grinned. He was admiring the gem as he held it up to the light. 'Highest quality, optimum clarity, and flawed by that one, single impurity.'

'I know all about the diamond,' Simon snapped. 'I'm the one who's selling it, remember?'

McGivern continued to contemplate its sparkling facets. 'It's even more beautiful than I thought it would be.'

Trying not to show his impatience, Simon took a deep breath. He was anxious to conclude their business and didn't want to waste time listening to McGivern wax lyrical over the stone. Once their deal was complete, he intended excusing himself so he could find out who his unknown visitors were. 'You consider the exchange to be fair?' he asked tersely.

'A number three for a number three. I think it sounds like the ideal basis for a swap.' McGivern wasn't looking at Simon as he spoke. He remained by the portal, holding the gem above his face and allowing it to freckle his cheeks with beams of whitened sunlight.

'If the exchange is fair, will you give me her papers?'

Abruptly, McGivern pushed the diamond out of sight. He stuffed it into his pocket and turned away from the portal. 'We have plenty of time to deal with the formalities. You said in your letter that discretion was vital.'

'We're alone on your private boat and speaking in whispered voices,' Simon reminded him. 'If we get any more discreet, one of us will have to leave.'

McGivern's smile was fleeting. 'You're acquiring this slave for the bull dyke?'

'Her name's Frankie.' Simon's firm tone articulated a warning.

'You're acquiring this slave for Frankie,' McGivern amended. 'But you don't want her to know that you've made the purchase.' His laughter was a malicious cackle that echoed from the walls of the pilothouse. 'Were you going to treat number three like a puppy? And tell Frankie that the bitch followed you home? Or were you going to say that you picked her up from the local branch of Slaves R Us?'

Simon chewed on his lower lip, struggling to keep control of his anger. 'Quite how I would have dealt with that is –'

'. . . none of my business,' McGivern concluded. 'And quite right, too. However, I anticipated that you might need a convincing cover story, and that's why these guests are arriving now.'

Simon went to the boat's portal and glanced outside. The harbour was filling with boats and he saw a third helicopter hovering above the maize field. He closed his eyes, made a wish that Frankie wouldn't see that one, then turned back to McGivern. 'These are your guests?'

'I've invited them,' McGivern allowed carefully.

'And what's the "cover story" that you mentioned?'

'A slave auction.'

Simon shook his head, not knowing whether to be outraged or disgusted. He rubbed his fingers against his forehead, trying to suppress the headache that lurked there. 'Are there any depths that you won't sink to?'

McGivern considered the remark, seemingly unoffended by Simon's hostile tone. 'Probably not. But don't get too comfortable with your position on the moral high-ground. These people are only here to make transactions like the one we've just made. And rather than insulting me, you should be thanking me.'

Simon considered him in stony silence.

'These people are arriving here expecting a slave auction.

There are buyers and sellers bringing a hell of a lot of stock with them. Frankie won't be able to keep track of all the sales and purchases that go on and, once it's all over, you can tell her that you acquired number three as a present. If that idea doesn't suit, you can say she got left behind as a piece of forgotten merchandise.'

'I preferred the Slaves R Us suggestion,' Simon said bitterly.

Simon had his own entourage of submissives and it was his practice to dominate them at every opportunity, but he also held each one of them in high regard. There was something about McGivern's cool indifference towards submissives that made Simon repulsed by his association with the man.

'It's too late to back down from it now,' McGivern said. 'There are some ruthless bastards out there and I wouldn't fancy your chances if you told them the auction had been cancelled.'

Simon was indignant. 'I'd be telling them that you organised it.'

McGivern shook his head. There was a veneer of satisfaction in his expression that Simon longed to shatter. 'I doubt they'd believe that. I thought the invitations would look more authentic if they had your name on them. These people are all expecting you to play host.'

'You bastard,' Simon whispered.

McGivern's grin widened and he shook his head. 'Enough flattery,' he said. 'I should be introducing you to some of your guests.' He reached out and placed his hand on Simon's elbow.

Simon shrugged his arm free.

'I'd like number three's deeds of indenture before we leave this room.'

'You have no faith in me, do you?'

Rather than replying, Simon flexed his fingers until the knuckles cracked.

McGivern's eyelids lowered and Simon was pleased that he had caused offence. He watched the man turn his back and pull an attaché case from behind one of the navigation consoles. After manipulating the dials, McGivern snapped both latches and flicked the lid open.

Peering over his shoulder, Simon saw that there were four rolls of cream vellum inside the case. Each one was circumnavigated at its centre by a blood-red ribbon.

'Deeds of indenture,' McGivern said, handing over a roll of paper. 'Like I told you before, and in spite of your pious hostility, it still seems like a fair exchange.'

Simon could hear the potential for deceit in McGivern's words. It wasn't a new timbre – he knew that the man always sounded like he was trying to wheedle some advantage for himself – but Simon was determined not to be misled. With a casual flick of his wrist he pulled the ribbon from the tube and unfurled the document.

'You really are an untrusting sod,' McGivern growled. He fastened the attaché case and slid it back to its hiding place behind the console.

Simon grunted. 'We both know that deeds of indenture are virtually worthless as far as binding contracts go.' He brandished the roll of paper. 'This thing wouldn't stand up in court if you grafted legs to it and put it in a pair of Wellington boots.'

'If you feel like that, then why are you verifying it?'

Simon scanned through the pages, making no attempt to conceal his suspicion. 'I'm verifying it because I've dealt with you before. I know the terms by which you do business and I'm going balls out not to be duped again.'

'Your words could hurt me,' McGivern said. 'But today I won't let them.' He stepped towards the portal and then turned back to Simon, his eyes shining with excitement. 'And you're wrong about the deeds being worthless. These people arriving now would soon you tell how valuable they can be. Come with me,' he said, starting towards the pilothouse door. 'Let me introduce you to some of them. I'm sure you'll get a kick out of it.'

Again he reached for Simon's arm and again Simon shrugged himself free.

'It says here that her name is Jane Smith.' Simon pointed

at the precise signature on the last page of the deed. 'Is that number three's real name?'

'You've already called it a worthless document,' McGivern returned acidly. 'Think how much more valuable it would be if it listed her name as number three.'

Simon considered this, knowing that McGivern was right, but still feeling sure he was being cheated in some way. 'You have another slave called Jane. That's quite a coincidence, isn't it?'

McGivern sighed wearily. He ran his fingers through his hair, making no attempt to conceal his exasperation. 'You're right,' he agreed, his tone thick with sarcasm. 'It's only the most common female name in the history of the western world and I have two of them in my entourage of twenty slaves. Next to those kind of odds, a lottery win looks like heads or tails.'

Without saying another word, Simon rolled up the contract and slipped the ribbon back over it.

'If you don't trust me, we can call this arrangement off now.' McGivern was reaching into his pocket and Simon could see he was about to retrieve the number three diamond. His tone had become defensive, as though he had finally grown tired of the constant slurs on his character. 'If you're going to tarnish my good name, then I'll let you have your diamond back and we can say –'

'We don't have to call it off,' Simon said quickly. It had taken a lot of soul-searching for him to decide that this was the right gift to acquire for Frankie. Now that the transaction had finally been made, he had no desire to go back on it.

It was only when McGivern moved his hand away from his pocket that Simon wondered if the man had been bluffing. An annoying voice at the back of his mind told him that McGivern wouldn't have returned the diamond anyway. It spoke with such conviction that he had to believe it. Hating the way that it made him feel cheated, Simon allowed McGivern to lead him out of the pilothouse and into the sunshine.

'Look at them,' McGivern said and grinned as he

stepped towards the side of the boat. There was a note of genuine reverence in his voice and his smile bordered on affectionate. 'These aren't just our peers, Simon. These are the dominatrices who hold us in high esteem because we own castles.'

Simon stuffed the deed into a pocket inside his frock-coat and followed McGivern to the railings. While they were talking in the pilothouse, the harbour had filled up. A fourth helicopter was hovering over the island and Simon guessed that it was struggling to find a place to land. Casting his eye over the brimming port, he studied the plethora of yachts and motorboats that now jostled side by side. An uneasy ball squirmed in his stomach and he tried to blame it on sea-sickness.

'How many did you invite?'

McGivern shrugged. 'I sent an open invitation to a dozen or so clubs. Aside from inviting a few personal friends, I also constructed a little web page that should have reached those who weren't on the A or B lists.'

'There are so many of them,' Simon whispered incredulously.

McGivern nodded, his eyes beaming excitedly. 'And they're desperate for a sale.'

Simon was shaking his head, trying to cope with the sight and all its implications. 'It's hard to believe you could get so many morally bankrupt souls together on one occasion.'

'Morally bankrupt?' McGivern sounded appalled. 'Dear God, Simon, where do you come up with these ridiculous ideas? These are the finest people on God's earth. These are the people who yearn to be our peers.'

Simon sniffed. 'They're slave traders,' he whispered. He shook his head unhappily, surprised by his own feelings of animosity. 'I felt bad enough swapping the diamond for number three, but right now I feel like a paragon of virtue when I see all these.'

McGivern shook his head. 'Your problem is that you think too much. You've lost perspective, Simon.'

'We're talking about the slave trade. What perspective is there to lose?'

'Try and keep step with the rest of us here in the twenty-first century. These slaves aren't being persecuted because of their race, creed or colour. They are men and women, blacks and whites, atheists and believers among them, with the same cross-section as their masters. They're all here for one simple reason. It's nothing to do with the exploitation of one section of society by another. These slaves and masters are here because they want to be here. This auction wouldn't exist if the stock weren't willing submissives.'

Simon knew McGivern was right but he still felt uncomfortable.

'The normal people do exactly the same thing when they grow bored with their lovers,' McGivern went on. 'If they don't try swapping or swinging, they test the waters of adultery. Our fellow dominatrices here have reached that same state of ennui in their relationships but they're dealing with it in a far more civilised manner.'

Simon considered this and decided McGivern was again probably right but he was loathe to voice such an opinion. 'I suppose that the promise of the auctioneer's privilege and a hefty commission had little to do with your decision to organise this.'

McGivern laughed. 'Those factors may have helped me to make the sensible choice,' he conceded. 'But let's not tarnish the day by talking about money. Let me introduce you to some of our fellow dominatrices. I'll soon assuage your fears about this venture.'

Simon sniffed unhappily. 'I'd rather not.'

McGivern wasn't listening. He was waving at the boat that rocked against theirs and calling for attention. Simon watched a submissive girl approach the side of the boat and stare across at them. She was down on all fours, a thick, spiked collar around her neck with matching cuffs at her wrists and ankles. The rest of her outfit was made up of figure-hugging Lycra, revealing all the swells and curves of her desirable frame. Placing her arms on the railing, she gazed across at them with an expectant smile on her lips.

'Permission to board?' McGivern called.

'I can't give you permission, sir,' the girl replied. 'I don't have the authority.'

'Now that's what I call servility,' McGivern told Simon. 'She knows her place, doesn't she?'

Simon shook his head in disgust.

'Fetch your master,' McGivern called. He wrapped an arm around Simon's shoulders and told the submissive, 'The organiser of this auction and I want to examine your stock.'

Simon felt a sickening lurch in the pit of his stomach. His nausea had nothing to do with being on board a boat. He watched the submissive climb down from the railings and scamper across the deck on all fours.

'There's going to be some marvellous stock here,' McGivern said cheerfully. He was rubbing his hands together and his gleeful anticipation should have been infectious. Simon was only thankful that McGivern was rubbing his hands.

'You can smell the quality in the air, can't you?'

'We've done our deal,' Simon said quietly. 'Can't we make an excuse and tell this lot to go away? I can find some other way of delivering my present to Frankie.'

McGivern was shaking his head. 'It's not that easy now. The wheels have been set in motion. Take heart, though. The auction should be finished by the end of today. Tomorrow morning you and the ...' He paused and checked himself. 'You and Frankie can talk about her present.'

Simon opened his mouth to speak. He had stayed silent for long enough. A barrage of insults was threatening to rush from him and now was the time to vent all of them. Before he could speak, a movement from the neighbouring boat caught his attention.

'And what can I do for you gentlemen?'

She stood in a splendour of scarlet PVC. Her hair had been coloured to a vibrant fire-engine red that complemented her figure-hugging outfit. The garish catsuit clung to every contour of her body, revealing broad hips, a narrow waist and massive breasts. Her face was hidden behind dark glasses and her crimson lips were set in an austere line. With her chin tilted upwards, and her nostrils flaring, she was a portrait of arrogance.

Simon grinned at her. The insults he had been about to release on McGivern were forgotten.

In one hand, she held three dog leads. Attached to each was a submissive scampering around her ankles. The submissives were all dressed like the one that McGivern had spoken to. Wearing only collars and cuffs with their tight-fitting uniforms, the trio stumbled around the deck. Simon could see that the two females were trying to behave for their mistress but the male was sniffing playfully at them and making a nuisance of himself. He continued doing this until the woman in red noticed. She hissed a command and the male cowered beneath her ferocious glare. With a surly expression, he lay down at her feet.

Simon watched the scene, wishing it wasn't so luridly fascinating. In spite of McGivern, in spite of Frankie's bad mood, and in spite of the hundred and one other things he needed to do, he could feel himself being drawn into the peculiar world of fetishistic domination on board the neighbouring boat.

'This is the organiser of today's auction,' McGivern called. 'He and I would like to inspect your stock.'

'Climb aboard,' the woman in red said simply. It was hard to gauge her mood through the impenetrable lenses of her sunglasses but Simon could sense disdain in her cool tone. 'You're McGivern, aren't you?'

McGivern's smile widened. His chest puffed out and he leaped over the railings to stand beside her. 'I see that my reputation precedes me,' he declared grandly.

The woman sniffed. 'If the things I've heard about you are true, then you shouldn't be so conceited.'

Simon was pleased to see McGivern momentarily deflated. He leaped over the railings and took the opportunity to introduce himself to the woman. With typical gallantry, he took her proffered hand and stooped to kiss it. Her fingers were long and slender and, once his hand was in her grasp, he found that she was unwilling to let go. She trailed her fingertips against the sensitive flesh of his inner wrist and teased the skin with a subtle caress. He realised that the animosity of her cool tone wasn't directed towards him and that made his smile widen.

'My friends call me Babs,' she told him. 'You're Simon, aren't you?'

He nodded, startled. 'How do you know me? Have we met?'

She shook her head. 'Your picture was on your web page.'

Simon cast a bitter glance at McGivern but it went unnoticed. McGivern was reaching down to pat the raven-haired head of a kneeling submissive.

'Do you live here alone, Simon?' Babs asked.

'Simon's something of a recluse,' McGivern said, glancing up. 'Aren't you, Simon?'

'I try to be,' Simon replied. He fixed McGivern with a meaningful glare.

'He doesn't usually allow guests on the island,' McGivern explained. 'So we can all feel highly honoured that he's allowed us to hold our auction here.'

'I already feel honoured,' Babs replied. She still held Simon's hand and her caress was becoming more intimate. He longed to snatch his fingers away from her but he knew that it would look like the height of bad manners. Now, as he studied the dark lenses covering her eyes, he felt sure he could see beyond them. The dark circles of her pupils stared back at him and, in that moment, he could see a promise gleaming in her shaded eyes. It was an exciting image.

'Tell us about your stock, Babs,' McGivern suggested. 'Are you selling?'

Babs sneered at him then turned to Simon with a smile. 'Do you want to hear about my stock?'

Her offer was tempting, not just because of the husky inflection in her words. There was something new and intriguing about Babs and her peculiar entourage. It offered a distraction from the minutia of day-to-day life at the castle and Simon found himself longing to hear whatever she had to say. Surprised by his own enthusiasm, Simon said, 'You possess a very obedient troupe, Babs. I'd be fascinated to hear all about them.'

Babs stepped closer to him and placed a hand around his waist.

For the first time, Simon noticed that her catsuit was designed with a zipper that went from her cleavage to her crotch. With his free hand, he could have teased the zipper's tag downwards. The idea had a lurid appeal and he had to will himself not to reach out for the tag between her breasts. The other thing stopping him was the certainty that Babs would have slapped his hand away.

'I train each of them personally and individually,' Babs told him. Her lips hovered close to his as she spoke. 'I know a lot of people who use cruelty to break a slave, but I'm not that perverse. I prefer to meet my goals with a system of kindness and rewards.'

'How noble,' Simon whispered. He knew that if he pushed his lips forward he could kiss her. The idea was hard to resist but he held himself just out of her reach, savouring her nearness. 'How noble and liberated.'

'Look at him,' Babs said, pointing to the boat's hull.

Simon glanced in that direction, wondering if she was gesturing at McGivern. McGivern had disappeared, and Simon found himself staring at the boat behind them. He didn't recognise the owner and at first he found it difficult to share Babs' antipathy. This wasn't the only vessel that bore a skull-and-crossbones flag. The boat was named *The Amazon Maiden* and the owner sat on top of the pilothouse, flanked by a pair of blondes with two brunettes kneeling by his side.

'They call him Captain Wilde,' Babs explained. 'He's got a wicked reputation. They say he's a real bastard.'

Studying him, Simon was touched by a chill of unease. Captain Wilde, sprawled in a thronelike chair, was basking in the adoration of his submissives. Although he looked like he was sunbathing, he wore black, leather pants and a matching waistcoat that accentuated his well-toned biceps. Each of the brunettes was performing a manicure on their master whilst the blondes massaged his shoulders and neck.

Catching the attention of one blonde, Simon winked at her.

He was rewarded by a sneer laden with contempt. Shrugging off the slight, he tried to find something about Captain Wilde and his crew that wasn't unsettling or dislikeable. Seeing the second blonde curl her lip at him, Simon realised it was going to be a fruitless search. From past experience, he knew that those masters who kept arrogant slaves were usually the most unpleasant. McGivern was one such master and, having known him for more than a year, Simon still had to find one likeable quality in the man's makeup.

'See, he's a real bastard,' Babs said. 'And cruel and malicious with it.'

Simon had to agree. It wasn't because the captain was dressed in black leather, or that he was tweaking the exposed nipple of one attendant slave. Black leather was *de rigueur* for most of the dominatrices that Simon knew, and his own pants, boots and frock coat were cut from the same fabric. Similarly, if Simon had wanted to watch slaves being abused, he didn't doubt that there were far worse atrocities happening on other boats. He could hear the whippings and the pleasurably punished wails from neighbouring vessels, and he knew that the cries were inspired by chastisements more severe than simple nipple-tweaking. But this man looked more menacing than was typical. Captain Wilde was casually employing a vicious brand of cruelty and it made Simon uncomfortable.

Casting a final gaze at the boat, he decided that there was simply some indefinable and unsettling aura about *The Amazon Maiden* and her crew.

'I don't think you can properly break a slave with cruelty,' Babs explained. 'I train mine with a reward system.'

Simon turned and regarded her expectantly. Her lips were painfully close to his and, as she spoke, he could feel the caress of each word against his chin.

'Do you want me to show you how I reward them?'

'I think that would be quite entertaining,' he said quietly. She was still holding his hand. He tried to draw it away from her but he found that Babs made a point of keeping hold of him. She was following his fingers to the swell of his erection. Behind the dark lenses of her sunglasses, he could see that her eyes were sparkling.

'I excite you, don't I?'

'I think we excite one another,' he replied as she traced the bulge in his pants.

She nodded agreement. Turning her face away, she called, 'Mandy. Here, girl.'

The raven-haired submissive was by her side in an instant. Simon barely cast a glance at the slave, content to watch Babs. He had seen Frankie force her will on to submissives, and the sight invariably aroused him. It was always the dominatrix – and not her charge – that fired his interest. There was something intriguing about watching a skilled dominatrix work a slave, and he doubted that Babs would disappoint him. The effortless command she had shown so far hinted at uncompromising authority. His stiffness grew more rigid.

'Does Mandy want a treat?' Babs asked the submissive.

Mandy nodded, her grin widening. She cast her gaze between her mistress and Simon. In her wordless expression, he could see she was desperate to please them both.

'Have you been a good girl?' Babs asked.

Mandy nodded again.

'Very well,' Babs allowed. She reached for the tag of her zipper and began to pull it down. 'If you've been a good girl, then you may have your treat.'

Simon watched, captivated by the naked flesh Babs was revealing. Her breasts were encased in a bra that looked too flimsy for its gargantuan task. The scarlet lace was straining beneath the pressure of her huge, rounded orbs. Like crescents over the delicate trim of each cup, Simon could see the dark shadow of her areolae. The thrust of her nipples distorted the lacy fabric and he found himself fascinated by the sight of her stiffening buds. His attention would have lingered there if he hadn't seen that Babs was pulling the zip down even further. Her exposed skin was sun-bronzed; her tan was unbroken. His erection grew harder.

She pulled the zip down even further, revealing the golden flesh of her stomach. 'Kneel like a good girl, Mandy,' Babs encouraged. 'Kneel like a good girl, and you may have your treat.' She had brought the zip down to the crotch of her outfit and Simon held his breath as he watched. The front panel of her thong was now visible and he could see it was the same vibrant scarlet as her bra and catsuit. Tendrils of crimson hair were curled behind the lacy fabric. What lay beneath those hairs was hidden in inviting shadows.

Babs took her hand from the zipper and reached for the front of her panties. She pulled the gusset to one side and revealed herself to the kneeling submissive. Simon was treated to a momentary glimpse of the woman's brightly coloured pubic thatch. As Babs raked her nails through the forest of hairs, he saw her pussy lips pouting open.

'Here's your treat, Mandy,' Babs whispered. 'Be a good girl and lap it all up.'

The slave responded without hesitating. She pushed her mouth forward and Simon could see she had slipped out her tongue in preparation. As she lowered her face, the slave's smile broadened.

Babs drew a deep breath and pushed herself towards him. The swell of her breasts pressed against his chest and he could sense the depth of her arousal. As the slave plunged her tongue into her mistress's cleft, Babs pressed her mouth over Simon's.

Her excitement was evident in the way that she kissed him and the depth of the tremors that shook her body. From the corner of his eye, Simon saw that the raven-haired submissive was nodding her head up and down, and he wondered how many hours she had spent perfecting her skill.

Babs held herself rigid and then shivered. Her tongue

slipped between his lips and she began to explore him hungrily. Simon left her hand resting over his groin where she playfully rubbed at his length. For the first time since they had shaken hands, Simon managed to extricate his fingers from her grasp. He reached for her breast and began to trace her nipple through the lace.

Babs released a shuddering sigh. She broke their kiss for a moment before calling, 'Rex. Here, boy.'

Simon blinked but before he could ask if she was talking to him, she had pressed her mouth back over his. His fingers slid inside her bra and her flesh began to yield beneath his caress. A man approached them, looking cowed and submissive.

'I've been training Rex to fellate,' Babs whispered. The huskiness of her voice had deepened and Simon could hear that she was swimming in a sea of euphoria. 'Would you like to try him?' She worked her hand against his erection as she asked the question, rubbing her wrist purposefully against the head of his hidden shaft.

'I'd like that,' Simon told her. He moved his mouth from hers and lowered his head to her breast. Deftly, he began to tongue the tip of her exposed nipple.

Babs gasped, then moved his head away. 'Simon, no!' she insisted. 'I have a girl to do that for me.'

She was speaking to him as though he was an inferior, but he forgave the indiscretion. Grinning broadly, he asked, 'Can your girl do it as well as I do?'

'She can do it better,' Babs said decisively. 'She can do it better because I've trained her. Tara!'

The second submissive appeared by her mistress's side. Taking in the situation at a glance, she moved her face to where it was needed and began to suckle on Babs' exposed breast.

Simon watched and, although he doubted the submissive could be doing a better job than he had intended, he conceded that Babs seemed to be receiving a good deal of pleasure from it. She moved her cerise fingernails back to his length and began to rub his erection to a state of full hardness. Immersing herself in pleasure, Babs pressed her mouth back over his and began to work on the zipper at his fly.

'My submissives know how to please their superiors,' she explained. She slid her tongue over his lips as she said the words. 'If you were a woman, you'd kill for the pleasures that Mandy and Tara can bestow upon you. And when you feel Rex's gorgeous little mouth around you, you'll agree that I have the most satisfying troupe of submissives in the world.' She tugged the zip down and her fingers snaked inside his trousers.

His erection felt like a burning poker against her cool fingertips but his stiffness didn't waver. Contrarily, he felt his pulse quicken as she tugged his cock out of his pants.

'Be a good boy and please the man, Rex,' Babs said absently.

Simon glanced down and saw Rex beaming up at him. He watched the man draw his tongue over Babs' hand. Rex's lips shifted over her index finger and then suddenly Simon was treated to the warmth of the man's mouth against his stiffness.

Stroking his hand against Rex's cheek, Simon allowed the pleasure to wash over him. He returned Babs' kisses with the same ferocity in which they were given. Rex had circled his lips around Simon's length. The pleasure was debilitating and Simon had to admit that Babs had been right about the skills of her submissives.

And yet, despite his bliss, Simon was becoming frustrated. Babs was exquisitely beautiful and he longed to touch and caress her properly. The stiffness of the nipple that still pressed into his chest was unbearably exciting and he longed to tease the bud with his tongue. He quelled an urge to push Tara away from Babs' breast, knowing that this would be unforgivable behaviour. Trying to resist his frustration, he contented himself with the pleasure of the dominatrix's kiss and Rex's fellatio.

Babs was moaning and Simon envied her mounting excitement. With only a little effort, he knew he could have given himself over to the moment and exploded inside Rex's mouth, but he knew his climax had the potential to be much more satisfying. A hunger began to grow inside him and he pressed his mouth close to Babs' ear. 'I want you,' he told her.

She laughed and shook her head. 'I doubt that you do.'

He studied her, surprised that she could say such a thing. 'I don't just want you,' he whispered urgently. 'Right now, I need you.'

Babs shook her head again and smiled evasively. 'Each of my submissives has wanted and needed me,' she explained. 'And they know that there's a price to pay for that pleasure.'

She was hinting at something, but with arousal nagging at his concentration, it was hard to guess what. 'What are you telling me, Babs?' He asked the question in between passionate kisses to her lips and cheeks. 'What are you saying?'

'I'm telling you that I don't fuck my fellow masters,' she said bluntly. 'Those who join me in my boudoir do it as a final act before submitting to me. If you want me for more pleasure than we're enjoying now, I'll happily allow it, but you'll spend the rest of your days on a leash, learning the arts of pleasure like Mandy, Tara and Rex.'

He contemplated her words, suddenly unmindful of the tongue against his shaft and the exciting kisses on his lips. 'How can someone so beautiful be so cruel?'

She shook her head and stroked a hand against his cheek. 'It's not cruelty. You'd have a life of constant rewards and delightful servitude, but I doubt it would suit your tastes.'

'You're right, but couldn't you make an exception for me? I couldn't be submissive to anyone, but I so desperately want to have you.'

Babs shook her head. 'I'm a dominatrix,' she reminded him. 'I don't know any other woman who bears that title and would give herself to a man without the promise of his submission.'

Her words threatened to spoil his mood. Rex was still sucking on his erection, alternating the pressure of his lips between gentle titillation and vigorous lapping. Without turning his head, Simon could see Tara's mouth teasing Babs' puckered nipple and, by lowering his gaze, he could watch Mandy's tongue plunging through Babs' crimson pussy hairs. But when Babs spoke, Simon found himself thinking about Frankie.

Frankie was a more intimidating dominatrix than Babs, and she and Simon had spent one glorious night together. More than being just a glorious night, it was an experience he had been longing to revisit. Hearing Babs now decry any female dominatrix who would allow such a thing made him feel distant from the woman.

Babs must have sensed his mood change because Simon could see a conciliatory edge on her smile. There was a measure of kindness inflecting her tone as she said, 'If you want to feel some pussy around that shaft of yours, I'll let you use Mandy. I've had many masters tell me that she has a gorgeous little hole.'

Before he could stop it from happening, Simon felt his shaft being pulled from Rex's mouth. The slaves were an attentive crew and they repositioned themselves with the minimum of fuss, guiding Simon into position while their mistress made herself comfortable by kneeling on the deck over Mandy, who continued lapping at her pussy. Rex and Tara went to either side of their mistress and pressed their mouths over her breasts.

Babs stared across at him, clearly savouring her position of authority and silently encouraging him to participate. Mandy had stripped herself of her Lycra uniform and lay naked on the deck. Her flesh shone with a lustre of sweat that was clearly part warmth and part excitement. Simon could see what was expected of him but he waited until Mandy had bucked her hips up before he kneeled to join the four of them. Glancing between the submissive's legs, he saw the sodden hairs of her pussy lips which were peeled open to reveal her arousal.

Simon moved between her legs and rubbed the head of his cock against the slave. She writhed beneath him and struggled to push herself closer to his threat of entry.

'Don't tease her,' Babs admonished. 'That's not nice.'

Simon laughed and, with a thrust of his hips, plunged into Mandy. The submissive's groans were muted between her mistress's legs and Simon watched her fists beat weakly against the wooden deck as he pushed himself deeper.

Babs leaned over the slave and pressed her mouth over Simon's. As she writhed over Mandy's face, she pushed her tongue into Simon's mouth. The pair of them savoured the intimacy as they both took pleasure from the woman beneath them.

Simon rode slowly in and out of Mandy's hole, pleased to hear her muffled cries of enjoyment. Babs made throaty sounds of excitement, reaching for his chest and caressing him through his shirt. Tara and Rex continued to suckle at her, fondly caressing their mistress as she hurtled towards her climax.

'Perhaps you should reconsider,' Babs breathed. 'You'd make a marvellous addition to my crew.'

Simon pulled his penis out of the slave and stroked his length along the lips of Mandy's wetness before plunging back inside her. He grinned at Babs and shook his head. 'I'm too much the dominatrix to be happy being subordinate.'

Babs was trembling and he could see she was losing herself in the throes of bliss. Mandy was squealing with pleasure beneath him and Tara and Rex were now grunting urgently. 'I'd make you more than happy,' Babs insisted. 'My slaves lead an idyllic life that makes them the envy of every other submissive.'

'I wasn't offering myself as a submissive,' Simon explained. 'I was just offering my services as a brief lover. If her mouth wasn't so full, I'm sure Mandy could tell you what joys you're missing.'

'You're a conceited bastard,' she told him.

He shrugged, sliding deeper into Mandy and relishing the groan of joy she released. 'I'm conceited but it's not misplaced. Perhaps you should reconsider my offer and allow me to become your lover.'

'You say things that tempt me,' Babs whispered. Her words were released through a fixed jaw as she fought against her orgasm.

'How strongly do they tempt you?'

'A lot.'

Simon moved his face from hers and lowered his mouth to Babs' breast. He pushed Rex out of the way and placed his lips over the rigid nub of her nipple, soon teasing the flesh between his teeth while his tongue danced against her bud.

'No! Yes!' she shrieked, shivering as the pleasure swept over her.

Simon heard the submissive beneath him groan again. Through a haze of excitement, he realised he had pushed hard inside her as he nudged Babs beyond the brink of her climax. As well as encouraging the mistress to her release, Mandy was trembling with her own orgasmic pleasure. Simon broke the kiss and stared expectantly at Babs. He slid his unspent erection from Mandy's wetness. Babs' gaze was focused on his length and he could read her thoughts as though she was an open newspaper.

'You want to play with me, but not become my submissive?' she reiterated.

'It's not such an indecent thing to propose, is it?'

'It's obscene,' she replied with a giggle. 'But you're tempting me.' With one hand she reached out and stroked his shaft. He was still slippery with the slave's arousal but that only added a delightful sensuality to her caress.

'Simon!' The voice came from the port in a harsh and desperate cry that cut through his good mood like a cleaver.

Babs studied him expectantly then turned her attention to the voice as his name was called again.

He glanced towards the port and saw who was calling him. Grace stood on the shore, glaring at him fixedly. She was embracing a weary-looking redhead, and Simon could see that she had a foreboding frown on her face. He stood up and fastened his trousers before waving a hesitant hand in acknowledgement.

'I'm going to revoke your bloody licence if you don't get here now, Simon,' Grace called. Her cheeks were flushed with furious spots of colour and her tone was outraged.

'I'm going to do that and a lot more, do you understand me?'

Simon glanced at Babs and gave her an apologetic smile.

Babs shrugged and said, 'I'll see you at the auction. Perhaps we can play again then?'

'I'll look forward to it,' he assured her. With a frown, he started towards Grace, wondering what could have inspired such fury and how he was expected to deal with it. At the back of his mind, he suspected that Frankie was involved, but he hoped his intuition was wrong. If Frankie had upset Grace, Simon knew there would be no way of placating the woman.

It never occurred to him to wonder where McGivern had gone.

Six

Frankie sat on a corner of the dining table, enjoying the leg of game that she had retrieved from the floor. After being macerated in a puddle of Chianti, its flavour was distinctly enhanced, and Frankie wondered if she had accidentally created a new recipe. It was only a passing thought; her mind was more occupied with the wealth of sensations that number three inspired as she nuzzled between her legs.

'I've been wanting to do this since we last saw one another, mistress,' number three told her. 'I didn't think I'd get the chance.'

Frankie swallowed a mouthful of pheasant and stroked her fingers through the slave's hair. 'I didn't think we'd able to, either,' she confessed. 'But it's happening now, so let's both enjoy it.'

'It'll never happen again, will it?'

Frankie shook her head and tried not to think of the finality in the slave's words. 'You still sound defeated,' she said. 'Take that tone out of your voice. If we're going to win, we have to think like winners.' She took another bite from the drumstick to show that she had grown tired of talking and splayed her pussy lips apart to encourage the slave to tongue the pulsing bud of her clitoris.

'Sage words, Frankie,' McGivern said, as he entered the room. 'Sage words indeed. And what is it that you're hoping to win?'

Frankie glared at him, pushing the slave away as she tried to cover her exposed body. 'You still haven't

102

mastered that trick of knocking on doors, have you?' she sneered.

Sprawling on the floor, number three stared from Frankie to her master, an expression of horror etched on her features. Frankie hardly noticed the slave's fright as she swallowed the remainder of her pheasant and tried to conceal herself from McGivern's lecherous gaze. Her sex still tingled with excitement but the arousal dissipated as her outrage grew.

'I think it's lucky for me that I haven't mastered the art of knocking.' McGivern grinned. 'Just think what I'd have missed if I had.'

Frankie's upper lip curled and her eyes narrowed into slits. Briskly, she smoothed her skirt down to cover her sodden pubic bush. Her leather jacket had been discarded as she and number three reacquainted themselves, and Frankie reached for it angrily. 'Don't tell me you've become a Peeping Tom these days.'

'Hardly,' he grunted. 'Although I have to admit, you do present a splendid figure. But that wasn't what I was referring to. You've committed a crime Frankie, possibly the worst crime that a dominatrix can commit against another master.'

Frankie had the good grace to blush, knowing that he was correct. 'You're right, and as much as it galls me, I have to apologise for that. I shouldn't have taken advantage of your slave without your consent. I'll make reparation for the injustice I've done you by sending you two of –'

'Let's not talk about reparation,' McGivern broke in. His tone was easy and his smile was unnaturally friendly. 'Reparation makes it sound as though we harbour antagonism for one another, and that's not the way things are between you and I, is it, Frankie?'

She looked at him warily. That she had wronged him didn't really trouble her, but she realised there was more at stake on this occasion. That was the only reason she had made an offer of reparation. McGivern moved closer and Frankie could see his smile was widening. She had shrugged her arms back into her leather jacket and fastened the zipper modestly over herself. Nevertheless, as McGivern stared at her, she felt sure he was able to see through the clothes and study her naked body. The sensation was so strong that she felt a shiver of revulsion. In any other circumstances, she would have told him to stop leering at her and fuck off. She hadn't yet given him permission to step on to the island and that reminder hovered on her lips. But she chose not to voice it.

'What is it that you're wanting, McGivern?'

'I want us to be friends,' he said quietly. 'That's not asking too much, is it?'

'Do you want me to answer honestly or politely?'

His smile vanished and the warmth in his eyes disappeared in a blink. With lightning reflexes, McGivern reached out and grabbed a fistful of number three's dark locks. The slave shrieked as he dragged her up from the floor to his side.

Frankie wanted to step in and help the slave but she knew she couldn't. Using a master's slave without his permission was a serious enough crime and alone could have seen her ostracised from those few sections of society she still chose to frequent. To intercede during a punishment was a far worse violation of the rules and would only make the situation worse. She remained seated on the corner of the table, watching McGivern and his slave and telling herself that she couldn't interfere. The impulse to stand up and free number three was so strong that Frankie trembled with the effort of self-control.

'You should have known better than to do anything for her,' McGivern growled. He had pushed his face close to number three's and his angry features were reflected in the depths of her eyes. 'It's a punishable offence and, as you know, I never miss an opportunity to punish.'

Number three regarded him silently. Frankie could see that her hair was straining at the follicles but her face remained inscrutable.

'You shouldn't be too hard on her,' Frankie broke in. She knew it was wrong to interfere but it was impossible

104

for her to sit on the sidelines and do nothing. 'She's done nothing wrong; she was simply obeying me. The whole incident was all my doing and number three refused repeatedly.'

McGivern didn't bother looking at Frankie. He stared menacingly at the slave as he spoke. 'Clearly she didn't refuse enough. She needs reminding who wields the whip in my household. There's only one proper way for her to learn that lesson.'

Frankie closed her eyes and wondered if there was a way of stopping this before it went any further. If number three had been her slave, she would have happily chastised her for any misdemeanour, but not in the way that McGivern was planning. If number three had been her slave, the punishment would have been meted out carefully, exactly as the slave needed it, and done so that it satisfied them both. Frankie could see that McGivern was struggling with a malicious rage and that he intended to make number three suffer. The realisation that she really couldn't intervene left Frankie feeling cold and impotent.

'I'm sorry, master,' number three whispered. 'Please forgive me.' She managed to say the words without any inflection of pain or apology and Frankie realised this was only going to antagonise McGivern further. Closing her eyes again, she tried willing the slave to make her plea sound more convincing but it was a futile effort and, when she opened her eyes, she saw that the situation hadn't improved.

McGivern shook his head, continuing to glower at his slave. 'It's too late for apologies and forgiveness.' Reaching into his jacket pocket with his free hand he retrieved a gag and pushed it into number three's hands. 'You know what to do with this.'

'This is unnecessary.' Frankie tried to make her tone placatory but it would have been a difficult task at the best of times. With her bad mood rising and her antagonism towards McGivern not having fully abated, it was miraculous that she hadn't screamed the words at him. 'Perhaps we can come to some arrangement?'

He glanced at her and there was something in his expression that Frankie found unsettling. If she hadn't known better, she could have sworn that he had been waiting for her to say those words. The twisting of his eyebrows and the knowing glint of his smile all hinted at his having anticipated this suggestion.

Reluctantly, McGivern shook his head and turned his angry frown back to number three. 'I don't think we could come to an arrangement. This is my slave and she's committed a punishable offence. We all know that there's only one way to deal with it, and that's just what I'm going to do.' He released his grip on the slave's hair and snatched the gag from her fingers. 'Seeing as you're making no attempt to do this, I'll do it for you, shall I?' Without waiting for the slave's reply, he started fastening the gag in her mouth.

Frankie had seen him use similar gags before. This was a large rubber ball, its size designed to fit perfectly in a submissive's mouth for absolute silence. He tugged the straps tight around the back of number three's head and fastened the small buckle. 'Put your hands behind your back,' he growled.

Number three did as he asked. With her back to him, she lifted her wrists as high as she could so that her master didn't have to bend to secure her.

Frankie watched, wishing she didn't feel so ineffective. The slave was obeying as though it was her destiny to suffer beneath McGivern, and Frankie knew that number three deserved a better master. This idea suddenly gave her the courage to speak out loud. 'What if she had a different master?'

McGivern glanced up from the handcuffs and again, Frankie was struck by the thought that he had been waiting for her to say this. There was no surprise in his expression, only that smug lilt to his smile which confirmed to Frankie that her suspicion was correct. 'What are you suggesting, Frankie?'

'What if she was my slave?'

'She's not,' he said simply. 'She's mine.'

'What if you were to sell her to me?'

He looked as though he was considering this, then shook his head. Turning back to the handcuffs, he snapped the last bracelet in place. 'I couldn't ask you to do that. You've apologised for your crime and I've forgiven you. I simply need to punish number three and then the matter will be over and done with. That's the way that civilised people like you and I deal with things, isn't it?' Glancing around the banquet hall, he asked, 'Have you got a spare whip or a crop in here?'

She could have said no but there would have been little point. Decorating one wall was a display of whips, crops and canes which McGivern was already admiring. Wearily, she pointed at them and he thanked her politely. He snapped an abrupt command at number three and the slave kneeled on the floor while he marched over to the mounted arsenal.

'This is quite a selection you have here,' he grinned. 'All right to use anything that takes my fancy?'

'Why can't we make a deal of some sort?' Frankie asked. She remembered her own plaintive voice telling Simon not to make deals with McGivern. But that seemed unimportant now. 'You don't have to subject her to this and since you've brought her to this auction of yours –'

'You know about the auction?'

'It's a small island and word travels fast,' she explained. If she had implicated Jane in this revelation, Frankie would have the suffering of two submissives on her conscience. Trying to sound amicable, she said, 'Let me acquire number three from you.'

'You want her badly, don't you?'

Frankie was stung by the comment. It was too close to the truth for her liking. Uncomfortable with the thought of revealing her feelings to him, Frankie shrugged and said, 'That's immaterial, isn't it? Can't you just treat my request like you would a normal buyer?'

McGivern reached for a cat-o'-nine-tails from the wall and pulled it down. He admired it for a moment, a smile teasing his lips as he toyed with its cruel strands. Curling his fingers around its length, he tested its weight and his smile widened. With a brisk motion, he flicked the whip through the air and its harsh tips scratched the tense atmosphere. 'Nice piece of equipment,' he told her. 'You keep a good stock here, Frankie.'

'Let me acquire the slave,' Frankie pleaded. 'We can call it my way of compensating for the injustice that I've done you.'

'You have a soft heart,' McGivern decided. 'But I also know that it's a lot stronger than your bank account. Even if I wanted to, I couldn't sell number three to you because you simply couldn't afford her.' He stepped behind the slave and stroked his hand over her bare backside.

His fingers caressed the jewellery that penetrated her pussy lips and Frankie saw that number three was still sodden with arousal. The sight of McGivern preparing to chastise the slave fuelled protective feelings that she had never experienced before. She couldn't physically intercede, but Frankie chewed her lower lip and tried to think of another gambit. 'I was thinking of taking you to court for the money that you owe Simon and me.' She tried to make the words sound firm yet conversational but annoyance was prevalent in each syllable. 'Let me have the slave and I'll forget all about the litigation.'

'I don't think so,' he laughed. 'You seem to forget that you have no case to pursue. I didn't sell this castle to you. You and Simon won it in a bet. If that's the best offer you can make, then I'd thank you not to interrupt me any more.' He tapped his hand against the peachlike orbs of the slave's backside and stepped back. Number three's cheeks trembled beneath his casual pat. Frankie watched the slave close her eyes in quiet preparation for the punishment.

Holding the whip behind himself, the muscles in McGivern's arm stiffened as he prepared to hurl the cat-o'-nine-tails at his submissive.

Frankie ground her teeth together and reached for a cigar. She glared at McGivern, wishing her frantic thoughts would present her with the best course of action.

He was still sizing up the slave's backside and, from her own experience in similar positions, she knew he was trying to decide which cheek to aim for. Number three kneeled on the floor, seeming resigned to her fate, and that only made Frankie feel even more ineffectual.

'Six of the best,' he snapped. 'Three for each cheek. I think that should be enough for starters, and then we can begin the punishment proper.' McGivern flexed his elbow and prepared to administer the first punishing blow. He was standing two paces away from the slave and, from Frankie's knowledge of the cat, she knew he had picked his position to inflict optimum suffering. After being thrown over a couple of paces, the tips of the whip could land with the force of bullets.

'What is it that you want, McGivern?' Frankie demanded. Without realising it, Frankie had taken hold of his wrist, preventing him from swinging the whip. She pushed her face close to his, unintimidated by the ferocity in his glare. 'You know I haven't got the money and I don't possess anything else I could offer you in exchange for the slave. So what do you want?'

'It depends how much you're willing to give for her.'

She tried not to show her exasperation and resisted the urge to ask if he was deaf or stupid. 'You already know that I don't have any money,' she growled. A suspicious thought crossed her mind and she asked, 'Is it my share of this castle? Is that what you're after?'

He snorted rudely and glanced around the banquet hall with a sneer of disdain. 'I was happy to get this millstone off from around my neck. Don't insult me by trying to throw it back at me.' With a wicked smile he said, 'Trust me, Frankie, it's not your share of this castle that I want.'

He stared at her meaningfully and, beyond his lewd appraisal, she caught sight of that expression again. He was smiling as though he had anticipated this conversation and she sensed that he had already worked it to its logical conclusion in his mind. With mounting frustration, she wished she shared his insight into where it was leading.

'I have nothing else to offer you,' she said thickly. The

109

gleam in his eye was chilling and Frankie had to resist the urge to slap his face. 'I have nothing else that you could possibly want.'

'You're far too modest,' he said stroking the back of his hand against her cheek. 'I'd love to let you take this slave off my hands but I don't think you'd feel comfortable acquiring her unless we made a formal exchange of gifts. Isn't there something you might want to give me in return?'

Frankie stepped back, frozen by the sparkle in his dark eyes. She swallowed and glanced from the whip in his hand to the slave on the floor. Number three had dared to look back over her shoulder and Frankie saw that her eyes were wide with a desperate plea. She knew that the slave wasn't begging for her own sake and Frankie took solace from the submissive's concern.

Frankie glared at him and said, 'You want a fuck, McGivern? Is that it?'

'You have such a coarse way with language,' he told her, shaking his head. 'And if you think that I simply want a fuck, then you're wrong. If I wanted a fuck, I could have one from any of my slaves. From you, I would want a lot more than a mere fuck.'

With a flick of his wrist, he brushed her hand from his arm and drew the whip behind him. His reflexes were fast and, before Frankie had the chance to intervene, he had sliced the cat-o'-nine-tails across number three's backside. The slave stiffened and made a grunting protest around her gag. The whip bit into her with the spatter of leather striking flesh and her arse cheeks were peppered with reddening marks. Number three's back trembled with the exertion of holding herself still.

Frankie stopped herself from rushing to the slave's side. 'There was no need to do that.'

'She's my submissive and there was every need to do that,' he growled. He tested a quizzical smile on her and said, 'That is, unless you want to acquire her.'

'What are you proposing?' Frankie demanded.

'Isn't it obvious?'

'Pretend that I'm really thick and I haven't followed all

your ambiguous clues and hints,' she snarled. She drew on her cigar and contemplated blowing the smoke into his smug face. Knowing that would antagonise him further only made her want to do it more.

'Explain this to you and pretend that you're really thick,' he repeated. 'That shouldn't tax my imagination too greatly.' He laughed into her deepening frown and said, 'I want your submission, Frankie. You want the slave, then you can have her. All that I ask in return is an afternoon's submission from you.'

Frankie glared at him, appalled at the suggestion. 'You can't be serious.'

'I'm deadly serious.' The mirth was gone from his expression and his firm gaze told her that he wasn't joking. 'Think about it for a moment Frankie. I'm sure you'll agree that it's a tempting offer. Think about it and let me know when you've made up your mind.' Turning his gaze away from her, he hurled the whip back behind him then flung it again at number three's exposed backside.

The slave gave a startled cry. She almost fell as the tips crackled against her buttocks.

'There must be something else,' Frankie insisted. She could hear a desperate plea in her voice but she was beyond caring. 'I can have three or four of my slaves do anything for you. I can have –'

'Your submission is the only currency that I'm prepared to accept for this transaction,' he snapped. 'But you have plenty of time to think about it. I still have to kiss her cheeks with the cat another four times. If you haven't come to a decision by then, I'll simply assume that you don't want to acquire her.'

She wanted to call him a heartless bastard but she knew that wouldn't help. She glanced at the slave and saw number three had dared to turn around again. Her eyes were wide with horror and she was shaking her head from side to side. If the gag hadn't been locked in her mouth, Frankie knew that the slave would have been telling her not to make a deal with him. Although she could read the words in the slave's features, Frankie doubted she would

111

have heeded such an instruction, even if it had been screamed in her ear.

McGivern drew the cat back again and branded the slave's backside with flawless accuracy. The tips bit loudly and Frankie saw the angst that etched number three's face as her inscrutable mask was shattered for a moment and she tried to force her body to cope with the indignity of McGivern's chastisement.

'Could you count these for me, Frankie?' McGivern asked slyly. 'Normally I'd have the slave do it, but she's unable to use her mouth. I'd count them myself but I'm too busy thinking about doing this to you.' He reached back with the whip and prepared to slice it through the air again.

Frankie stopped his arm, resting her fingers on his bicep. 'An afternoon's submission in exchange for the slave.'

'Are you taking me up on my generous offer?'

'When?'

'Today. After the auction and before the party.'

'Party?' This was a new development. She wondered if she had missed something. 'What party is this?'

He waved a dismissing hand over her fears. 'There's always a party after these auctions. They turn into such a social occasion that everyone will be expecting it.'

Frankie brushed the party from her mind. It was galling that McGivern could march on to the island having organised an auction and a party without consulting her, but she couldn't waste valuable time thinking about that. She assumed Simon had been in on the rest of the arrangements. Turning her thoughts back to McGivern's proposition, she said, 'What would you expect me to do?'

'I think you know what I do with my submissives,' he laughed. 'Or did you want me to explain so you could get all excited?'

She ignored his deliberate baiting, determined not to commit herself to anything without knowing exactly what he had planned. She drew on her cigar, trying to rationalise her thoughts as she savoured the thick flavour. 'Before I consent to anything, I want an exact itinerary of what you have in mind. I recognised some of those boats in the harbour and I know that a lot of them are your friends. I'm not having you introduce me as your concubine so I can be the subject of a gang bang.'

His face was earnest and he was studying her with more lechery than she had ever seen before. The fact that she was considering his suggestion had obviously excited him and Frankie could see the proof in the bulge at the front of his trousers. 'I wouldn't subject you to anything so vulgar,' he told her. He licked his lips, his eyes never wavering from hers. 'If I got the chance to use you as my submissive, I wouldn't share you with anyone.'

Number three made a protesting sound. The noise broke the silence that had settled between them and Frankie and McGivern turned to her in unison. The slave was shaking her head from side to side again and beseeching Frankie with a heart-wrenching plea.

With a casual flick of his wrist, McGivern snapped the whip at her backside. 'That's for insubordination,' he growled. 'I still owe you two more blows. Now, face the other way and allow us to converse without your garbled input.'

For one moment Frankie thought the slave would defy him. Number three fixed her with a last appeal to refuse. Her eyes were glassy with tears and she continued to shake her head from side to side. When McGivern started to raise the whip again, number three turned away from them. She resumed her kneeling position but now her shoulders were set in a defeated arch.

'Do you want to accept the exchange?' McGivern asked. 'This slave for an afternoon's submission?'

'You haven't told me the itinerary yet,' Frankie reminded him. 'What would you want from me?'

His smile was sickening. He was already studying her as though she was naked but now she could see his imagination had moved further on. In the glimmer of his eyes, she could see he was picturing her bound and degraded as she submitted herself to him.

'There are so many things I've always wanted to do to you, Frankie,' he whispered. 'I'm not sure I'd know where

113

to begin. I've already promised you that it would just be you and me, with no third party involved. Can't you just trust me?'

'I'm contemplating being your submissive for an afternoon,' Frankie reminded him. 'Don't stretch my credulity too far by making me pretend I can trust you.' She could see that the insult stung him but she was beyond caring about his feelings. Drawing on her cigar, she met his deepening frown. 'Tell me what you want from me and I'll consider it.'

He snatched his gaze away from hers and glared at number three's backside. 'That's not the deal I'm offering. You either submit blindly, or you can join the rest of the trash at the auction and watch number three go under the hammer.'

Frankie bunched her fingers into fists, then released them. She could see that there was no option available to her but her mind was still racing to find some alternative. Over the past few months she had contemplated making many sacrifices to attain number three but she had never envisioned herself considering an offer like this one. In a perverse way, she thought McGivern was being uncharacteristically generous. From the little she knew about buying and selling slaves, the stock seldom went cheap and in that respect, his asking price was more than reasonable. However, in a real sense, it was far too high. The idea of having McGivern degrade and humiliate her was so galling it was almost impossible to entertain.

The crack of the whip landed against number three's backside, snatching Frankie's thoughts back to the room. McGivern grinned at her, his eyes beaming with lusty appraisal. 'Have you come to a decision yet?' he asked quietly. 'I'm about to deliver the last blow, and when I've done that, you'll be out of the bidding. I'll be clearing this room and getting it ready for the auction.'

'You're a heartless bastard, McGivern,' Frankie growled.

'Sticks and stones will break my bones –' he began.

'Shall we test that supposition?'

114

His grin widened. He cast his gaze over her body for one final time then shook his head. 'You obviously didn't want her that badly did you? Say goodbye to number three, Frankie. The next time you get a chance to talk to her, she'll be serving under another master.'

It was now or never, Frankie realised. If she didn't submit now she could see that his pride wouldn't allow her a second chance. Although the idea of spending a minute's submission beneath McGivern was sickening and contemplating an entire afternoon left her numb, he was offering such a great reward that she knew she had to accept. Number three had visited her daydreams and attended her night-time fantasies since Frankie first met the slave. Now that she had the chance to own her, it would be madness to miss the opportunity.

McGivern prepared to deliver the final blow. The slave's backside was a sea of blistered red and Frankie tried not to think of the torture that the submissive had already endured. She saw McGivern's muscles flex as he was about to brand her with the cat.

He raised his arm in a sweeping gesture and the whip began to make its descent.

Frankie reached out and stopped him.

McGivern glared at her expectantly.

'An afternoon's submission in exchange for the slave,' she growled. Her cheeks burned crimson as she said the words. 'Is that the deal?'

'Are you accepting my generous offer?'

'If I want the slave, I have no other option, do I?'

He shrugged, a wicked smile teasing his lips. 'You could always leave me alone and hope that someone buys number three as a gift for you.'

'Don't toy with me,' she said scathingly. 'I've agreed to your terms. An afternoon's submission was the price. Let's get the unpleasantness over and done with.'

He shook his head, his grin growing ever broader as he studied her. 'I have an auction to organise first and I'd thank you not to call it unpleasantness, Frankie. It's only going to be unpleasant for one of us.'

115

Seven

Elle watched the scene with apprehension, thankful that Frankie wasn't there to make things worse. Her mistress had a way of exacerbating situations like this one and Elle was grateful that Simon, with his gentle manner and considerate ways, was dealing with Grace.

'I think you should calm down a little, Grace,' Simon said quietly.

'I've just found my daughter, stripped naked, tied to a plough and toiling like a farm-hand,' Grace squawked. 'Don't tell me to calm down, Simon.'

The daughter in question was shivering inside her mother's jacket. The collar was turned up and its long-line cut concealed her buttocks, but Elle still thought she looked like an enticing vision, a desirable figure that Elle had already had the chance to admire. Her long, coltish legs were bare and she hadn't bothered to push her arms into the jacket's sleeves, seeming happier to hold herself protectively as she feigned distress and unhappiness for her mother's satisfaction.

'I'm not just unhappy about this, Simon,' Grace told him. There was an icy edge in her voice. 'I'm annoyed. Extremely annoyed.'

Simon was making a determined effort to console her. He raised his hands in a soothing way and, when he spoke, his words were conciliatory and reassuring. Elle could see it was having no effect on Grace but she admired his persistence.

'I'll find Frankie and see what sort of explanation she has to offer.'

'She can't have any explanation,' Grace screeched. 'Only a madwoman would inflict indecency like that on another human being and madwomen don't give explanations.'

'I think we could deal with this more easily without the hysteria,' Simon said firmly. Elle could see that Grace was bristling at the remark but Simon seemed unmindful. 'Wait on your boat and I'll come back to you once I've found out what happened.'

'We're coming with you,' Grace said firmly.

Elle watched Simon roll his eyes and empathised with his exasperation.

'I don't think that would be wise.'

'Why? Are you wanting to concoct a story while I'm out of earshot?'

'No. I'm thinking of you and your daughter.'

Grace snorted but Simon ignored her rude interruption.

'We have guests at the moment and their appearance and behaviour might be a little more outlandish than you're comfortable with.'

'Outlandish?'

Simon gestured towards the boats in the harbour behind them. Several of the crews were setting down gang-planks and leaping on to the port. Casting her eye over those disembarking, Elle saw a handful of slaves assisting a leather-clad dominatrix from a nearby boat. The dominatrix carried a short, mean-looking paddle and by way of a thank you, he made two of the submissives bend over and suffer a smack to their backsides. There were others climbing from their vessels, but Elle was sure this would be the incident that Grace was looking at. It was an exciting scene, hinting at a world of punishment and retribution that Elle would have loved to explore. However, she doubted that it had inspired the same dark intrigue in the prim woman by Simon's side.

'That's more than outlandish,' Grace whispered. 'That's obscene.'

'Outlandish was the kindest word I could think of,' Simon admitted. 'And I'm sure you'll agree that it's not really the type of company that you, or your daughter, would want to be associating with.'

'We've already associated with that type of people,' Grace said. She scoured him with a meaningful expression. 'That's the reason I'm so unhappy.'

Elle bit her lower lip, sure that the woman had just pushed Simon too far, and fearful of seeing him lose his temper.

'Wait for me on your boat, Grace,' Simon said firmly. 'I'll get Frankie and we can try and discuss this like adults.'

'I'm coming with you. My daughter will wait on the boat but I'm not letting you and that mad bitch construct some wishy-washy excuse to try and placate me.'

Simon rubbed his fingers through his hair. 'If that's the way you want it,' he agreed tiredly. He snapped his fingers and Elle realised he was gesturing for her to approach him. She smiled, pleased that he had noticed her and eager to do whatever he wanted. Unmindful of her own nudity, she stepped quickly towards him.

'Escort Grace's daughter to her boat.'

'That woman's naked,' Grace hissed.

Simon silenced her with a steely flicker of his grey eyes. 'How astute of you to notice. Elle knows how things work on this island and she has the common sense to get your daughter safely to your boat. Would you rather she went there alone?'

'You have a peculiar way of doing things on this island.'

'And because it's an island we normally manage our peculiar ways with very little criticism.'

Elle could hear the cutting inflection in his words and she saw that Grace had the humility to blush. Simon no longer seemed bothered if his words sounded cold or hurtful. His manner was now brisk and his tone had become officious and businesslike. 'If you insist on helping to find Frankie, you'd better follow me, Grace.'

Elle watched the pair of them walk towards the castle and exercised a wary smile on Grace's daughter. Feeling sure that some sort of introduction was called for, in spite of their having met in the cornfields, she said, 'They call me Elle.' Trying to make the gesture appear normal, she offered a welcoming hand.

Grace's daughter returned a scornful sneer. 'I don't care what they call you, and don't think you'll get my name out of me that easily. I already told that nasty woman with the tattoos that I wasn't giving you my name.'

Elle shrugged, unoffended by the antagonism. 'Are we going to the IHS craft?'

The redhead nodded curtly.

Elle started in the direction of the boat, not waiting for her to follow. The harbour was brimming with more boats than she had ever seen and the port was quickly filling up with a menagerie of different people. If Simon hadn't given her an instruction she would have found the time to study the newcomers and gain a little enjoyment from the variety they seemed to offer. As it was, she was happy to admire the beautiful people and their charges from a distance as they climbed from their vessels.

'I'm going to ruin her, you know? I'm going to make her suffer for what she did to me.'

Elle glanced back but said nothing.

'Who does she think she is, abusing people like that?'

'She is the woman who owns fifty per cent of the castle and fifty per cent of the island,' Elle explained. 'Since we are out of the jurisdiction of most countries, I suppose you could say that she is the law and the executioner on this island.'

'I might have known that you'd defend her,' Grace's daughter growled. 'You and she are lovers, aren't you?'

Elle stopped and turned to face her. 'I would thank you to take that sneering tone out of your voice when you speak about the mistress. What she and I were doing in the cornfields was no different to what you were doing with the maid.'

'I wasn't doing anything with the maid. And if you repeat that lie to anyone I swear I'll –'

'What?' Elle barked. 'You will not tell me your name some more?'

They studied one another in silence and Elle could see that the redhead was struggling to understand the argument she had involved herself in. Anyone less arrogant

119

might have deserved her sympathy but Elle could only feel contempt for the spoilt creature in front of her.

'All right,' the girl agreed, starting back towards the boat. 'Perhaps I was wrong to say that, but I'm still going to make that bitch pay.'

Elle said nothing, following quickly and struggling to keep her feelings of contempt to herself.

'She violated me and abused me and –'

'And you did not start complaining until she suggested you do some work for her,' Elle observed dryly.

'I'm not a pervert,' Grace's daughter growled. She stopped walking again and turned to glare at Elle.

'I do not suppose that you are any worse than the rest of us,' Elle allowed. 'When mistress Frankie caught you in the cornfields, you were excited by it, and when she teased you with those corn cobs –'

'I don't want reminding of that.'

'Why not? Are you scared that you will get excited again?'

They considered one another in menacing silence. Elle could see that the redhead was angry by the sparks of fury that fired in her green eyes. She knew it was her position to be submissive but rather than simply quivering beneath the anger of Grace's daughter, she found her loyalty to Simon and Frankie made her defiant on this occasion.

The redhead was the first to break their silence. 'Perhaps you're right,' she said. 'Perhaps it did excite me. But I'm still angry with that woman –'

'Mistress Frankie,' Elle offered.

'Frankie,' she agreed, deliberately omitting the title. 'I'm still angry with Frankie. But I shouldn't take it out on you, especially when you're right about the pleasure involved.' She turned and nodded at the craft behind them. 'This is my boat. Would you care to join me on board for a drink?'

Unhappy with the sudden mood change, Elle stumbled for an excuse. 'I have other chores to perform at the castle,' she began hesitantly.

'Do I have to invite you, or order you?' The redhead's grin widened and she reached forward to caress her hand against Elle's neck. 'You look like you might respond more favourably to an order,' she added thoughtfully.

There was a glint in her green eyes that now replaced her fury. Elle could see the promise of excitement in her smile and, as the redhead raised her arm to reach for her face, she was afforded a glimpse of her concealed nudity. Most of her body was still shrouded in the shadows of her jacket, but Elle made out the shape of her nipples. Both were standing firm and erect. Her obvious arousal hinted at the promise of more than a drink and Elle was torn by a moment's indecision. Her hesitancy quickly passed as she studied the wicked smile she was being graced with.

'Just one drink,' Elle said quietly.

Grace's daughter slowly moved her fingers away, seeming to extract inordinate pleasure from the last moments of the caress. Shaking her head, as if to clear her thoughts, she stepped past Elle and reached for the rope-ladder that hung from the side of the IHS craft. She pulled herself swiftly on to the boat, shrugging the jacket from her shoulders when she reached the deck.

Knowing that she was obliged to follow, Elle climbed up behind her.

'My friend and I are going below deck.' The girl was talking to the boat's captain and her firm tone and offhand manner showed that she was used to speaking down to inferiors. 'We are not to be disturbed while we're down there, do you understand?'

The captain regarded her naked body greedily. Although he was making a determined effort not to study her nudity, his cheeks had turned red and an embarrassing bulge was distorting the front of his pants. 'Very well, miss,' he agreed. 'Will your mother be joining us soon?'

'I neither know nor care. Just follow my instructions and see that we're not disturbed.' She reached out and wrapped an arm around Elle's waist, pressing her naked body close.

Elle swallowed nervously, wondering where all this was leading and trying to decide if she should extricate herself from the situation before things developed any further. She knew that Frankie didn't approve of submissives doing

121

anything without permission, but she was also aware that Frankie wasn't on hand to offer or withhold approval. The pleasure awaiting her might be worth the penalty of Frankie's unhappiness. Her decision was made when the redhead leaned closer to kiss her cheek.

Warm lips caressed the lobe of her ear and Elle gasped, surprised by how responsive her body was to such subtle stimuli. She knew that the captain was still watching and she saw his stiffness grow as he leered at their intimacy.

'See that we aren't disturbed, and I might show you my gratitude later,' Grace's daughter told him.

'Very well, miss,' the captain agreed, wiping his hand over a sweating brow. 'I'll look forward to that.'

Elle caught a final glimpse of his face: he was contemplating their naked bodies with lurid intent. Then she was dragged from the deck and taken through the main hatch to the quarters below. Acting as an obliging host, the redhead poured drinks for them both before urging Elle to join her in a padded chair barely large enough to accommodate the pair of them. They squeezed close and Elle was acutely aware of her host's body touching hers. Their thighs pressed together and their arms constantly nudged as each girl sipped her own wine.

Clearly content with this arrangement, the redhead asked, 'What sort of things do you do here on the island?' She half turned for an answer, and one nipple casually stroked against Elle's bare body.

Elle couldn't decide if the gesture was accidental or deliberate but she had no problems assessing its effect. Her body was suddenly tingling with anticipation and, judging from the glint in her host's smile, she didn't think her hopes would be disappointed. 'We do many things here on the island,' she began. 'There is work to do in the fields and Frankie and Simon both require many chores to be performed.'

'That's not what I meant.' The redhead moved her face closer.

The boat's gentle rocking motion gave their every movement a rhythm that was disturbingly exciting, subtle but sufficient to make their bodies sway together. For Elle, each second of casual contact reminded her of their nudity.

'You work for Frankie, yes?'

Elle nodded.

'But your relationship seems more sexual than a normal employee and employer relationship.'

'Of course,' Elle said, surprised that something so simple needed to be explained. 'Frankie is a dominatrix. I am one of her submissives.'

The redhead's eyes widened. 'Like you read about in the books and see in those seedy films?' To make herself more comfortable in the chair, she draped her arm around behind Elle's neck. Her fingers were tracing small circles on Elle's shoulder and moving purposefully down towards her breast.

Elle shrugged, trying not to think of the arousal in the casual caress. 'I am not sure but I think we are talking about the same thing.'

'That sounds terribly exciting.'

'It can be.'

'And is it all pain? Or is there some pleasure involved?'

Elle swallowed thickly, aware of a burning need between her legs. She could see exactly where this was all leading now and she longed to reach the moment. Their lips were so close she could smell wine-scented breath with each word. Every shiver of her body reminded Elle that there was a naked breast carelessly touching her exposed flesh. 'There is always pleasure involved, no matter how unbearable the pain is. Did you not learn that when Frankie used the corn cobs on you?'

'I said I didn't want reminding of that,' the redhead growled. 'That was a humiliating experience.'

Elle could detect an unexpected shift in her host's mood and she wondered if she had spoilt the amity that had been growing between them. 'Humiliation is part of the fun,' Elle explained quickly. 'The embarrassment makes you feel more aware of the indignity that you are suffering.'

'I'll take your word for it,' the redhead decided. Her unease seemed to mellow as she voiced her thoughts. 'I think if I was to try something like that again I would want to be in the dominant position.'

Elle studied her, excited by the meaning she detected behind those words. 'What are you suggesting?'

'Isn't it obvious?'

Before Elle could think about the repercussions she found herself surrendering to a kiss. A wine-chilled tongue plunged into her mouth and her lips were cooled by a lingering exchange. It was the exact response that Elle had been hoping and fearing would happen. Not sure of what she should be doing, she listened to the voice of her awakening appetite and gave in to those sensations that coursed through her. An intense burst of pleasure made her muscles stiffen and she realised then that she had dropped her wine glass.

They both gasped as the chilled Chianti splashed on to their legs. Elle couldn't apologise fast enough. No sooner was the kiss broken than she was babbling 'sorry' and trying to brush the icy liquid from her host's legs.

Standing up quickly, the redhead glared down at her. 'What would your mistress do if you'd been this clumsy in her presence?'

Elle closed her eyes, trying not to think of how Frankie would respond. The image of her mistress's wrath was always an exciting one and Elle didn't need any more stimuli to fuel her arousal. In a meek whisper that only hinted at the real truth of her need, she said, 'Mistress Frankie would be angry.'

'Would she make you clean up your mess?'

'Yes,' Elle whispered.

'Would she make you lick it up?'

Instinctively, Elle kneeled on the floor. She found it easy to fall into the role of the cowed submissive. She knew that she should really have been waiting for Frankie's permission before she submitted to anyone else, but the moment wouldn't allow for such niceties. With her burgeoning need justifying everything, Elle could also see how her obedience might help things. If Elle administered enough pleasure now, Grace's daughter might forgive

124

Frankie for the humiliation she had suffered in the cornfields.

'Yes,' she agreed, licking her lips and trying not to grow too excited at the prospect of what lay ahead. 'Mistress Frankie would certainly make me lick up the spilt wine.'

'Then do it, slave. Do it.'

Elle held her breath, surprised by the urgent rush that the command inspired. She lowered her head and tried to focus her thoughts on the situation's requirements. The Chianti had trickled down her host's ankles and, knowing that would be the best place to start, Elle touched her tongue against the sweet liquid. Savouring the flavour of mingled wine and sweat, she stroked her tongue further upwards, pausing when she reached one finely sculpted knee. Deliberately relishing the pleasure, and determined not to rush things, Elle began to use her mouth on the other leg.

'You have a very delicate kiss.'

Elle mumbled a thank you, moving her mouth over the knee and up to the inner thigh. She moved her tongue even further up until her nostrils were nuzzling the fiery, orange hairs of the girl's pubic bush. The wine hadn't splashed this high and Elle could only taste the deliciously salty flavour of sweat, but that pleasure proved to be its own reward. Unable to resist the temptation, she buried her nose in the forbidden curls and inhaled the musky scent. Stopping herself from indulging in a pleasure that hadn't been permitted, Elle moved her mouth back down to the other knee and began to lick the spilled Chianti again.

'You're a very good submissive,' the redhead purred. 'Are you getting a lot of pleasure from that?'

'Yes,' Elle whispered, not daring to move her face away from the knee she was lapping at. Experience beneath Frankie's merciless hand had taught her the necessity of doing a job properly and she was determined to make sure that every droplet of wine had been lapped up before she stopped. Her tongue traversed up to the upper thigh and, although she could find no trace of Chianti so high up, again she couldn't resist the opportunity of nuzzling the mound of wiry curls.

125

'There's no wine there.'

Elle gasped and moved away. She was still kneeling and from her position, it looked as though Grace's daughter was frowning down at her. 'No,' Elle whispered. 'You are right. There is not any wine there.'

'But we both think there ought to be, don't we?' Not waiting for a response, the redhead reached for the bottle of Chianti and tipped it towards her pubic thatch. Elle watched the wine splash through the curls, soaking them, then cascading down her thighs. Droplets spattered against Elle's face and breasts and she shivered as the liquid chilled her.

Without moving from her position above Elle, the redhead put the bottle back on the table and grinned down. 'Now lap up the rest of that wine, slave. Lap it up or suffer a severe punishment.'

Elle moved her face closer and buried her nose into the wine-sodden cleft. The idea of suffering a punishment was distinctly appealing but she knew that Frankie would definitely not approve of that. Her thoughts were a jumbled torrent as she tried to work out how she had fallen into this position and whether or not she should try to get out of it before things developed any further. But there was no escape right now, and she happily submitted herself to the task of trying to give pleasure.

The wine had soaked the wiry curls and each time Elle moved her mouth against the hairs, she was treated to its invigorating flavour. Beneath that taste, and infinitely more appealing, she could detect the intoxicating scent of arousal. Daringly, once she had sucked all the Chianti from the pubic bush, she tested her tongue against the heated cleft the curls concealed.

The redhead moaned and a tremor coursed through her body.

The sound came so loudly that Elle knew it had been lingering at the back of the girl's throat. Spurred on by the noise, she moved her tongue to press deeper between the yielding pussy lips. The flavour of the Chianti was gone and she was treated to the delicious taste of excitement. As

126

she breathed in, the scent of arousal coloured every inhalation, and Elle felt her own elation rushing to a pinnacle as she empathised with her lover's need.

'Here, slave,' the redhead snapped. She pushed her hand down to her pubic bush and delved her fingers into the thatch of hairs. Splaying her sex lips wide open, she bucked her hips forward and teased her clitoris in front of Elle's face. 'Tongue this; that's what I need.'

Elle acted without hesitation. She pushed her tongue forward and lapped at the rigid nodule. It was always an exquisite sensation to feel the pressure of a clitoris in her mouth, and this one seemed more responsive than any she had tongued before. She worked against the pulsing nub of flesh, her arousal growing as she listened to the appreciative words echoing around the cabin. Spurred on by the praise, Elle sucked and nibbled more fervently on the excited pearl.

'Enough,' the redhead ordered breathlessly.

Elle moved away instantaneously. She stared up with a concerned expression, hoping she hadn't done something wrong. 'Was I not doing it correctly?'

'Too correctly, slave.' A smile twisted her lips but again there was a mischievous glimmer in her eyes. 'You were very naughty spilling that wine, and I need to punish you, don't I?' Not waiting for Elle's response, she stepped away and snatched a hairbrush from a nearby table. Her grin came from somewhere between playful and wicked as she studied Elle and tested the weight of the brush against her palm.

'I am Frankie's submissive,' Elle said quietly. 'I am not sure that it is right for someone else to be punishing me.'

'You didn't spill the wine on Frankie, did you?'

Elle shook her head, unable to argue this point.

'And considering the way Frankie treated me, I doubt she'd offer permission for me to punish you. Yet I still need to make you sorry for your clumsiness.'

'I am sorry,' Elle whispered.

The redhead shook her head from side to side. 'The word sorry isn't good enough, slave. I don't just want you to say sorry; I want you to feel sorry.'

127

There was an intimation in her sentence that made her meaning clear.

'Turn around and bend over.'

Knowing there was no other choice, Elle did as she was told. She had assumed the position for Frankie so many times that there was no hesitancy in her actions. Still kneeling, she turned around and lowered her face to the floor while thrusting her backside high in the air.

'Is it usually six of the best?' The redhead was trying to keep her tone conversational but Elle could hear a husky excitement colouring her words. Her breathlessness hinted at an arousal that mirrored Elle's. 'Is it usually six, or am I confusing that with boarding school?'

Elle swallowed thickly before responding. 'Six is usually sufficient,' she replied. The familiar tingle of embarrassment was reddening her cheeks and she could feel the heady tug of desire warming her inner thighs. She had no idea how severe the punishment would be from a relative stranger and that added even more excitement to the moment. The hairbrush looked like a wicked implement to be spanked with.

Before she had time to properly contemplate any of these thoughts, the first blow landed against an exposed cheek. Without thinking, Elle cried out in surprise. Frankie would never have tolerated her making such a noise and would have doubled the punishment for such a breach of protocol. Grateful that Grace's daughter wasn't aware of these conditions, Elle savoured the pleasure that the hairbrush delivered. One cheek of her arse was a stinging expanse but she took comfort from the warmth it transmitted to her cleft.

'Was that painful?'

'A little.'

'Only a little? I must try harder.'

There was more to her words than idle banter. Elle heard the hairbrush make a whistling descent and then felt its punishing sting against her other cheek. There was more weight behind this blow and the explosion of pain was deeper, more intense. Resisting the urge to voice her

128

discomfort, Elle bit back her anguished cry and remained silent.

'You didn't shriek.'

Elle took a slow breath before daring to reply. 'No,' she agreed, aware that her voice was strained in its attempt to sound normal. 'I did not shriek.'

'I obviously didn't do that hard enough. Let's see if I can make this third one even harder for you.'

As good as her word, she smacked the hairbrush against Elle's backside with malicious force. Elle chewed her lower lip, unable to stop the protesting cry welling at the back of her throat. She turned around to glance at her tormentor and watched the hairbrush make its fourth descent to her bruised arse. This time the blow was a little less severe but because she saw it falling, Elle felt it more acutely.

The cheeks of her arse were glowing and although the warmth had now spread to the lips of her sex, she was touched by the thrill of shame that always enhanced her pleasure during punishment. Smiling fondly, Elle silently begged for the fifth bite of the hairbrush.

The last two strikes were delivered in swift succession, one for each cheek and with no leniency. They landed at the tops of her thighs, pricking at the sensitive flesh and leaving Elle giddy with the need for release.

'Now that you've been punished, slave, you can get back to what you were doing before.' The redhead tossed the hairbrush to a corner of the cabin and dropped back into the leather seat.

Because Elle was still kneeling, her face was on eye-level with the girl's lap. Needing no more instructions or threats of retribution, Elle pushed her face forward and tongued at the exposed cleft. The arousal she had tasted before had been satisfying, but since then it had become more intense. Suspecting that this was due to the thrill of dominating a submissive, Elle grinned contentedly to herself. She placed a hand on each thigh and tried to bury her face closer in an attempt to work her tongue further between the pussy lips.

The redhead thrust her hips up so that Elle could tongue

129

against the slippery labia. Once she had tired of that pleasure, she teased her fingers through her pubic thatch and encouraged Elle to work at the nub of her clitoris.

Not thinking of any repercussions, and revelling in the joy she was administering, Elle worked more urgently. She drank the syrupy wetness, slurping greedily when she heard cries of delight from above her.

The redhead lifted her legs and hugged them to her chest so that Elle could get closer. This new position allowed Elle to reach the taut rim of her anus and, even though she hadn't been asked to do it, she pushed her mouth over the puckered arsehole.

'No!'

Elle paused, moved her mouth away, and looked up uncertainly.

Panting and clearly trying to come to terms with the new sensation, the redhead gave her a dazed grin. 'All right then, slave. Go on.'

Eagerly, Elle pushed her mouth back into place and plunged her tongue into the forbidden depths. She was aware of delighted squeals ringing in her ears which matched her own excitement. The thought that she was introducing her host to a new experience left Elle giddy. Her own arousal was nearly orgasmic but she forced herself to ignore it. Revelling in her submissive status, she knew that before she could attempt to enjoy her own release, she had to satisfy her superior.

She worked her tongue deep into the redhead's forbidden confines and, at the same moment, nuzzled against her sodden cleft. The bridge of her nose rubbed over the clitoris and, hearing a scream of delight, Elle pushed the redhead beyond the brink of orgasm. A spattering of pussy honey doused her nose and eyes, wetting her cheeks and chin.

Determined to administer as much pleasure as she was able, Elle continued to work her tongue against the redhead's arsehole. Her face was pushed away by a lightly shaking hand.

'Suck my breasts now, slave.'

Elle obeyed the instruction without hesitation, pressing her body over Grace's daughter. They were both slick with sweat. Elle relished the sensation of slippery, nubile curves gyrating beneath hers and moved her mouth over an exposed nipple to tease it between her teeth.

As they writhed together, their sighs grew from a whisper and built towards another crescendo. Feeling sure this might be the right moment to say something in Frankie's favour, Elle trilled her tongue against one stiff bud and used her fingers to stimulate the other breast. She then placed her lips close to the redhead's ear and tried to think of how best to phrase a plea for leniency, placing a series of gentle kisses against the girl's neck and then nibbling at her lobe.

'Perhaps now,' Elle began. 'Perhaps now you might reconsider your anger with my mistress?'

'Reconsider?' The redhead's words were laboured with satiated passion. 'Reconsider how?'

'You said you were going to make Mistress Frankie suffer,' Elle reminded her. 'Perhaps now you might forget your thoughts of litigation and compensation and think of forgiveness?'

Grace's daughter shook her head, a gleeful smile broadening her lips. 'Not a chance in hell,' she decided happily. 'If anything, I'm more determined to beat the bitch than I ever was before.'

Elle frowned, unable to believe she was hearing this. That everything she had just done had been for nothing was a galling thought.

'I'm going to take the bitch to court if I have to and I won't stop until she gives me half the castle as compensation.'

'You cannot mean that,' Elle gasped.

'I can mean that and I do,' the redhead assured her. 'By the time I'm finished with your mistress Frankie, I'll own her share of this castle and I'll have all of her slaves under my command.'

Eight

Jane could see the argument brewing for half an hour before it occurred. McGivern had been making preparations for the auction and his mood was annoyingly inconsistent. He clapped her on the shoulder and confided that he was about to enjoy the sweetest conquest he had ever known. His high spirits were infectious and she relished a sparkle of excitement when his fingers cupped her breasts and caressed her concealed nipple. His way of touching her always stirred her arousal and she invariably responded, regardless of the situation or circumstances.

This time, before she could contemplate doing anything about her excitement, McGivern had turned away from her. He was tearing a strip off number seven, pushing his face into the blonde's and screaming at her maniacally. He complained that the beluga tasted as though the flavour had already been chewed from it, then Jane saw him raise a hand, threatening to slap the submissive's cheek. At the last moment, he changed his mind, preferring to exercise his merciless grip on the semi-hard nub of the slave's nipple.

Jane had seen enough of his mood swings before. These extremes of temper were typical of him. She had also seen enough of his high spirits to know that they invariably ended with someone's suffering and, determined not to be a victim of his elation, she distanced herself from him.

Using cajolery and charm, McGivern playfully teased two slaves before instructing them to place the banquet table in the centre of the hall. In a more menacing tone, he

132

screamed at number three and made her kneel on the banquet table.

Number three was naked, save for the ball-gag in her mouth and the handcuffs around her wrists and ankles. She bore the marks of a recently administered whipping and her arse cheeks blushed painfully. With a critical eye for detail, Jane realised that the slave wasn't simply kneeling on the table. McGivern had secured her hands to her ankles and instructed her to keep her chin and breasts in contact with the tapestry tablecloth. Studying the scene, Jane thought the slave looked like a piece of skilfully prepared poultry, laid out in readiness for the impending feast.

Determined not to suffer the wrath he was so eager to vent, Jane took the chance of door duty as soon as it came up. Number eleven, McGivern's redheaded submissive, was helping, although the impending auction seemed to have soured her usual good mood. She stared unhappily in the direction of her blonde lover while Jane did most of the work, welcoming the guests as they entered the banquet hall.

The crowd was a strange collection of dominatrices and fetishists, each one making no secret of their intimate peccadilloes. Six months earlier their presence would have terrified Jane but a lot had happened since then. She had met many of McGivern's colleagues at his new castle and grown used to the sight of flamboyant dominatrices and their charges and she could feel the warm tingling of excitement and intrigue colouring her mood as she greeted each new face this time.

A woman in red entered the banquet hall with two submissives scampering on all fours behind her. The submissives were dressed in tight bodysuits, complemented by matching collars and cuffs. The Lycra was snug against their skin, not disguising their curves or bulges to any degree, but this was modest amongst the gathering crowd. Jane thought that the submissives could have been naked and nobody would have raised an eyebrow. Nudity was so commonplace in the banquet hall, it was almost passé.

She whispered seating instructions to the dominatrix and

watched her glide elegantly into the hall. Before her gaze could follow the woman any further, Jane realised there was a new arrival to be greeted and she turned her attention back to the door. She found herself staring into the unsmiling face of an austere figure, dressed all in black and escorted by two ice-cool blondes.

'This is Captain Wilde,' one of the blondes explained. 'I expect you have a seat specially reserved for him?'

Jane shook her head and hoped that her response didn't antagonise. Captain Wilde had an unnerving look that told her he could be vicious if the mood took him. 'There are no specially reserved seats at this auction,' she explained.

Rather than appearing upset, Captain Wilde smiled at her. He placed his hand against her face and brushed a couple of stray curls from her forehead. 'You're very pretty,' he murmured. 'Will you be involved in the auction?'

His dark eyes were appraising her in a way that was distinctly unsettling. Jane caught a startled breath in the back of her throat and shook her head quickly. 'My master is here as the auctioneer,' she explained. 'He isn't selling me.'

'A pity,' Captain Wilde whispered. 'I would have bid high for you.'

She swallowed and said a brief prayer of thanks that good fortune had spared her. The man looked disturbingly sinister and the idea of being his submissive left Jane feeling cold but as he walked into the hall and joined the growing crowd, she realised there was no time to dwell on it. She turned to greet more of the auction's potential bidders.

McGivern had told her that management of the auction was an exercise in simplicity. Buyers were to remain on one side of the banquet table, where they were expected to wait patiently until the auction began. Sellers were to deposit their slaves behind the banquet table before joining the growing crowd of buyers in the larger part of the hall. Jane had passed these instructions on to a dozen or more people when she heard a raised voice approaching.

'Leave it with me, Grace.'

Jane recognised Simon's voice instantly but the note of frustration that coloured his tone gave it a new timbre. 'I'll find Frankie and then we can sort this out together.'

'It's not going to be that simple.' Jane could hear bitter determination in the woman's tone. She frowned and glanced at number eleven, wondering if she could offer any enlightenment on the angry exchange.

The redheaded submissive seemed oblivious to the argument. Her gaze was locked on to her blonde friend and, even as she instructed another dominatrix where to stand, number eleven wasn't concentrating on her words. Jane strained her ears to hear more of what was happening.

'Things never are that simple, are they?' That was Simon again, still sounding uncharacteristically disgruntled. He was a lot closer now.

'I can revoke your licence, Simon. It's not too late in the day for that.'

'Go back to your boat and wait for me there. I understand that you're upset and I sympathise with your distress, but there's nothing I can do about it until I've found Frankie and got her side of what happened.'

There was a disgusted snort followed by the words, 'Let me come with you.'

'You won't want to do that.'

'Why not?'

Simon burst through the doors, his cheeks tinged with an exasperated flush. He was glaring at the fiery-looking woman by his side and struggling to control his anger. With a sigh, he glanced around the room and pointed his finger directly at number three. 'See her?' Simon demanded, singling out the bound and gagged slave kneeling on the banquet table.

A handful of the bidders turned to stare at him but Simon ignored their curious expressions. He was glaring angrily at the white-haired woman as he pointed towards the slave.

Jane followed the direction of Simon's finger. Number

135

three's posture would have been humiliating enough if she had been alone on the table but Simon had chosen to enter the room at the moment when McGivern was kneeling between her legs to adjust the piercings at her labia and his meticulous attention made the slave's bondage seem infinitely more demeaning.

'Do you see her?' Simon demanded.

The woman beside him swallowed and a flicker of revulsion passed over her face. She raised a flustered hand to her throat and said, 'I see her.'

'Good,' Simon barked. 'Follow me around this castle and you'll see a dozen or more sights exactly like that one. If you don't want to witness things like that, you'll join your daughter back on your boat and wait for an hour until I've found Frankie.'

'An hour?'

'Quicker if I can manage it.'

The woman considered him with a sullen frown before nodding her grudging assent. She raised a warning finger and pointed between his eyes. 'If you're not at my boat in one hour I'll come looking for you, regardless of these indecencies.'

'Thank you for being so understanding,' Simon replied sardonically. Turning his back on her, he marched on into the banquet hall. He glanced at the redhead and frowned at her vacant expression before turning to Jane. 'Have you seen Frankie?'

'Not recently,' Jane told him. 'There isn't a problem is there?'

Simon shook his head. 'No worse than she usually causes. Is this where the auction is being held?'

Jane nodded.

'Then let's hope McGivern gets it over and done with quickly.' He looked as though he was about to say more when he looked at the submissive on the banquet table and did a double-take. Jane could see that when he had pointed at number three earlier on, he hadn't recognised her. As the slave's identity finally registered with him, a look of outrage twisted Simon's face.

136

'What the hell is she doing there?' Simon demanded loudly.

Unable to think of an appropriate response, Jane was silent. She glanced at number eleven but the submissive was oblivious to everything except her own melancholy. Her gaze was turned towards her blonde lover and her smile was tinged with a sadness too depressing to contemplate.

Simon's words had cut through the atmosphere of expectancy in the hall and now the eyes of every potential bidder were turned to study him. Climbing off the banquet table, McGivern raised a hand and waved nonchalantly at Simon from across the hall.

'What's the matter, Simon?' Jane whispered.

'More than I would want to deal with at the moment,' he said flatly. 'I should have listened to Frankie and never dealt with this bastard.' As he spoke, Simon was glaring at McGivern. Jane could see the venom in his expression.

'What's he done?' she asked. 'What's going on?'

'As soon as I find out, I'll let you know.' Simon started towards the banquet table.

Reluctant to leave her position at the door but determined to find out what was happening, Jane asked number eleven to cover for her, then followed him.

'She's my slave, McGivern,' Simon bellowed. 'What the hell do you think you're doing with her?'

McGivern smiled. 'Calm down, Simon. We have guests and we don't want to air our grievances in public, do we?'

'I'm at the stage where I'm beyond caring,' Simon informed him. Despite his words, he lowered his tone so that Jane had to step closer to eavesdrop on their conversation.

'Why is number three on the table? We had a deal. You sold her to me.'

McGivern glanced warily around the hall and Jane could see that he was trying to work out who had overheard them. Apart from herself, there was no one else within immediate earshot. A smile of relief passed over her master's features, the exact opposite to the confused expression twisting number three's face. Normally a picture of self-composure, she turned her head from Simon to McGivern as though this was a revelation to her.

'I haven't reneged on our deal,' McGivern assured him. 'But you wanted to give this gift discreetly. This will help you to accomplish that.'

'It should have been a simple exchange,' Simon hissed. 'That was all I wanted: the diamond for the slave.'

Jane stopped a shocked cry escaping her lips. She could accept that McGivern had sold number three, but she was astounded to hear that Simon was the purchaser. Her small squeak wasn't heard as number three released a frustrated groan. Jane glanced at the slave. Again, unusually for her, number three was frantically losing her composure. Her eyes were wide and horrified and she grunted around the ball gag, clearly trying to summon attention.

Both men ignored her.

Simon was still trying to impress his outrage on McGivern. 'Instead of a simple exchange, I end up with a string of unwanted guests, a bloody slave auction and the lead role in some farce that you're producing.'

'I can give this back to you now,' McGivern said, reaching into his pocket. He pulled out the small, black jeweller's box and pushed it under Simon's nose. 'If you want this back, just take it off me now and we can pretend that we never did business together.'

Simon pushed the hand away. 'I'd like nothing better than that but I don't want the diamond. I want the slave.'

'And you want to give her to Frankie discreetly,' McGivern added.

Jane stepped closer to the pair, aware that they were lowering their voices as more guests flocked into the banquet hall. She strained her ears to catch snatches of their conversation, not sure that she understood everything they were saying.

After glancing surreptitiously around, McGivern began to speak more swiftly, sounding as though he was impatient to get things explained to Simon and continue with more important matters. 'Number three will be the grand prize in a treasure hunt tonight.' Talking over Simon's protests, he said, 'I'm going to arrange it so that Frankie will be the one who gets first prize. That way everything will be sorted.'

Simon rubbed his fingers through his hair. 'There's never a dull moment with you, McGivern, is there? You've turned up here, having organised a slave auction. You've invited your own guests and, as if that's not bad enough, you have to hold a rigged game for their entertainment.'

'All games are rigged, Simon. That's the only way that I enjoy playing them.' He was still holding out the jeweller's box. 'Do you want this back? Or do I go ahead with my plan? I'd like an answer, because if you don't want number three, I can sell her at the auction.'

Jane leaned closer, listening intently.

'You're not using number three as the prize in a rigged game,' Simon said firmly. 'This is an auction and I take it you'll be playing to auction house rules.'

'Of course.'

Jane had no idea what auction house rules were, but McGivern's tone made it sound as though he was honour-bound to conform to them.

'Then you won't use my submissive to deceive these people,' Simon told him. 'I have no intention of suffering the penalty, and if the idea appeals to you, I'd thank you to find a way of doing it that doesn't implicate me.'

'There's no danger of either of us suffering the penalty,' McGivern protested.

'I know there isn't,' Simon agreed quickly. 'Because number three won't be a part of this auction. Get her off the table and keep her safe until I return.'

There was unquestionable authority in his voice and Jane could see that McGivern wasn't going to challenge him.

'Get her off the table and then get this auction over and done with,' Simon hissed. 'I have other things to attend to, and if I have to deal with this again, you won't like the consequences.' He turned his back on McGivern and started towards the door, accidentally pushing Jane to the floor as he stormed away. Ordinarily, Simon would have apologised and chivalrously helped her up. This time, Jane was surprised to see that he ignored her.

'You were listening, weren't you?' McGivern's voice was an icy growl.

Jane stared up at him, frightened by the menace in his eyes. She nodded dumbly and tried to think of words that might pacify him. Nothing sprang to mind as she studied the void of his sullen expression. Her thoughts were a frenzy of repercussions and impending punishments.

'Not that it matters,' McGivern decided. 'You don't know everything that's going on around here, do you? And I'd thank you not to discuss my transactions with anyone, unless you want to really suffer my displeasure.'

Number three made a grunting sound that echoed around the hall like a squeal of protest.

'I think she wants to say something,' Jane said quietly. She glanced at the slave, then turned back to McGivern.

He grinned and helped Jane from the floor with his hand extended. 'I can imagine that she wants to say quite a lot,' he agreed affably. 'But she's to remain bound and gagged until I say otherwise, and there will be severe retribution if that order isn't obeyed.'

'Do you want me to do as Simon asked?' Jane ventured hesitantly. 'I can take her somewhere safe until after the auction.'

'Number three is staying put throughout the auction. She'll be the grand prize in tonight's treasure hunt.'

Jane frowned. 'But Simon said –'

'I heard what Simon said,' McGivern replied loftily. 'And the day that I take instructions from him and his sort is the day that I roll over and die. Number three stays where she is and you keep quiet about everything that you've heard, do you understand?'

Jane could hear the threat in his voice and she nodded meekly. She cast a final, apologetic glance at number three, then turned away, unhappy with the helpless desperation she could see in the slave's eyes, an expression so pained that, for the first time since she had become a submissive, Jane felt guilty for obeying her master.

'Join me behind the table,' McGivern said. He still held her hand and he tugged on Jane's fingers, forcing her to go with him. 'I'm about to begin the auction and I'm sure you could provide valuable assistance.'

Knowing that she had no option other than to obey, Jane allowed him to lead her behind the banquet table.

'We'll get proceedings off to a quick start,' McGivern called, his voice booming around the hall as he addressed the gathered crowd. 'None of you want to hear me ramble on for an hour when there's important trading to be done, so I'll reiterate the usual terms and conditions of auction house rules, and then we'll begin.'

'Just get on with it,' a voice called from the audience.

Surly laughter followed this heckling but McGivern treated it with more good grace than was normal for him. 'I'll get on with it in good time,' he laughed. 'But first we need to discuss currency . . .'

Jane wasn't listening to him. She briefly acknowledged the full hall. Standing close to number three, she could see that the slave was glaring at her. Taking a step closer to number three, she frowned and silently shaped the words, 'What's wrong?'

Number three shook her head and sighed heavily. Her eyes were glassy with the threat of impending tears but she blinked them away.

McGivern was busy explaining the rules of currency and Jane could hear a disinterested murmur travelling through the crowd. She stepped closer to the bound slave and repeated her question, this time as a hiss. 'What's wrong?'

'. . . ranky . . .' number three gasped.

Jane frowned and pressed her face closer. She cast a hesitant glance in McGivern's direction to make sure that he was still involved with his audience. He was busy reciting his instructions. She dared to move her ear close to the slave's face. 'Say it again. I can't understand a word.'

The slave closed her eyes and Jane could see a

concentrated effort on her face. 'Ranky if eyeing hee . . .' The miserable grunts were made unintelligible by the gag.

Jane cast another glance at McGivern. He was still revelling in the limelight before his audience. Daringly, she reached for the buckle at the back of the slave's neck and began to unfasten the gag.

'. . . and with finances sorted out, I should also mention the other rule that governs our trading today,' McGivern told the audience.

Jane surreptitiously guided the strap through the buckle and began to tease the metal clasp from its hole in the leather. When she saw the slave's eyes widen, she pressed a silencing finger to her own lips and cast another wary glance in her master's direction.

'Honesty, ladies and gentlemen. Honesty. I don't doubt the integrity of any of you, but I think you should all be aware that there are repercussions for anyone involved in underhand dealing.'

'Get on with it, McGivern,' the heckler cried again. 'We're tired of your voice now.'

McGivern ignored him. 'Anyone found to be involved with unfair trading will be punished by the traditional penalty of auction house rules,' he said. 'And for those of you who don't already know, that means three things. Sequestration of stock, punishment by peers and a final sentence of servitude or exile.'

'We know the rules, McGivern. Get on with it.'

McGivern glared at the owner of the annoying voice. 'I have a ball-gag here,' he said, pointing to number three. 'It's in use at the moment but you're beginning to look like a more worthy cause.' He glanced down at the slave and blinked rapidly when he saw that Jane was trying to ease the gag from the submissive's mouth.

Jane stared up at him, horrified to have been caught in an act of obvious disobedience.

'Fasten it.' His words were spat from between clenched teeth.

Jane obeyed without hesitation. She caught sight of the pained expression on number three's face and tried to

142

dismiss it from her thoughts as she tugged the strap back into position.

'I'm sorry,' Jane whispered. 'But she –'

McGivern grabbed a fistful of her platinum locks and pulled her on to the table with him. Jane wanted to scream but she knew better than to make a sound when McGivern was demonstrating his mastery in front of peers. She tried to ignore the bolts of pain from his grip and stood humbly beside him.

As though he had planned this, McGivern turned to his audience and said, 'You all know that sequestration means handing over your slaves and submissives. You all know that exile or servitude means either giving up your association with us, or enduring a period of servility, but Jane here will help me to illustrate the punishment aspect of the penalty.'

'Please don't,' Jane whispered.

McGivern acted as though he hadn't heard her. He reached for her blouse and pulled the garment open. With a flick of his wrist the fabric was rent and Jane began to blush as her bared breasts were exposed. However, rather than trying to cover herself modestly, she endured the attention of the crowd. She had tried to conceal herself on previous occasions and soon learned that McGivern didn't take kindly to such behaviour.

McGivern suddenly snatched the zipper at the side of her skirt and pulled it downwards. The garment fell from her hips and pooled at her ankles, revealing her completely naked. Jane's cheeks were fully flushed crimson as she stood beneath the audience's expectant gazes. A couple of wolf-whistles greeted her nudity and she heard a spattering of applause from near the door.

'Many of you may be familiar with the punishment ritual,' McGivern began. 'But I think it's important that we demonstrate it for those who aren't aware of how severe it can be.'

'Please, don't,' Jane begged. She had so far silenced her qualms about enduring most of the indignities that McGivern foisted upon her, but this was taking things too

143

far. Although she had no idea what fate awaited her, a morbid fear twisted her stomach muscles as she basked beneath the lecherous faces of the audience. Her blushing cheeks had triggered an automatic reaction between her legs and she could feel a glorious wetness growing there. As her nipples grew harder, she warned herself that this punishment would be more severe and humiliating than anything she had previously experienced. 'Please, don't,' she repeated.

'Too late,' McGivern grinned. 'I'm about to make an example of you.'

He pushed her forward and Jane stumbled from the banquet table. She managed to find her feet at the last moment and, instead of falling over, she landed clumsily.

'I want you on your knees,' he growled.

Jane started to obey but he was still tugging at her hair. Realising she wasn't properly adhering to his instructions, she cast an unhappy glance at him.

'Keep your back to the audience, face the table, and prepare yourself for a punishment like you've never known before.'

Jane groaned and did as he asked.

'Who's first?' McGivern declared cheerfully. 'The set-up is simple enough. You can each deliver six blows using whatever is available. Those of you who don't have a cane, crop or paddle can pick one of the implements hanging from the wall.'

Jane groaned again but the desperate sound was lost beneath the crowd's approving chatter.

'I think I'll start the ball rolling,' McGivern said cheerfully. 'And for those of you who are thinking I'm a heartless bastard, I'll show a little kindness and just use my hand.'

As the first slap of his hand landed against her buttock, a solitary tear began to trickle down Jane's cheek. The pain at her arse was short, sharp and brief, more stinging than uncomfortable. The second one landed on exactly the same spot, warming her backside and spreading its glow towards her sex lips. She wanted to ignore the arousal of this

144

humiliation but she knew that McGivern wouldn't be so lenient.

He shifted position to deliver the third and fourth blows and threw his open palm against her other cheek. Jane tried not to tremble as she endured his wrath. She bit back the cries for him to stop, knowing they would go unheeded. A second tear followed the line of the first and she shivered miserably.

McGivern hurled all his weight into the last two blows, one for each cheek. Although she couldn't see the flesh, Jane could picture its bright, crimson hue in her mind's eye. With the same knowledge of experience, she could envisage the display that her exposed cleft presented to the banquet hall. The lips of her sex would have peeled open and her most intimate crevices were being studied by a hundred unknown faces.

'That's got her reddened up,' McGivern told the audience. He rubbed his hand over her punished orbs and Jane wished that her libido wasn't responding excitedly to his touch.

'Who's next? Babs?'

Jane closed her eyes and shivered.

'I have no intention of punishing anyone,' Babs replied. Jane couldn't see the woman but she could hear the haughty disdain in her voice. 'I don't train slaves by punishing them. I use a reward system.'

McGivern's tone was a derisory sneer. 'What a waste,' he told her, dismissing the woman. 'Are there any more takers, or is this the only punishment a cheat can look forward to if they suffer the penalty?' he asked the audience.

Although she knew it would go unanswered, Jane made a silent prayer that no one would respond to his prompt. Footsteps behind her indicated that already someone had and she braced herself for an onslaught from the stranger. The crowd was silent with an expectant hush but however much Jane strained her ears, she could hear no clue to the identity of the person behind her. Her reddened cheeks had passed their peak of discomfort and were now subsiding to a dull but tolerable ache. She contemplated glancing back over her shoulder to see who was standing over her, but she didn't entertain that thought for more than a moment. McGivern was already furious with her and he would use any excuse to make her punishment even more unbearable.

A sharp whistle sliced through the air. Jane stiffened as she heard the sound but its impact arrived before she had a chance to brace herself against it. A razor of pain exploded across both buttocks and, without thinking, she released a scream of dismay. Before her body had a chance to contend with the sensation, a second whistle sliced the air and Jane suffered another cruel blow.

The pulse between her legs beat faster and her nipples throbbed with the need for attention. As the third strike landed, she contemplated caressing herself, then realised that is was something she shouldn't attempt. With so many people present in the hall, someone was bound to notice. McGivern would be outraged if he thought she was extracting enjoyment from this humiliation.

The fourth and fifth blows landed with such quick succession that Jane barely had a chance to cry out. Her breathing had trailed off to miserable sobs and she managed to gasp only a little air through hitching cries.

'Stay silent,' McGivern growled. 'You've already embarrassed yourself enough. Try to retain a little dignity.' He made no attempt to mask the threat in his words and Jane nodded her surly agreement of his instruction. When the sixth blow of the crop struck her backside, she suppressed the urge to cry out, fearful of further repercussions.

Before she had a chance to recover from the crop she felt the familiar weight of a studded paddle landing against her exposed cheeks. It was hard to believe that her bruised flesh could be so sensitive as to distinguish between implements but even if she had dared to turn around and study her torturer, she wouldn't have been able to see the instrument of punishment more clearly. In her mind's eye she saw a flat expanse of leather, its plain surface broken by uniform steel rivets that were designed to pepper her cheeks painfully.

The six blows from the paddle were followed by a bare hand. After that, she felt another crop, then a light, multi-thonged tawse. McGivern had punished her backside on many occasions but he had never inspired a fire like the one that now burned in her arse cheeks. Tears of shame rolling down her cheeks were forgotten as soon as she revelled in the most intense heat that humiliation had ever introduced. She bit back her cries as the pain proved too severe, and she stifled groans when her body's response seemed too wanton. Through a misty haze of arousal, she knew it was a most degrading punishment. She could see why it was part of the penalty for a breach of the auction house rules. Admittedly, Jane was able to glean some satisfaction from the degradation but she doubted any of the dominatrices would be able to extract anything other than shame and misery.

More hands slapped her bare backside and she was acutely aware of how intimate the slaps were becoming. Her arse-cheeks felt numb with the flames that exploded beneath each blow and her concentration seemed focused on the inquisitive fingers teasing at her pussy lips. Each caress intensified her arousal. She knew it wouldn't be long before her body succumbed to the growing orgasm.

Not for the first time, Jane decided that life had treated her fairer than most. It would have been easy to hate McGivern for the indignities he administered, but that would have been the wrong emotion to harbour. The pleasure that she was extracting from this group spanking was exquisitely humiliating. Knowing that he was angry with her, yet still allowing her to enjoy such intense excitement, left Jane choked with gratitude. She could understand the worry that plagued her fellow slaves of McGivern's entourage. If she had thought he was selling her, Jane would have been equally upset. Like her, they all thrived on his cruel affection and without him, their lives would be missing something very special.

Another hand slapped her backside, dragging her thoughts from their adoration of McGivern and his discipline. This was special: this was her master's hand. She imagined she could feel the echo of his voice through his slap.

'Penetration!' McGivern called.

Jane felt giddy with a combined rush of desire and loathing. This looked set to be the ultimate degradation of the penalty and she could imagine how tortuous it would be for any dominatrix. Grateful that her own submissive status was allowing her to relish the moment, she braced herself in readiness for what was about to happen. McGivern's hand remained on her backside and the pressure of his thumb weighed heavily over her anus. She couldn't decide if it was her imagination or the thrill of this punishment, but it felt as if he was trying to ease the digit inside her. When the thumb pressed beyond the ring of her sphincter, Jane growled happily.

'This is a lesson by example,' McGivern declared. 'None of us are here to tolerate cheats and we can prove that to one another now. Unless we show what we'll do to anyone caught in the act of unfair trading, we could be encouraging someone to deceive us.'

His thumb squirmed deeper as he spoke and Jane curled her hands into fists. He had told her to remain still, but now the task seemed gargantuan. All she wanted to do was collapse on the floor and let events overtake her. However, she knew that if she did, McGivern would simply haul her back to her knees and make her endure the punishment from the beginning.

The weight of something round and bulbous fell against her sex lips. Her body instinctively tried to draw away from it but she stopped herself. Knowing that any movement might cause the removal of McGivern's thumb, Jane tolerated the shameful indignity.

It was a dildo of some description, she thought vaguely. The sensation was all wrong for this to be anyone's cock. The domelike end was too large and felt too smooth and cold to be human flesh. It spread her wide and filled the channel of her sex, leaving her breathless with the threat of her explosion. Her mind was racing to imagine exactly what this was as burning tears rolled down her cheeks. The length worked its way back and forth, fuelling her heat and promising to send her towards a dizzying climax.

When the shaft began to tingle, she realised the item was nothing more unusual than a large vibrator. But the thought was only a passing one as the tremors began to rack her frame. She grunted back her mounting excitement, fearful of McGivern's response if she began to wail with pleasure. Before the vibrator could transport her to a plateau, it was snatched away.

She felt a moment's regret, wondering how phenomenal the release would have been if she had simply given herself over to it. Before the regret could turn into anything more profound, a second weight pushed against her gaping hole. This time the end wasn't domelike or smooth. This felt misshapen and twisted and threatened unbearable stimulation against her aching sex lips. Suddenly, the shaft plunged into her sex and she was treated to a cruel battering from the gnarled sides.

Her breath had started to come in guttural cries from her shuddering lips. She tensed herself against the thrill of an orgasm, knowing that it was inevitable now that she was being abused in this way.

And then the second phallus was removed. She prepared herself for the insertion of whatever else the throng had planned for her, despising her body's hunger for this predicament. The idea of enduring a thick cock had begun to formulate in the back of her mind, and she was suddenly aware that her body wasn't going to be satisfied until it had been forced to accept that pleasure. With her need mounting urgently, Jane wondered if McGivern would deign to punish her with his length before the ordeal was over, and this idea sent shivers cascading up and down her back.

McGivern removed his thumb from her backside and squatted down so that his face was close to her ear. Another phallus penetrated her sex and Jane coughed back the scream of euphoria threatening to burst from her throat.

'You were a naughty girl, Jane,' he whispered. 'I trust

that in the future, you'll remember which of us is in control?'

There was no recourse other than to nod her agreement. She could imagine the bedraggled spectacle that her image presented and she was grateful that there was no mirror nearby to reflect the depths to which she had sunk. It was enough that she could see his displeasure in the crease of his frown.

'I could have sold you at this auction,' McGivern reminded her. 'But I chose not to. I have a special fondness for you, Jane, and I don't think you realise how badly hurt I am by your disobedience.'

The phallus was plunging deeper and her body's response was threatening to drown out McGivern's whispered words. She coughed back a scream of delight and dared to meet his eyes. 'I'm sorry, master,' she whispered meekly.

He nodded and pushed his thumb under her nose. 'Lick this clean and we'll say no more about it.'

Without hesitating, Jane thrust her tongue forward. Six months earlier the idea would have repulsed her. She could still detect the sour-sweet musk of her own anus. The notion of using her tongue to clean it from him should have sent her screaming with indignation. But she was his slave and she was enduring this punishment because he had said so. Jane placed her tongue against the extended thumb and then began to suck on it without thinking about her own base situation. Using her lips on his hand, she found her excitement was threatening to take her beyond the brink of elation, and she worked her mouth harder. The phallus between her legs was working faster than anything else she had experienced so far at the auction. The rush of her climax was almost upon her.

A hand slapped her backside, surprising her with the force of the blow.

The phallus was tugged away, leaving her feeling empty and unfulfilled. She needed to feel something else penetrating her and her libido had already decided that it didn't matter where; both her arsehole and her sex were

150

desperate to feel some sort of intrusion. If McGivern hadn't already told her to be silent, she would have screamed this declaration around the banquet hall.

But there was something about the way that her arse had been slapped that told Jane the penetration was now over.

McGivern slipped his thumb from her mouth and stroked her hair to dry himself before stepping away. From the corner of her eye, she saw him smile a greeting to whoever was holding her backside.

A second slap landed, harder than the first and, she noted, slightly more vicious. Rather than simply striking her, the hand clutched at her buttock. The fingers were merciless, clawing at her aching cheek as though they were trying to rip the bruised flesh away. Jane felt a thumb tease against the ring of her arsehole and she shallowed a cry of elation. The other hands and crops had been cruel but the punishments they administered had been given with some degree of tenderness. This hand was different: it seemed determined to inflict pain. She could feel her arse-cheeks being pinched between fingers and thumbs that were tipped with razor-sharp nails.

'I want this one. I want to buy this one.'

Jane flinched from the words as though they had hurt her more than the brutal fingers. She dared to glance over her shoulder and saw that she was being caressed by the foreboding Captain Wilde. He wasn't looking at her; his attention was directed towards McGivern. Jane glanced at her master, wondering how he would extricate her from this potential sale.

'Jane's not for sale,' McGivern said firmly.

Captain Wilde reached into his wallet and produced an impossibly thick sheaf of notes. 'I think you'll find she is for sale when you hear what I'm offering.'

With a sickening lurch in the pit of her stomach, Jane could see McGivern hesitate as he contemplated the money.

Nine

Frankie leaned between the crenellated embattlements, smoking a cigar and staring out towards the horizon. From the island, the horizon was an unbroken expanse of blue, glittering beneath the descending sun. The top of the west keep was ideal for soul-searching and introspection and Frankie began to wish she had hidden herself somewhere else. The monotonous view gave her nothing to distract her thoughts from the impending submission to McGivern and, as the moment grew nearer, her doubts were beginning to surface.

'Thinking of tossing yourself off?'

She whirled around, not overly surprised to see Simon standing behind her. His opening line was the first half of a joke they often shared whenever they caught one another leaning over the embattlements. She was meant to reply with the line, 'No. I just had my hands in my pockets to keep them warm.' The first time they had made the exchange Frankie had almost choked on her cigar as she laughed and she had cackled for hours afterwards. Now, she was struggling to curl her lips into a smile.

'I could be angry with you, Simon,' she told him. 'But I'm not. I'm just disappointed.'

'I could say the same thing to you,' Simon agreed. 'But it wouldn't be true. I'm absolutely livid with you.'

At this, Frankie started. Although Simon knew nothing of the arrangement she had made with McGivern she still expected his sympathy and understanding. Mentally back-tracking over the morning, she could think of nothing that she had done which deserved to incur his wrath. 'And what the hell have I done?'

'Why did you have that redhead working on your plough this morning?'

Frankie didn't meet his gaze. She turned back to the horizon and tried to ignore the fact that he was glaring at her in anger. Her own outrage was forgotten and, as she waited to hear exactly what wrong she had done, she spoke in an apologetic tone. 'At the time, I thought there might be repercussions,' she confessed.

Simon came to stand by her side to study the empty horizon with her. 'That was quite perceptive of you,' he said carefully. 'And when the notion of repercussions occurred to you, what exactly were they? Civil prosecution from the IHS? A charge of indecent assault from the woman you were abusing? Or is there something else you haven't told me?'

Frankie smoked her cigar and said nothing.

'I'm meant to try and appease that girl's mother,' Simon told her quietly. 'Can you think of anything I should say that might pacify the situation?'

'Spare the rod and spoil the child?'

'Can you think of anything more constructive?'

'I could give her a box of oranges and some sweetcorn if you think that might help.'

'I can't see that working,' Simon said. The patience was ebbing from his voice. 'We're beyond the "oranges and sweetcorn" stage now. Grace is after blood at the very least, and if she can't have yours, she'll want mine instead.'

Frankie turned, unable to control her temper any longer. 'Should I go down to her boat and open an artery?' she demanded, glaring at him. 'Because if that's what you and Grace want, right now I'm just about prepared to do it.'

Simon stared at her uncertainly, clearly surprised and concerned by her outburst. She tried to turn away but before she could move, Simon had grabbed her chin and was forcing her to face him. 'You've been crying,' he observed. The words came out in a flat voice, as though he was almost too stunned to express his incredulity.

'Don't be stupid,' she hissed, brushing his hand away and wiping at any treacherous marks that lingered on her cheeks. She turned back to the horizon and said, 'I'm a dominatrix. I don't cry.'

Without saying a word, they looked at the horizon together. The day was cooled by a mild breeze which blew more fiercely at the top of the embattlements. Long, dark tresses of Frankie's her hair were teased by the wind and she brushed the wayward strands from her face with an irritated hand. In the thick silence that rested between them, Frankie could almost hear Simon's thoughts. They seemed to catalogue a volume of unspoken questions. Knowing that he deserved some sort of explanation, she ground her teeth together and tried to think of the best way to tell him what had been happening. 'I think I'm losing it,' Frankie whispered eventually.

Simon studied her uncertainly. 'Losing it?'

She nodded.

'Losing what?'

'Losing it,' she said. She was beginning to grow exasperated because he hadn't read her thoughts and made sense from her words already. 'I think I'm losing my ability to dominate. I think I'm losing my ability to control submissives and underlings.'

He shook his head. 'I don't think you've lost those abilities. Perhaps you've just lost the knack of knowing when certain things are acceptable and when they aren't.'

She sniffed, doubting that his explanation would suffice for all the self-recriminations tumbling through her thoughts. 'No,' she said firmly. 'I'm definitely losing it. There was a time when I used to be able to dominate without giving it any thought. There was never any hint of insurrection from submissives. And there was never any of this crap about legal or civil prosecutions. I'm losing it, and I'm beginning to think that I deserve most of the shit that the rest of the day has in store for me.'

'Come on,' Simon began. She could hear that he was trying to cajole her from her unhappiness but she doubted he could say anything to help her flailing spirits. 'I'm sure you can handle things if you put your mind to it. You've just had a crap day. You're a fighter, Frankie.' He placed his arm around her shoulders and gave her a reassuring squeeze.

Even if his words offered no solace, she was pleased that he allowed his arm to linger there. It was comforting, and she pressed herself into his embrace. Taking a final draw from her cigar, she hurled the stub over the side of the embattlement and tested a wary smile on him. 'Was this IHS thing important to us?'

He nodded.

'Very important?'

'We'll keep the castle for a while longer,' he explained. 'But if our licence of approval is revoked, or if we get caught up in some lawsuit for assault, I can see the castle becoming a casualty.'

Frankie sighed heavily and wished she hadn't thrown her cigar away. News like that deserved to be mellowed by the taste of a Havana. 'Then I'm sorry if I've fucked things up. If I had any skill as a dominatrix, I might attempt to sort things out, but the way my abilities are failing me at the moment, I think I'd make things worse.'

'You're on a hell of a downer, aren't you?'

'Don't worry,' she said, trying to smile. 'I've got a feeling my day's going to get a lot worse before it gets any better.'

'What else is happening?'

She shook her head. For a moment the idea of telling him was distinctly appealing. If she explained to Simon that McGivern was on the verge of selling number three, Simon might offer to step in and save the situation. It was a tempting scenario, and she could see it saving her from her afternoon's submission, but she knew it was not an option. Simon already had a lot of work to do as he tried to appease Grace and her secretive daughter. Having him deal with McGivern would reinforce her own unsettling suspicions that she was an inadequate dominatrix. She was already close to believing that was the truth. It would only take one more knock to her confidence and she would be wallowing in the role of a submissive for the rest of her life.

'Come on,' Simon pressed, squeezing her tighter. 'Tell me all about it. What else is the matter?'

She shook her head again and said, 'You don't want to know.' She had to get away from Simon before he got the truth from her and she leaned towards him, meaning to give him a kiss on the cheek and thank him for his concern. They were close friends as well as one-time lovers and she didn't think the gesture was inappropriate or overly familiar. She moved her mouth towards his cheek at the exact moment that he turned to face her.

Their mouths met.

Frankie could see that he was as surprised as she was. That wasn't the most powerful emotion that struck her. As their lips came into contact, she was touched by a spark of excitement that banished McGivern and the auction from her mind. Rather than thinking of the repercussions of her morning in the cornfield, her concentration was focused on the intimacy of their melded mouths.

Simon broke the kiss, panting lightly and studying Frankie with wary hesitation. 'You kissed me,' he whispered.

She bit back her laughter, happy to see he was as stunned by the moment as she was. 'You kissed me,' she returned belligerently. 'I was just trying to kiss you on the cheek before I told you to fuck off and stop pestering me. You kissed me.'

'Do you want to try it again?' he asked.

She did. Frankie pushed her mouth on to his and the pair of them began to explore each other with their tongues. Simon moved his fingers to her face and caressed her temples lovingly as they shared the moment. Determined not to be overpowered by him, Frankie grabbed his head. She held him firmly against her face as she plunged her tongue between his lips. With their mouths locked together, she was lost in a blissful world without problems. Simon's closeness filled her with an excitement she hadn't known in ages. Her body began to respond to him with a need that went beyond desperate.

'You're exciting me,' she growled, only breaking the kiss long enough to spit the words at him.

He grunted dourly. 'You started it.'

She moved one hand away from his head and reached for the crotch of his pants. The bulge of his excitement pushed against his leather trousers and she felt him gasp, as the pressure of her fingers sparked a burst of pleasure.

By way of retaliation, Simon reached inside her jacket and found her breast. Frankie made no attempt to stop him, and she pushed her chest towards his inquisitive fingers. With unfailing accuracy, he caught one nipple between his finger and thumb and began to tease the bud.

Frankie drew startled breath, amazed by the giddy sensations. Simon's hand went to her other breast and Frankie groaned as he filled her with even more intense pleasure. Determined to allow him unfettered access to her body, she shrugged the jacket from her shoulders and pressed closer to him.

His shaft was still in her hand and now she was aware of its pulse. The dull beat was muted through the leather, but she could sense his excitement as clearly as she could taste his kiss.

The last time they had shared this sort of intimacy, Frankie knew she had been too drunk to appreciate it fully but she hadn't been so senseless as to forget the overwhelming pleasure. This time they were both sober and clear-headed and she was determined to enjoy every sensuous second. With fumbling fingers, she tried to tug his zipper downwards, eager to get closer to his arousal.

He moved her hand away and silenced her protests with a serious expression. His need for her was apparent in his shining, grey eyes, but he moved a full step backwards so they could study one another properly. 'Should we be doing this?' he asked.

'Probably not,' she conceded. 'But that's not going to stop us, is it?'

He shrugged and, with the same carefree attitude, they fell into each other's arms. There was no hesitancy in their embrace and, as their mouths met, each made a swift attempt to undress the other.

Frankie allowed him to snatch the skirt from her hips,

happy to feel the cool breeze against her naked buttocks. She tore his shirt open, eager to explore the magnificence of his chest. Simon had a beautiful body, each muscle well-toned from the hours he spent in the east keep's gymnasium. His chest was broad and, as soon as she had bared it, Frankie pressed her lips over his exposed nipple and bit.

'Bloody hell!' he gasped. The exclamation came from the world between pain and pleasure. 'That hurts, you bitch. You're going too hard.'

She laughed, unoffended by his outburst. Glancing up at him, her lips still hovering over the bruised bud on his chest, she grinned and said, 'Don't tell me you didn't like it.'

'If you're going to play rough, you shouldn't expect me to go easy on you,' he warned. His tone was severe but she could see the excited sparkle twinkling in his eyes.

Her laughter deepened to a throaty chuckle. 'If that's a threat, I look forward to seeing you carry it out.' She pushed her lips towards his left nipple and tongued the ball closure ring before daring to place her teeth around the pierced flesh. He held himself rigid in her embrace and Frankie felt a thrill of euphoria as she realised how much excitement she was giving him. Teasing the sensitive nipple with her tongue, she began to unfasten his trousers.

'You're going too rough,' Simon complained.

'I can't be,' Frankie assured him. 'You'd have told me before if I was.'

She pulled the belt from his waistband and tugged open the button above his fly. She had already unfastened his zip, and so in one swift movement, was able to pull his trousers down to reveal his erection. 'I really have excited you, haven't I?' she exclaimed. It had been a while since she had seen Simon naked and she wondered how she could have forgotten that he was so well built. His massive length filled her hand and, as she gently squeezed the erection, she was pleased to feel his pulse beat faster.

He stepped out of his thigh-length boots and tugged the trousers away from his legs. Pushing his naked body against hers, Simon took Frankie in his arms and kissed her again. His hands were cupping her buttocks, exciting a need that grew quickly inside her. The pressure of his length pressing against her bare stomach burned like a branding iron.

'I want you,' he told her.

'Like it's not obvious,' she grinned. She moved to hold him tightly. He was taller than her, and sex in this position wasn't just impractical, it was virtually impossible. But she relished their closeness all the same and her fingers moved over the mounds of his arse, caressing and cupping the cheeks as a crude exploration. Simon was handling her with the same callous ferocity and she knew that whatever else their intended love-making promised, it would be passionate and deeply satisfying. Without thinking about it, she pressed her mouth over his chest and bit hard at his flesh.

He gave a surprised grunt and pushed her away from his embrace. Her teeth had left a circular imprint on his chest, just above his pierced nipple. 'You're a vicious bitch,' he growled.

'I don't think you'd want me any other way,' she grinned. She moved towards him again, intending to match the bite mark on the other side. He stopped her, pushing one hand between her legs. His fingers made no attempt to comb through the curls of her pubic thatch but reached purposefully for the lips of her sex.

Frankie caught her breath, startled and excited by his casual control of her body and his obvious appreciation of her needs. She held herself still as he teased her pussy lips apart with two fingers and brushed the nub of her clitoris with another. The shiver of pleasure was so strong, she could feel herself melting against him.

Simon pressed his lips over one breast and tongued her nipple furiously. His fingers continued to work on the pulse between her legs and Frankie felt him pushing her towards a thrilling climax. Not wanting to rush the moment, and determined to savour every second of their time together, she tried to move away, but her body was

159

reluctant to forsake the pleasure of his intimacy and she couldn't find the strength to move. His tongue circled the areola of her breast then he teased his teeth against the rigid bud of her nipple.

Her shivers grew more profound, and she knew that they weren't because of the cooling breeze. When he moved his mouth to the other breast, she swallowed her cry. She was desperate for him to satisfy her. The need between her legs had grown out of all proportion and she yearned for more.

'Why haven't we been doing this more often?' he asked.

It was as though he had read her thoughts. She glanced into his face, surprised to see that he had asked the question in earnest. 'We're both incredibly stupid hedonists,' she told him. 'We take our pleasure wherever we think we can get it, and act surprised when we discover our ability to please one another.'

He nodded. 'That's what I thought.' Not wasting any more time on words, he wrapped his arms around her and lifted her off her feet.

Frankie was torn between surprise and indignation as the floor was snatched from beneath her but she made no protest as he carried her to the castle's wall. He placed her gently in the dip of a crenellation and smiled down at her. His shaft was at eye-level and, although Frankie was willing to taste his arousal, she made no attempt to move her head forward. She could see that his foreskin had peeled back and the purple end of his length was revealed under a gleaming polish of pre-come. His cock twitched for her with an eagerness that matched her own heartfelt need.

'We should definitely do this more often,' he decided.

She reached for his shaft and circled it with her fingers. Firmly, she pushed downwards so that he had to kneel between her legs. 'We should do this now,' she corrected. 'We can talk about "more often" afterwards. Right now I have needs and you're going to satisfy them.'

He grunted dry laughter as she guided his shaft towards her hole. His hardness filled her hand and she bit her lower lip as she anticipated the moment of his penetration. 'That sounds like the instruction of a dominatrix,' Simon told her. 'Not a bad one either, considering that you claim to be losing it.'

She frowned, not sure how to take the remark. But it wasn't important, and she tugged him closer and said, 'Stop talking, Simon. If you need to do something with your mouth, just kiss me.'

He laughed again, and she could see that he was thinking of making another comment about her dominant attitude. Instead of voicing his thought, he did as she instructed and bent to kiss her. She placed the head of his length over her sodden hole and rubbed gently. Her pussy lips were slippery with excitement and the friction of his dome against her vulva sent a thrill coursing through her body. Her exclamation of euphoria was drowned in his kiss as their tongues entwined. She rubbed him more firmly against her cleft.

'Are you determined to make me beg for it?' he asked her.

'Would you?' she teased.

He shook his head and smiled tightly. 'I don't think so.'

'Then let's not waste time trying to make you.' She rested the head of his shaft against her pussy and bucked her hips forward. In the same moment, as though he was perfectly attuned to her needs, Simon pushed into her. With one marvellous lunge, he filled her. In one swift movement, the length of his shaft was splaying her inner muscles and hammering at the neck of her womb.

His face twisted into a grimace of elation. He held himself rigid inside her and she tensed her muscles around his shaft. As though uncomfortable with the pressure, Simon began to pull himself away from her, but it was only to push back inside. His rhythm was brisk but unhurried, and she raised herself to meet him, amazed by the pleasure he evoked.

Their kiss broke and at once, he used his mouth against her breast while his shaft continued riding in and out of her. Frankie gasped, surprised by the intensity of his passion. She was touched by a moment's hesitancy as she tried to decide which part of her anatomy to thrust towards him, and then the indecision was gone. As her body found its natural position, joining with his, it seemed like she had been made for this moment. Their hips worked in fluid motion, pushing and pulling together. His mouth moved from one breast to the other, exciting each tip with a firm kiss. When he moved away, Frankie took full advantage of the moment to suckle against his single piercing.

Their cries were little more than rasping pants as they gave themselves over to pleasure. Frankie knew she was hurtling towards a climax that outshone anything she had experienced recently. A part of her mind wanted to ask Simon if his enjoyment was as intense, but her need for satisfaction forbade her from speaking and breaking the mood. Instead, she simply rode herself harder on to him and chewed more deliberately at his pierced nipple.

'Turn over,' he gasped. She could feel his hands at her arms as he tried to reposition her. His rigid length was sliding from her sex lips and she felt a wave of despair as he threatened to pull the shaft away. She grinned up at him and asked, 'What if I don't want to?'

'I could force you.'

'I'd fight,' she said defiantly.

'You'd lose.'

'You'd have lost your appetite for sex by the time you made me turn over,' she warned him.

He shook his head, his smile weary but nonetheless affectionate. 'I wish your spirit had been cowed,' he growled good-naturedly. 'You might be easier to handle. Are you going to turn over or not?'

'Do you want me to?'

'Yes.'

'Then say please.' She knew it was wrong to play power games with Simon. She had been looking forward to a chance of reliving their passion since their first experience and the voice of her conscience told her it was unforgivable to tease him like this. But there was a gleeful spirit inside her that needed to exert some control and, even though this was Simon and she had been desperate to savour his caresses again, it was crucial to her enjoyment that they made love on her terms.

'You want me to say please,' he repeated. 'I should be grateful that you're not making me beg.'

'Don't put ideas into my head,' she warned him. 'Just say please and I'll turn over. And hurry up about it. I'm as horny as you are.'

'Please,' he spat sharply.

She grinned again and twisted around on the stone. Her breasts were touched by the sandpaper caress of the crumbling masonry but that only added to her arousal. Reaching behind her, she tried to catch hold of Simon's length and tease him again before allowing him to penetrate. He slapped her hand away and pressed the head of his shaft over the glistening lips of her sex. Rather than being able to prolong his excitement, he was now torturing her with the same threat of penetration that she had used on him.

The dome of his penis weighed heavily against her yielding lips, but he held it carefully and didn't allow it to plunge inside her. Working the end up and down, he traced a path from the edge of her perineum to the pulse of her clitoris. The pressure was firm, and with a growing need welling inside her, Frankie cried out, stopping short of begging him to enter her. 'Do it, Simon,' she demanded hoarsely. 'Do it now.'

'Say please,' he chided.

Frankie sucked lungfuls of air and half turned to study him. 'Just do it.'

Simon obeyed. The entry was deeper from this position and Frankie could feel herself being propelled forward as he tried to force his entire length into her tight confines. She could feel every tingling instance of his penetration and, as the climax that had been building threatened to burst in a gargantuan rush, she tried to focus her thoughts on the faraway horizon in an attempt to stave off her orgasm.

Seeming oblivious to the intensity of her response, Simon pushed deeper, then withdrew all the way from her wet channel, allowing the end to fall from between her sex lips. With a sharp thrust of his hips, he suddenly plunged back inside, and Frankie stifled the scream of elation of approaching orgasm.

Repeatedly he teased her in the same way, allowing her to think that he was pulling all the way out, then forcing himself back into her with a passionate rush. The effect was debilitating and if she hadn't been laid across the stone, Frankie would have collapsed on to it. She heard herself cry out, her voice growing louder and more distant in the same instance. He was taking her to a new level of pleasure, and it was only a determined effort that stopped her from succumbing to the magnificent release his love-making offered.

'We're going to have change positions,' he gasped. 'I want more from you.'

He sounded breathless and Frankie sympathised with his exhaustion. She had been lying down and allowing him to do all the work while she revelled in the glory of their passion. Usually, when submissives entertained her Frankie spared no pity for their weariness. But this was Simon, and her conscience told her that she should be making more of an effort to please him. Trying to turn, she grinned at him and said, 'You've got no stamina. Lie down.'

He shook his head and placed a firm hand on her back. 'I didn't mean that. I said I wanted more.' His shaft had eased itself from the lips of her sex and he rubbed it against her as he spoke. Then, to emphasise his exact meaning, he rested the head against the rim of her anus.

Frankie moaned softly, surprised by the excitement evoked by his suggestion. She contemplated asking him to say please again, but instead, pushing her hips backwards, tried forcing herself on to his length with her arsehole.

Simon held his shaft rigid and muttered a growl of satisfaction.

Frankie was momentarily aware of his length plundering her forbidden depths but the sensation was almost lost as the orgasm swept through her. He was large, a fact that her quivering pussy muscles bore witness to, and she had

164

anticipated at least some discomfort in having him penetrate her backside. However, she hadn't expected the pleasure to be so exhilarating.

Waves of joy coursed through her and left her sobbing. She was aware that Simon was fighting against his own explosion, but that thought was peripheral as she found herself achieving peak after peak of marvellous excess and he probed deeper. She felt his hands hold her hips as he tried to draw her towards him. The knowledge that her body couldn't accommodate much more of him was unimportant compared with her desire to experience as much of him as she could.

With a bitter sigh, she heard him groan, and then she knew that he had lost the fight against his own inevitable need. Her entire body trembled and, as the pulse of his ejaculation echoed through her, the final wave of her own pleasure flooded her body. For the briefest, sweetest of moments, her consciousness was fading as the strength of her orgasm knocked her senseless.

A few seconds later, she managed to focus her mind back to the real world as Simon slid his shaft out of her. He was leaning forward, planting kisses against her shoulders and whispering words of affection. Frankie half-turned and met his mouth with her own. Her body was trembling as after-echoes of her pleasure continued to tease her, but the intensity of the climax was now passed.

Simon worked his mouth against Frankie's breast and she pushed herself towards him. As he sucked on the nipple, she stared up at the azure sky and reminded herself that the world wasn't the bleak place she had thought it was. Perhaps she would have to endure some unpleasantness with McGivern but it was for a good cause, a cause worth making some sacrifices for. She also realised that once McGivern and his guests had left, she and Simon would be alone on the island with only the submissives for company. Contemplating the pleasure that lay ahead for them both, Frankie shivered excitedly.

Simon glanced up from the nipple he was sucking. There was a frown creasing his brow and Frankie wished she

165

hadn't seen it. His obvious consternation reminded her that the island wasn't really the paradise she had just been imagining. 'Does this change things?' he asked.

Frankie stared at him, surprised he had voiced thoughts that reflected some of her own reservations. 'You tell me.'

'Perhaps we can work out the answer together?' he suggested.

His hand moved towards her stomach and she could see his fingers were easing their way purposefully down to the mound of her pubic bush. She stopped him from going any further and shook her head. It wasn't that she didn't want to enjoy the experience of having Simon again. Being totally honest, she would have wanted nothing more at this precise moment, but she knew that was an impossibility. Having seen the way the sun had moved across the sky, Frankie knew that there was little time left before she had to submit herself to McGivern.

'Maybe we can work it out tonight,' she said quietly. 'I have a small business matter to attend to this afternoon.'

'You have to help me deal with Grace,' Simon told her.

Frankie shook her head. 'You'll have to deal with Grace for me. If she insists on seeing me, then I'll try and deal with her when I'm finished.' Simon looked as though he was unhappy with this situation but she could see he was prepared to accept it. The realisation that his generosity extended beyond his love-making made her smile.

'I need to check on McGivern before I next see Grace, but I'll do what I can.' He paused and studied her hesitantly. 'What is your business matter?'

She shook her head. 'I can't tell you now, and I probably won't tell you afterwards. Just trust me when I say that it's something I have to do.'

'It concerns McGivern, doesn't it?'

She nodded, but refused to meet the scrutiny of his questioning expression.

'I was a bloody idiot for inviting that man here,' Simon said angrily. He slammed his fist against one of the stone embattlements and Frankie saw him grimace against the pain. 'What the hell was I thinking of?'

166

'Fuck knows,' Frankie said quietly. 'But it's done now and I suppose we'll learn to live with it.' They were optimistic words and as she watched Simon start to dress himself, she wondered if she would feel so generous once the day was over.

Ten

'Bend.'

Captain Wilde spat the word like an insult and Jane couldn't stop herself from obeying him. His hand fondled her arse-cheeks with a brutal disregard for the beating she had just suffered. Harsh fingernails stroked her ravaged orbs and she flushed crimson as he then began to tease them against the warmth of her cleft. She knew the touch should have been exciting – his manner was calculated and his authoritative tone was so severe he made McGivern sound indecisive – yet she could feel nothing but antipathy for this dominatrix. Even when he pushed a stout index finger into the confines of her sex, Jane couldn't admit to feeling turned on by him.

He was obviously a competent master, and clearly a powerful authority figure, but Jane's appetites needed something more than that. Her body needed the initial spark of attraction before it would allow her to enjoy the whole exciting process of submission.

'Spread your legs wider.' This instruction was followed by the lightest of spanks to one bruised arse-cheek. The mild blow rekindled the burning embers of her arousal, but that was the closest he had come to exciting her so far. As Jane obeyed him, sullenly spreading herself wider beneath his intrusive hand, she glared at McGivern.

It didn't surprise her that McGivern was avoiding her gaze. His concentration was fixed on the wad of banknotes he had just accepted. He was holding each one up to the light before silently declaring it satisfactory and stuffing it into his pocket. Each time his gaze flitted to meet hers, he widened his smile and gave her a reassuring wink. Before Jane could turn her surprised features into a scowl, McGivern was looking away again and studying the validity of another banknote.

The finger between her legs was joined by a second one and Jane felt both digits plunder deep into her sodden depths. Their wriggling inspired an unexpected tickle of pleasure and she swallowed her surprise as she experienced the first real flicker of arousal. Her enjoyment was made more intense because it felt so darkly shameful. Not only had she taken an instant dislike to this dominatrix, but he was also examining her in front of a hall of leering masters and slaves. The humiliation of the situation, and her body's treacherous response to it, filled Jane with a growing excitement that she was loathe to acknowledge.

'She's tight, wet, and built with exceedingly good muscle control,' Captain Wilde decided.

The fingers were snatched from her sex and she heard him sniffing like a connoisseur. Without needing to turn and see, Jane could picture him inhaling the fragrance of her pussy honey from his dripping fingers.

'She also has a good bouquet,' he declared. 'And I think she'll make an excellent addition to my staff.'

His low growl of approval should have been comforting. Instead, Jane's revulsion for the man was rising. For the past six months she had been happy to tolerate life as McGivern's plaything. She had given herself freely to him and his colleagues and the rewards of that shared pleasure had always been satisfying. But the idea of submitting herself to this stranger left Jane feeling cold and frightened. He looked more suited to administering pain than pleasure and she needed to enjoy that combination of sensations in equal measures. There was something sinister about his manner that chilled and unsettled her.

'I haven't finished with her just yet,' McGivern said. He was speaking above Jane, barely acknowledging her presence as he addressed her new owner. 'You don't have any objections to my retaining her services until after the auction?'

169

Captain Wilde nodded stiffly. Staring at McGivern, he said, 'You're her master until after the auction, but for no longer than that. You can give me her deeds of indenture then, and she will become my possession.'

'Of course,' McGivern agreed. His voice sounded distant and Jane could see he was concentrating on the money rather than the arrangement. Bitterly, she wished his indifference towards her wasn't such an aphrodisiac and a spur to the dark arousal that squirmed in the pit of her stomach. Her need for satisfaction began to grow.

Captain Wilde snapped his fingers and Jane realised he wanted her to stand up straight. Unhappy with having to obey him, but fearful of the retribution that he might inflict if she didn't, she reluctantly eased herself from her undignified position.

His fingers went to her nipples and Jane tried not to step away as he caressed the sensitive tips. He was placing a finger and thumb on either side of her nubs, and she braced herself for the public indignity of having both breasts teased. The pressure was gentle at first, tolerable and exciting enough to quicken the pulse between her legs. She dared to meet his eyes and saw that they were shining with cruel intent. As his grip tightened, his grin grew broader. She could feel her composure threatening to collapse as his fingers squeezed against her excited flesh.

Flares of protesting pain were sparking from her breasts and she quelled the urge to slap his hands away. Her nipples had grown excessively responsive while she had endured the group's punishment. Her pussy lips had been teased and caressed by a dozen unseen hands, and her arse-cheeks had been taken to a level of discomfort that made them too tender to touch again. But throughout that ordeal, her breasts had been ignored and their need for attention had grown. As the captain began to twist her nipples, Jane met his gaze with defiance. Although she was determined not to give him the pleasure of seeing her excitement or her unease, that resolution began to melt when his fingers pressed more tightly together. The tingling coursing through each orb was making her gasp with pleasure.

He released her abruptly, snatching his hands away and tugging down in the same instance. The movement left her shocked and she could feel herself about to crumble beneath a wave of orgasmic pleasure. For an instant she was sure she had cried out with pained elation. In the tense silence of the hall, she realised that the cry had come from someone else, and she silently thanked the unknown person for their empathy.

The captain studied her silently, raising a hand to her face before drawing his fingers against her cheek. The smile he flexed was menacing and, as she stared into the bottomless depths of his black eyes, she was struck by the realisation that he was a cold-hearted and merciless bastard. There was something in his smile that showed him to be far more barbaric than McGivern could ever hope to become.

As though he had read her frightened thoughts, the captain's grin broadened. 'This one and I are going to have fun together,' he growled happily, glancing at McGivern. His fingertips were ice cold as they trailed against her skin, and Jane steeled herself against shivering beneath his touch. She closed her eyes, fearful he would see the loathing in her expression. When she dared to open them, the captain had returned to his place amongst the rest of auction crowd. Without caring whether or not her actions defied her submissive status, Jane stepped over to McGivern and pushed her face close to his. 'How could you do that to me, you bastard? How could you?'

He shrugged indifferently. 'You're stock. I didn't want to sell you but he made me an offer I couldn't refuse. What's an entrepreneur supposed to do in a situation like that?'

There weren't words to express her contempt at his question. 'You're nothing but a heartless mercenary,' she spat.

He was unmoved by her anger. 'It's nice that we understand one another. Now, be a good girl and make sure all the transactions are sorted out properly. I wouldn't want things to go awry at this auction because of some fudged technicality.'

171

She glared at him incredulously. How could McGivern be so arrogant as to think she would obey any instruction after suffering the indignity of being examined and sold? However, he seemed to take her acquiescence for granted. 'Why the hell should I do anything you ask?' she demanded.

His smile was wicked. Glancing in the direction of her new owner, he said, 'Right now, I think you'd do just about anything to delay putting yourself into Captain Wilde's hands. So, be a good girl and do as I've asked, or I'll tell him to take you down to his boat right now.'

Jane glared at McGivern, knowing she had no option other than to obey him. Trying not to think of the new life that awaited her after the auction, she took a seat behind the table and prepared to perform her final tasks as McGivern's submissive.

McGivern stepped back on to the banquet table and clapped his hands for attention. He was holding a cloth bag high in the air and Jane dreaded to think what significance it might have for the coming events.

'Clear a circle,' McGivern cried. 'Clear a circle so we can prepare the running order.' He glanced back over his shoulder and grinned at the waiting slaves. 'Submissives, come to the front of the table, if you please. We're about to try something that they did at one of the Borgia's soirées.'

Jane watched warily as the slaves trouped in front of the table. The majority were women; their different sizes and shapes made for an eye-catching feast. Each one had been stripped to some state of undress that ranged from scantily clad to total nudity. There was a shameless display of bared breasts, pierced nipples and intimate tattoos. A handful tried modestly to cover themselves from the gaze of the crowd, but most stood proudly defiant.

'Clear a circle,' McGivern called again, gesturing for his fellow dominatrices to step backwards. They moved reluctantly and Jane guessed that they were unused to being on the receiving end of instructions. 'We're going to sort out the running order,' McGivern told them. 'And this

172

is the fairest way I can think of doing it.' He held ↗
cloth bag and said, 'I've got numbered marbles in h
Each of the slaves will collect one from the floor and tha.
will be used as her lot number.' Casting his frown on the
row of submissives, McGivern said, 'Any slave who takes
longer than two minutes will suffer another example of the
penalty. Do I make myself clear?'

Jane watched the row of submissives nod with varying
degrees of reluctance.

'And any slave who doesn't have a marble will simply be
given away.'

The expressions in the row turned serious and Jane
could see that this threat frightened most of them more
than the idea of the penalty.

McGivern grinned and, with a flick of his wrist, he
hurled the marbles into the hall. They sounded like
hailstones against the stone floor and before the spatter
had subsided, the submissives fell on them.

In a rush of naked flesh, they scrabbled on hands and
knees in their hasty attempts to follow McGivern's
instructions. Jane could see that the room had become a
mass of squirming bodies, with backsides and breasts being
casually displayed to anyone who cared to look. The
dominatrices applauded with approval as they kicked stray
marbles back into the crowd of slaves.

Jane watched a pair of submissives snatch their prizes
from the floor, then hurry back to the corner of the room
that McGivern had allocated. The writhing throng began
to diminish as each slave retrieved a marble and went to
join the others. Before McGivern's two-minute deadline
had elapsed, there was only one unfortunate brunette left
in the centre of the room and Jane could see that she was
chasing the final marble. A pair of dominatrices were
gleefully kicking it between one another, laughing as the
submissive stumbled in her attempts to catch it, each one
taking a turn at spanking her bottom when they had
kicked the marble away.

Unhappily, Jane realised that one of these malevolent
beasts was her new owner, Captain Wilde. This made her

loathe him even more, and she tried to shut out thoughts of her new predicament.

With growing fear, the brunette submissive began to cry as she continued lurching between the pair. Her arse-cheeks bore the fresh, red marks of both men's handprints and her breasts quivered as she tried to control her sobs.

'Let her have it,' McGivern snapped.

'But –' Captain Wilde glared angrily at him and Jane could see that the man didn't enjoy being the recipient of such commands.

'Just let her have it and then we can begin.' His tone was a warning but Jane knew he wasn't trying to assist the submissive because of chivalrous motivations: he was giving the instruction because he was desperate to start the auction.

Churlishly, Captain Wilde bent down to the floor and picked up the marble between his finger and thumb. He held it out for the brunette and she approached him hesitantly. As she reached out for it, the captain snatched the marble away. Jane was struck by the wickedness in his broad smile.

'Give it to her,' McGivern growled.

Glaring at him again, Captain Wilde tossed the marble in the air.

The brunette stumbled in her attempts to catch it and the marble slipped through her fingers. She plucked it from the floor and turned a meek expression on McGivern, clearly aware that she had exceeded his two-minute deadline. Rather than instigate the punishment he had threatened, McGivern simply nodded his head in the direction of the waiting slaves. The brunette rushed to join the others.

McGivern cast a final, challenging glance in Captain Wilde's direction, then cleared his throat and allowed his smile to resurface. 'Bidding is underway, ladies and gentleman,' he declared theatrically. 'Just one final word of warning to you all: a slave is for life, not just for Christmas.'

He barked for the first number and seemed mildly

surprised to see number seven raise a reluctant hand. He took a quick side-step and reached for her arm. The submissive looked unhappy at being dragged into the limelight, but she responded to her master's instruction as obediently as any of McGivern's entourage. She cast an unhappy glance in the direction of number eleven and then both of them looked away in different directions. The blonde's cheeks flushed crimson and she studied the expectant crowd fearfully.

'This is the first lot we have on offer, and it's one hell of a fine specimen,' McGivern told his audience. 'She's blonde, female and exceptionally submissive. She's moderately obedient and has a decent backside that blushes well when spanked properly.'

Jane glared at McGivern, trying to hate him and wishing she didn't find his natural exuberance so exciting. The tingle between her legs was beating at a swifter pace as she made herself ready for the auction. Jane wasn't surprised by her libidinous response. She doubted there could be a more humiliating experience than being examined and sold and, before she would allow the full implications of her new predicament to sink in, she was determined to enjoy the effects of watching this indignity.

McGivern's concentration was fixed on his sales pitch and Jane knew that the bidders were only interested in the slave he was exhibiting. Despite the fact that she was sitting at the front of the room, no one was looking at her.

Slowly, she stole a hand between her legs. The lips of her sex were slippery with excitement and she wondered how she had managed to contain her explosion for so long. The punishment and penetration of the penalty had brought her close to orgasm, but not close enough. As her fingertips caressed the wet flesh, Jane could feel her climactic needs bristling. The pleasure of the entire day flashed through her mind's eye, and she stopped herself from crying out loud as her body prepared to vent an enormous release. The bite of the riding crop that McGivern had used on the boat as they approached the castle was still fresh enough in her memory to make her smile. Number three's caresses against her punished backside and the recent group chastisement were all catalysts to her growing desire. Even the hateful examination by Captain Wilde added fuel to her fire, and Jane bit back a groan as her body revelled in its arousal.

To Jane's left, between her seat and McGivern's, number three was still bound and gagged in her undignified position. The slave's buttocks were facing her and, as she surreptitiously studied her, Jane's arousal deepened. The bondage had clearly excited the slave and Jane could see that the submissive's pierced pussy lips were sodden and gaping. The tiny steel balls on each of the closure rings shone with a slick coating of pussy honey. It occurred to her that one of the piercings looked a little unusual. This piercing behind number three's clitoris was almost lost in shadows but from her position facing it, Jane could see that it sparkled. She pushed her hand more firmly against herself and savoured a rush of pleasure.

The slave's flushed, hairless cleft was glistening and Jane wished the two of them had been afforded a moment's privacy. The sight of the slave's pierced labia was always thrilling to her and Jane could picture herself tonguing number three's wet hole and teasing the tiny, steel rings. That image alone would have been sufficient to hurl her beyond her restraint, but Jane fought against it, determined to savour the exquisite pleasure of a slow release.

'. . . going to start the bidding?'

She couldn't be bothered with listening to McGivern; her concentration was focused on the eager fingers that slid against her sex. With the sensation of her own hand frigging the nub of her exposed clit in subtle, yet deliberate thrusts, Jane reminded herself of the indignities that the day had brought upon her and her body grew weak with the need to explode.

Reluctantly, she turned her gaze away from number three. There would never be the chance for them to share anything ever again and she was unwilling to sour her

176

excitement by dwelling on this thought. Casting her eye over the gathered crowd, she let the casual displays of submission and control add to her fantasies as she pushed her body towards its long-awaited release.

Bare backsides were flushed pink beneath slapping hands and sexual punishments were being exacted in full view of anyone who cared to watch. Jane saw a meek brunette bent before her master and taking his length in her mouth. She worked her ripe lips over his shaft, sliding a dark tongue occasionally against his balls. When the brunette took the dome from her mouth, Jane saw a shaft silver with saliva, the end leaking a string of pre-come. The master's grin was thin, almost disinterested, as his submissive took his length back into her mouth and began to suck greedily on him.

A dark-haired male, kneeling at his mistress's feet, kissed the toes of her boots. His erection was tied by leather straps and stainless-steel rings and Jane could see the shaft straining furiously against its restraints. An expression of tortured bliss twisted the man's face as his mistress bent down and clawed cruel nails against his buttocks. Punishing, red lines were etched against the pale flesh of his arse-cheeks and the sight reminded Jane of the ache that still throbbed in her own backside.

Yet it was the indignity of the sale to which Jane's thoughts kept returning. The woman in red – Babs, Jane remembered – had taken an interest in number seven. She was studying the submissive through her opaque sunglasses, caressing the blonde's figure. The dominatrix spat out a handful of stark instructions and the slave complied obediently. Jane could see that number seven was unhappy with the indignity but empathising with the submissive only made her more aware of her own arousal.

Her pussy lips had peeled open, and she used one hand to keep them apart as the other reached again for her clitoris. The moment of unfettered contact sent a spasm coursing through her and she held herself rigid, fearful that someone would see if she started to thrash and undulate at the banquet table. Her future was already looking bleak and she doubted it would be improved if her life under a new master began with a punishment for self-indulgence. Unable to stop herself from the course she had already started, Jane tried to keep her upper body motionless as her fingers worked against her nub.

Babs made number seven parade around on all fours and the blonde was managing the task with guileless grace. Jane saw that the submissive was now responding excitedly to the humiliation, and in spite of number seven's evident arousal, Babs appeared to be pleased by the submissive's efforts and nodded grudging approval.

Jane closed her eyes and stole her finger deeper against her sex. Next, she managed to slide two fingers into the gaping lips of her hole and was thrilled by the rush of pleasure. McGivern's use of her that morning had been satisfying to a degree but it had still left her body with an unfulfilled ache which had grown throughout the day and, as she had endured excitement and punishment, her need for release had grown beyond all measure. Now, as she pushed her fingers deep inside herself, she could feel all that pent-up arousal threatening to burst.

Bidding had started on number seven and Babs was intent on acquiring the submissive. However, Jane wasn't watching or listening. Her sex was hot and moist and her need to climax nagged relentlessly. She avoided touching her clitoris, knowing that the tactile nub would only need to suffer a little more pressure before her orgasm struck. Instead, she slid the fingers deeper, savouring the slippery wetness of her excitement.

McGivern repeated the bids, cajoling the crowd into raising the stakes by making the submissive turn, kneel and bend to display her assets. His attention was focused away from her and Jane felt as if she could have screamed with excitement and not been noticed.

A handful of applause and McGivern's hearty cheer sounded the end of the first sale. Through a hazy mist of pleasure, Jane saw that Babs had been victorious in her bidding. But this realisation was distant. Her fingers were working more furiously, her orgasm only moments away.

178

She feigned interest in her surroundings, barely acknowledging Simon's return to the banquet hall. From the corner of her eye, she saw number eleven take her place in front of the bidders, but the impending thrill of release was a whisper away and Jane could think of nothing that would drag her thoughts from that pleasure.

Simon placed himself next to Babs and allowed her to hold his hand as she made her bids. Instead of watching the bidding, or McGivern, he glanced impatiently around the hall. If anyone was likely to spot her lapse into indiscretion, Jane knew it would be Simon, but she was beyond caring. Besides, Simon had the decency to treat his submissives with compassion and she hoped that if he did see what she was doing, he wouldn't draw any attention to her.

The moment of release was approaching all too quickly. Jane knew that she needed to keep still when the orgasm struck and she was also fearful of voicing her climax, but still she continued to slide her fingers in and out of her sodden cleft. As the rush of the climax came nearer, Jane wondered how she could accomplish such an act in front of a crowd of people and go unnoticed. Her head was pounding as adrenaline coursed through her veins. The slurping sound of fingers at her sex was so loud, she felt sure it should be heard by those dominatrices who stood at the back of the banquet hall.

Yet still no one seemed to have noticed that she was pushing herself towards the brink of a gargantuan climax. Discovery was bound to happen if she didn't change positions, so Jane slid her chair closer to number three. The idea of hiding behind the slave would have seemed almost comical if her thoughts hadn't been so fogged with arousal. But there were also other impulses driving her: the impetus for her climax only needed one more thing. Jane had to have it before she gave in to her last orgasm before submission beneath another master. Grateful that no one had noticed her change in position, she edged her chair still closer to the bound submissive.

'Going once,' McGivern cried. He glanced around the

banquet hall and Jane held herself rigid, fearful that he would see her.

'Is Babs the only one who's going to walk away from here with a freshly bought submissive today?' When there was no response to his question, he cried, 'Going twice,' and cast his gaze around the hall again.

Even though the world was blurred by heady splendour, Jane could see that there would be no final bidders as McGivern relented and called, 'Three times and gone. Sold to the lady in red.'

As the bidders murmured excitedly in the break between lots, Jane moved towards the cleft of number three's sex. Before she allowed her body its elation, she wanted to savour the taste of the slave's sex. It was a flavour she had yearned to experience since she had first met the submissive. That morning on the boat had been the closest that either of them had come to exploring their mutual attraction. She knew that there would be repercussions if anyone saw, but she was so far beyond caring, the thought seemed immaterial. As she pushed her nose closer to the open lips of the slave's sex, Jane felt her release building to a delicious crescendo.

McGivern was selecting another lot for the auction and the crowd was falling into dutiful silence as he gave a brief description of the submissive's merits. Jane heard everything as though it was being spoken through a tunnel, her attention totally devoted to reaching the bound submissive's hole. Her face was hidden from view and, taking advantage of the discretion, Jane pushed her tongue forward. The cloying scent of arousal filled her nostrils and she savoured the taste of the slave's excitement. Number three grunted slightly and, shifting her head away, Jane saw that the slave was trying to look at her. Not daring to make an obvious display of what she was doing, Jane pushed her tongue deeper and lapped greedily at the slave's wetness. Pushing her fingers hard against her own wet hole, she knew it would be impossible to stave off the climax for an instant longer.

Thrusting her fingers deeper than before, Jane felt her clitoris being pressed between her hand and her pelvic bone. The climax was debilitating. A spray of pussy honey spattered into her palm and she could feel its copious flow wetting the tops of her thighs. The orgasm swept through her with unstoppable force. She struggled not to shriek as every nerve-ending was scoured with an electric thrill that left her dizzy. She rocked from side to side in the chair, burying her nose deeper into number three and willing the delightful shivers to subside before she dared begin to move away. Each inhalation was filled with the slave's dewy musk and this only prolonged Jane's agonising, blissful moments. As the waves of euphoria began to recede, she finally found the energy to pull herself away. Her fingers felt numb after rubbing so hard and her body ached with the delicious after-echoes of enjoyment but common sense told her that she couldn't stay where she was any longer. After giving the slave's hole a final, grateful kiss, Jane tried to shake off the thrill of her orgasm and regain her composure in case anyone noticed her.

Another hearty cheer went through the crowd and McGivern slapped his hand casually against number three's backside to finalise the deal. Jane saw his fingers land against the wetness where her mouth had just been and she shuddered when she saw how close she had come to being discovered. The thought gave her a devilish thrill and she tried not to dwell on it, fearful of where such lewd imaginings might lead.

'We still have plenty of sales to get through,' McGivern told his audience. 'But if any of you were thinking of leaving early, I should tell you, you'll be missing one hell of a party afterwards. And just to add to the fun, I've organised a little game with a marvellous prize. The prize is this slave here.' He slapped number three's backside again to show exactly who he meant.

Number three flinched, surprised by the blow. She stared unhappily up at him, her sultry brown eyes begging for release. Jane felt a pang of guilt twist in her stomach like the blade of a knife.

McGivern didn't bother to look at either of them. He was intent on imparting something to his guests and wouldn't have noticed any distraction at that moment. 'Somewhere in this fine castle, I've hidden a precious stone: the number three diamond.' He waited for the audience to fall silent before he continued. 'For those of you who don't know about the number three diamond, it's a simple gemstone, with a rather attractive flaw that makes it unique. The game is a simple treasure hunt: find the diamond and you can have the slave. I'll tell you now, it's hidden somewhere in this room, so you don't have to pillage the entire building. The first person to locate it gives it to me, and I let them take possession of this slave.'

An excited murmur went through the hall, but it was almost dwarfed by the sound of someone shouting, 'No!' Jane saw Simon struggle to free himself from Babs' embrace, march through the crowd of bidders, and grab hold of McGivern's arm. 'You can't sell number three,' he hissed. 'She's not yours to sell, she's mine.' His voice was cold and clear and it echoed around the banquet hall.

There was a stunned, expectant silence and Jane realised that everyone was watching with lurid grins. She switched her gaze between McGivern and Simon, sickened by the animosity between them.

'I told you it's going to be a mock treasure hunt,' McGivern hissed. 'Frankie will win the prize, she'll get her slave and we'll all be happy. Now, get back to your seat and don't make me embarrass you.'

'And I told you that I'm not going to con these people,' Simon spat back. His grey eyes had hardened to the colour of tempered steel and he studied McGivern with the glower of a predatory animal. 'Unfasten number three and put her in my charge.'

'Should we discuss this in private, Simon?' McGivern said in a low whisper. 'Just you and me, so that the rest of our peers can't eavesdrop?'

Simon shook his head. He made his voice louder than normal, deliberately trying to defy McGivern's suggestion. 'You've done enough private transactions today. This one is going to be done in full public view so that everyone can see what a cheating bastard you really are.'

McGivern gave an indifferent shrug, a smile growing broader over his face. Jane gritted her teeth, knowing that this was the defiant smile McGivern always gave when he was still confidently in charge of a situation. 'If that's how you want it,' he said. His voice was as loud and theatrical as Simon's. 'Why don't you prove publicly that this is your slave?'

Simon reached into his pocket and took out the tube of vellum. 'Number three's deeds of indenture,' he said triumphantly. 'I think you'll find that they are still in order as when you sold them to me this morning.'

McGivern took the tube but made no attempt to open it. He casually handed the vellum to Jane and said, 'Can you see if this gives Simon's claim any validity?'

Jane lifted a reluctant hand from beneath the table and took the offered paper. Her fingers were still sodden with spent excitement. Only after wiping her hands dry on her bare thighs did she carefully unfurl the roll of vellum. With a practised eye, she glanced through the contract, leafing through to the final page.

'Well?' Simon demanded. 'That proves she's mine, doesn't it?'

Jane drew a startled breath. She tried not to cower beneath Simon's frown and wondered how angry he was going to become when she told him the truth.

'Doesn't it?' he demanded.

Jane shook her head. 'These aren't number three's deeds of indenture,' she explained meekly. 'These are mine.'

She saw his frown deepen and a thunderous fury crossed his brow. He turned to McGivern and curled his hands into fists.

'Don't even think about causing a scene,' McGivern warned him. He kept his tone so low that Jane had to strain to hear what was being said. She barely managed to catch all of the conversation and felt certain that no one else in the crowd could hear McGivern's words. 'We have a crowd of dominatrices here and they're working to auction house rules. You can either be a good boy and do exactly as I say, or I can ask them to inflict the penalty on you for trying to cast disrepute on my name.'

'I'm not happy with this, McGivern,' Simon growled. In spite of his words, Jane could see that he had uncurled his fists. The threat of violence had passed, for the moment.

'Pardon me for not giving a fuck about your happiness.' McGivern laughed quietly. 'Just be warned: if you embarrass me again you'll have to deal with this lot.' He raised his voice and turned to the audience. 'Good news, good news,' he cheered loudly. 'Now that the little misunderstanding has been cleared up, our host here is going to take over the auction. I'm going to leave you in his capable hands and I'll try to join you again before the end of the party.'

'Where are you going?' Simon asked.

McGivern's smile grew broader. 'As much as I'd love to tell you, I don't think it would be wise for you to know too much.' Jane saw that his grin was tainted by his typically malicious brand of mirth. 'Perhaps I'll tell you after I've finished,' he chuckled. 'Although that might make you want to become all physical again.' Without another word, he waved a cheerful farewell to the auction and started towards the door.

'Where does this leave us?' Jane asked quietly.

Simon was glowering at the door, his concentration focused on McGivern's back as the dominatrix disappeared out of the room. 'It leaves me regretting that I ever did business with that bastard,' he whispered. 'And if I ever get the chance to settle the score . . .'

He didn't need to finish the sentence. As Simon reluctantly organised himself to take charge of the auction, Jane agreed that she knew exactly how she felt.

184

Eleven

Frankie glared at McGivern as he walked into her bedroom. He was holding a carrier bag and riding crop in one hand and a large jug of orange juice in the other. Her fears immediately focused on the riding crop rather than the two innocuous items he held. Her body was suddenly coated with gooseflesh and she strained her thoughts, desperate to find a way out of the situation. But knowing it was a futile effort, she resigned herself to the fate she had been anticipating throughout the afternoon. She had promised to submit to him and he had promised her number three in return. It was an adult exchange and she considered herself mature enough to be able to cope with it. The knowledge that it would undoubtedly be the most humiliating experience of her life didn't make Frankie feel comfortable with the situation.

McGivern marched past her and placed the crop and the orange juice on her dressing table. Turning to face her, he graced her with a sneer of contempt. 'No, no, no.' He was shaking his head unhappily. His voice was didactic and his frown looked tired and exasperated. 'This isn't how I want you at all.'

Frankie glanced down at herself, surprised that he could find anything wrong with her appearance. She had found a pair of fishnets for this occasion and was wearing a fresh leather mini. Simon's seed had soiled the skirt she wore earlier and in a spirit of uncharacteristic kindness, she had decided to make some effort towards appearing present-able for McGivern. The leather bra she wore beneath her biker's jacket was tight yet flattering, and she could think of no other way to enhance her appearance for him. 'What's wrong with me?' she asked sullenly.

'I want you to get changed,' he snapped. 'I want you to get changed now, and I want to watch while you do it.' He fixed her with a meaningful glare and said, 'We don't have long together this afternoon but I'm determined to make your suffering drawn out and memorable for the both of us.'

'You want me to get changed into what?' Frankie asked. The air between them was thick with expectancy and she tried not to contemplate the degradation that lay ahead. 'In case you didn't know, I should tell you that this is pretty much the same as everything else I have in my wardrobe.'

McGivern sniffed and she could hear a note of genuine disgust in his tone. 'I thought that might be the case. That's why I took the precaution of bringing these for you.' Using his whip hand, he hurled the bulging carrier bag towards her.

Frankie caught the bag and began to rummage through its contents. As she identified each item of clothing, her unhappiness deepened and she turned to face him with a sneer of contempt. 'This proves what I've always thought,' she told him. 'You're a twisted bastard.'

McGivern took a step closer and waved a threatening finger in front of her face. 'One more comment like that and this whole deal is off. You're meant to be submitting to me, not offering unsolicited opinions on my mental health.'

Frankie considered saying something else, then thought better of it. She began to pull the clothes from the bag and hurled them, item by item, on to the foot of the bed. A pair of white, over-knee socks went first, followed by a pair of frilly, cotton panties. Next to those she dropped a plain, white blouse and a pleated, grey skirt that was longer than those she normally wore. Beside the sensible shoes, the plain, white bra and the straw boater, she threw the final item for the ensemble: a silver and purple school tie.

Looking at it as it rested on top of the uniform, she shivered with revulsion.

'You should also find a box of make-up in that bag,' McGivern said. He grinned at her deepening scowl. 'I know that make-up is usually something that women wear, but I'm sure that on this occasion, we can make an exception.'

It was one barb too many and she could hear her anger rising up like an explosion. 'You're an offensive –'

He held up a silencing finger. 'Remember not to antagonise me, Frankie,' he warned. 'Another outburst like that and our deal's off.'

Frankie chewed her lower lip and resisted the urge to spit at him. 'I'm really not happy about having to wear this lot,' she said, pointing at the pile of clothes on the bed.

McGivern nodded, gracing her with a smile of artificial sympathy. 'Of course you're not happy with them,' he agreed. 'I tried to think of a way of making your submission enjoyable but then I realised, I didn't want it to be like that for you.' His smile was twisted by a malicious lilt. 'I want you to loathe every moment of this, Frankie,' he explained gleefully. 'I want you to hate every minute of it because watching you suffer is how I'm going to extract most of my pleasure.'

'You –'

He held up a warning finger and she could see from his expression that it really was the last chance he would allow. Glaring sullenly at the mound of clothes, she shrugged the jacket from her shoulders and began to undress.

McGivern jumped on to the bed and watched as she stripped off. His attention was riveted on her body as she slid the skirt from her hips. He leaned forward as she eased herself out of her bra and Frankie could see he was licking his lips. She wished there was a way to stop his hateful study of her nudity but common sense told her there wasn't. She tried to turn her back on him but as soon as she moved, he coughed angrily and told her to face him as she undressed.

'I want to admire all of your charms, Frankie,' he whispered. 'Don't try and hide them away from me.'

She fixed him with a scowl and watched him grin again with anticipation. Her cheeks darkening, she tugged her bra open and released her breasts.

'Aren't you just the loveliest sight?' McGivern grinned. Although he was forcing his tone to sound inordinately cheerful, she could hear a genuine appreciation in his voice. She glared at him, unable to conceal the loathing that burned in her eyes.

'I could look at you all day like that,' he said. 'But I don't think I will. Kick off your stockings and boots and get dressed in that uniform.'

Without a word, Frankie removed the final items and began to sort through the clothes he had brought. She climbed into the unflattering cotton panties first, hating them the moment they touched her skin. Having spent so many years without wearing knickers, these felt uncomfortable and awkward against the lips of her sex. The gusset caused a dry friction between the cheeks of her arse while her pubic curls scratched like wire wool as they were held tight against her pelvis.

'Very feminine,' McGivern said sardonically. 'Now the bra.'

She said nothing and merely picked the garment from the foot of the bed. It wasn't the perfect size and by the time she had struggled to press her orbs inside they were threatening to burst over the cups. Nevertheless, she adjusted herself inside the stiff cotton and glanced down to enjoy the sight of a heavily emphasised cleavage.

'Very, very pretty,' McGivern exclaimed. 'Who would have believed there was such a pretty girl lurking beneath that bull dyke exterior of yours?'

She could feel her face burning a hateful red. That she was dressing like this to please McGivern added fuel to her outrage and she was torn between thoughts of hating him or loathing herself. The idea of reneging on the deal was constantly at the forefront of her mind but reminding herself that she only had to endure this humiliation for a few short hours was enough to calm the rising flames of her outrage. The knowledge that she could take possession of number three after suffering this indignity had a calming effect and she took solace from it.

Trying not to meet McGivern's hawklike gaze, she tugged the socks on, pulling them over her knees and turning them down smartly. She then snatched up the skirt and blouse and finished dressing, trying not to notice McGivern and his lecherous study.

His smile was coarse and mocking and she could see the enormous bulge that pushed at the front of his pants. The thought that she had excited him did nothing to raise her spirits and his lechery only worsened her acute embarrassment. She stepped into the shoes, pushed the boater firmly on her head, and fastened the tie loosely around her neck.

'There,' she said decisively. Unable to stop herself, she stood before him in an unconsciously arrogant posture. Her hands were balled into fists, resting on her hips, and her legs were slightly apart. 'Was that you wanted?'

'It's a start,' he conceded. 'But you haven't put the make-up on yet.' Speaking as though the idea had only just occurred to him he said, 'And we still need to discuss the way you address me.'

'I won't call you master,' she told him defiantly. She reached for the knot of the tie at her throat and glared at him with furious determination as she loosened it. 'I don't care if it does sour our arrangement. I won't call you master. Not today. Not ever.'

'I wasn't going to suggest such a thing,' he said quietly. 'But I do insist that you call me sir.'

Frankie glared at him, hating his manipulative smile and despising the leer in his eyes. 'Sir,' she spat.

'Very good,' he told her. 'Now put your make-up on and let's see what you look like with a pretty face.'

For the briefest of moments she thought that applying the make-up might offer some reprieve from her unhappiness. It would mean that she could sit down at her dressing-table and be away from McGivern's invasive stare. Her hopes rose at the prospect. However, those hopes were quickly dashed as soon as she settled herself at the table because the mirror presented her with a new aspect on the situation: McGivern's face caught in the mirror over her shoulder. He was stroking the bulge in his trousers and the sight was a constant reminder that she was there under his scrutiny.

When she concentrated on her own reflection, Frankie's despondency grew darker. Her face was held beneath the shadows of the boater's brim and her cheeks were darkened by a mortified blush. Instead of seeing her own familiar features, she was studying the reflection of a woman who looked as though she had been thoroughly cowed.

'Make-up,' McGivern said encouragingly as she hesitated in front of the glass. 'I think the scarlet lipstick and the black mascara should be sufficient to get the right effect, don't you?'

Those weren't the thoughts at the forefront of Frankie's mind, but she didn't dare give voice to the ones that really lurked there. Examining the jumbled collection of make-up in the bottom of the bag, she saw the items he was referring to and made a fumbling attempt to apply them. Aside from the occasional experiment with nail polish, it had been a long time since she had worn make-up of any description. Her mirrored image seemed to be obeying different instructions to those she was giving to her face and she knew the task would have been less difficult if she had been more practised. On more than one occasion she slipped artlessly and smeared a thick red line towards her cheek. Wiping the excess away with a tissue, she tried not to think of the subtle stimulation that the make-up's perfume provided. She had always found the scent of lipstick arousing and it invariably thrilled her when she tasted it on a submissive's lips. Because the scent was so intrinsically linked with intimacy and lovers, she wasn't surprised to find herself responding to its sensuous fragrance.

Modestly pleased with the coating of lipstick, she reached for the mascara and shook the tube before opening it. The action was so natural that she was touched by a moment's surprise when she realised she had done it but trying not to think of the innate skills that were a natural

190

part of her femininity, Frankie snapped the lid off the mascara and took a deep, steadying breath. The dark liquid was scented with a feminine perfume that made her stomach churn uneasily.

She had expected McGivern to make this episode uncomfortable, humiliating and degrading, but she hadn't expected him to do anything that would arouse her. The knowledge that she was starting to enjoy this position left Frankie feeling sick with self-loathing. Her hand was shaking as she moved the mascara brush to her eyes and she forced her fingers to hold the handle firmly. Agonising moments passed as she painted her eyelashes so that they became thick curls. When she dared to glance away from her own reflection, she could see McGivern sitting behind her, silently encouraging her to continue.

The temptation to call off the deal struck her again but she had already gone too far to turn back. She replaced the lid on the mascara and eased herself from her chair. Standing away from the mirror, she was able to see the overall impression of her new clothes and make-up. She knew she couldn't have passed for a schoolgirl under anyone's interpretation but the outfit didn't look too ridiculous. The skirt stopped just above her knee and there was the tiniest sliver of lower thigh visible between its hem and the tops of her over-knee socks. The blouse wasn't particularly tight but it stretched against her bust and the shape of her overfilled bra was clearly visible beneath it. She was surprised to see how well she had applied the make-up after all and took a moment to admire her glossy, crimson lips and dense, dark lashes.

Not taking too long in front of the mirror for fear that McGivern would see she was pleased with the first part of his plan, she turned to face him. 'Is that good enough for you?'

'You forgot to call me sir.'

'Is that good enough for you, sir?'

'That's wonderful,' he said. His eyes widened and he put a hand over his mouth in a gesture of pantomime shock. 'But Frankie,' he exclaimed. 'You're wearing make-up and we all know that schoolgirls aren't allowed to wear make-up.'

She glared at him. 'Is this part of your sad fucking game?'

'Play along, or we call it off,' he growled. 'And the next time you forget to call me sir, I'll think of another way to make things a damned sight more uncomfortable.'

'Is this part of your game, sir?' she reiterated.

He allowed his smile to resurface and nodded. 'You're a very naughty girl. Do you know what happens to naughty girls who wear make-up?'

Frankie bit back a sardonic retort and shook her head.

'We have to remind them that they're still girls and punish them like girls. I'm going to have to spank your bottom.'

Frankie drew a deep breath. She wished she could have had a cigar but she already knew McGivern hated the smell of them and she felt certain that he would make his punishment worse for a naughty girl who was caught smoking a Havana. Ignoring the craving, she met his gaze and whispered, 'Very well, sir.'

He swung his legs from the bed, sitting on its edge. 'Place yourself over my knee, you naughty girl,' he grinned. 'I've been wanting to spank your bottom for a long, long time.'

Frankie hesitated, not wanting to put herself through this humiliation but seeing no other way of getting what she wanted. Her initial suggestion of a simple fuck would have been a lot easier to tolerate. At least that unpleasantness would have been over and done with quickly and she could have expressed her contempt for him as their bodies met. This was a far more punishing price to pay and Frankie knew McGivern was gleaning huge satisfaction from her discomfort.

'Come on, you naughty girl.' He slapped his own legs, encouraging her to bend over his knees. 'I need to smack your naughty bottom and I'll make the punishment more severe if you keep me waiting.'

She swallowed and took a faltering step towards him.

His grin was hateful and she loathed him with a vengeance. She lowered herself to the floor and draped herself over his knees, her thoughts shrieking at her to reconsider. McGivern was too close, her startled mind screeched. She was actually touching him as she bent over his knee and the subtle fragrance of his cologne was now filling her nostrils. The pressure of his erection was pulsing against her side and, without needing to think twice, she knew she was wholly responsible for his arousal.

'How many of these do you think you deserve, Frankie?' McGivern asked.

'None, sir,' she said flatly.

He made a tut-tutting sound and she could tell he was shaking his head. He had one hand between her shoulder blades, holding her in the servile position. The other caressed the backs of her legs and then drew the skirt slowly away from her thighs. The sensation of being exposed heightened her feeling of vulnerability and she felt a moment's gratitude towards the white, cotton knickers covering her sex. When she felt his fingers traversing the stiff fabric she tried to ignore the shameful thrill of excitement from his touch.

'I think you need six slaps to your backside,' he decided.

'And then may I go, sir?' she asked. It was a futile hope but she couldn't resist voicing it.

'And then we can begin to play this game properly,' he corrected. Without another word, he allowed his hand to fall against her bottom. The pressure was harsh enough to sting but the cotton knickers protected her from the discomfort she had anticipated. Her arse-cheeks trembled and she tried not to think too hard about the pulse in his erection. Because she was bent over his knee, her waist was pressed firmly against his lap. His excitement was obvious and she could feel it prodding into her ribcage, twitching firmly each time his arousal was inspired anew.

The second blow landed more firmly than the first. Frankie guessed that each slap was going to grow more uncomfortable as he progressed, and she closed her eyes against the sting of shame that burned her cheeks. She could tolerate pain of most descriptions but this was not pain: this was humiliation. More than that, in making her dress up like a naughty schoolgirl, McGivern had found a way to demean her that was far worse than she would have believed possible.

The third blow landed so heavily it left her backside trembling. She drew a startled breath and tried to glance back at him but at the last moment, Frankie stopped herself, knowing how much it would excite him if he thought that he had caused any suffering. Unwilling to give him that pleasure, Frankie kept her gaze focused on the carpet and reminded herself that there were only three more slaps to follow.

'I don't think these panties are helping,' McGivern decided. 'You need to take them off.'

She refused to give in to the thrill that his suggestion evoked. Hissing the words, 'Yes, sir,' she reached to her hips and started to tug them down.

His fingers stopped her with a brutal smack. 'I'll take them down for you.'

She didn't want him to but she knew better than to resist. Her pleated skirt was pushed all the way up her back and his fingers began to explore the elasticated waistband of the cotton knickers. His hands were warm and the subtle intimacy was annoyingly arousing. As he pulled the garment away from her backside, Frankie was struck by an unwanted glimmer of excitement. It didn't help that he was deliberately stroking her buttocks, or that his hands were coming into contact with her sex. His casual caress lingered at her pussy lips and as the thrill stole over her like an unwelcome intruder, she squirmed against the response he was inspiring. He made no attempt to penetrate her and his touch was so soft it felt as though he was only teasing the curls of her sex lips.

She had almost acclimatised her body to the embarrassment when his hand fell again. The sound of flesh striking flesh rang in her ears and a bolt of surprise travelled up from her backside. Frankie stiffened and tried to brace herself for the next blow but this one landed with a force that caught her properly unaware. She swallowed a growl of annoyance and again fought against her body's urge to enjoy the chastisement. The final slap was too harsh and, before she could stop herself, she had released a low grunt of discomfort. McGivern's cock twitched hard against her side and she was touched by a sickening wave of arousal as she shared his excitement.

'All six over and done with,' he said cheerfully. 'That wasn't so bad, was it?' He still had one hand between her shoulder blades, pinning her down. The other was casually stroking her smacked bottom, each subtle caress evoking the memory of the punishing slaps he had just administered. As his fingers travelled towards her cleft, Frankie tried to clench the cheeks of her backside close together. McGivern moved too quickly for her and, before she could stop him, she felt the gentle touch of a finger at her pussy lips. The sensation was annoyingly exquisite.

'I don't think it was all discomfort for you, was it?' he asked as he stroked his finger up and down. She knew he was making no attempts to penetrate her but that didn't make her humiliation any less intense. Her treacherous body was responding to him with an eagerness that she would never have believed. More than that was the fear of what might come next. She had spanked her own submissives in similar ways and knew that once they had been aroused with a chastisement, it was customary to have them taste their own excitement. Now McGivern was likely to moisten his finger against her sex, then press it against her mouth. The prospect left her shivering.

'You've made my finger all wet,' he said, sounding mildly surprised.

The words came as though her thoughts had prompted them. Frankie closed her eyes, wishing she wasn't so knowledgeable about how these games were played. Her lips had parted into an anticipatory pout. She could almost savour the hatefully servile flavour of her own musk as, in her imagination, she licked it from his finger.

Instead, he wiped his hand clean on her inner thigh, close to the top of her leg but not so close as to touch her cleft. As he rubbed at the soft flesh, she could feel the sticky residue of her arousal daubing the intimate skin.

'Put your panties back on,' he said quietly. 'Now we can begin to play.'

Unable to believe he had let her off so lightly, Frankie eased herself away from him and pulled the panties back into place. Her buttocks were mildly uncomfortable but it was an ache that she knew would subside within half an hour. If that was the worst thing he intended to throw at her, she knew she could have coped with it. But she suspected there was more to come. His wicked grin confirmed her fears and, as she brushed the hem of her pleated skirt down, she waited to hear his next instruction.

'Fetch my crop and the jug of orange juice,' he said, pointing at the dressing table. 'And it might help if you brought a glass as well.'

Remembering that she was meant to be submissive, Frankie nodded and whispered, 'Yes, sir.' She handed him the riding crop and gave him the glass before pouring the drink for him.

'This is for you,' he said, handing the glass back to her.

She put down the jug before accepting it and held the glass as she waited for his next instruction. She had broken enough submissives to know that being given a drink wasn't the same as being allowed to drink it. Simon had once said that being a dominatrix was the realm of the truly pedantic and it was often like playing a cruel variation of the game 'Simon says'. Frankie brushed the memory from her mind. Why was she having thoughts of Simon as she prepared to submit herself to McGivern again?

'Go on,' he encouraged. 'Drink it. Then pour yourself another.'

'I'm not that thirsty, sir.'

'Drink it.' There was a layer of granite in his tone that grew thicker with her insubordination. 'I don't care whether you're thirsty or not. It will help you.'

'Help me do what?' she asked. As soon as she had asked the question she realised it was a stupid one. She frowned

196

and opened her mouth to protest at the idea of such an indignity but before the words were out she saw he was enjoying her discomfort.

'Drink it,' he instructed. 'Then pour yourself another and drink that one.'

Knowing that she had no other recourse available, Frankie put the glass to her mouth and swallowed. She drank the orange juice, ignoring its flavour but realising that it did actually quench her thirst. As soon as she had finished, she poured a second glass, drank it, then poured a third.

'It's not affecting you already, is it?' McGivern asked quietly.

Frankie glared at him, hiding her scowl behind the glass as she drank more juice. She wanted to tell him that she wasn't a tap and she thought of sarcastically explaining her body's normal processes of digestion and filtration. Knowing that he would take umbrage at either of these responses, instead, she simply drained the third glass and poured a fourth. She didn't need the fourth glass but it meant she could enjoy a moment free from the threat of McGivern's dominance. When he had entered the room, she had been contemplating visiting her en suite garderobe but the situation since then hadn't allowed her the opportunity. As she drank the fifth glass, she realised that her stomach was unwilling to accept any more. She put the empty glass on the floor, already feeling the growing urgency in her bladder, and was surprised by how quickly the juice had affected her.

'What do you want me to do, sir?' she asked.

'I want to watch you piss your pants,' he said, grinning.

The words made her stomach lurch uneasily. She had been expecting as much since he asked her to pour a glass of the orange juice. Hearing his instruction being said out loud somehow made the threat real. 'What if I don't want to go?'

'Then you'll drink more until you do,' he said simply. 'And for each minute that passes without you pissing, I'll stripe your arse.' He tested the crop through the air and its whistle sang starkly.

Frankie glanced at the empty tumbler, knowing that she couldn't manage a sixth glass. She dreaded the humiliation of degrading herself as he had suggested. There was no alternative. With his threat of chastisement for each dry minute that passed, she was torn between the choice of punishments. Knowing that she would eventually have to suffer both, she gritted her teeth and tried to prepare her body to do as he had asked. 'Do you want me to do it anywhere in particular?'

He shrugged. 'Where you're standing will do fine.' He glanced at his wristwatch and said, 'Your first minute begins now.'

Frankie willed her bladder to release. The position felt unusual, not just because McGivern was leering at her. As she wasn't used to wearing knickers or feeling the gusset in constant contact with the lips of her sex, her body revolted at the idea of having to relieve itself in such a way. As soon as she told herself she had to do it, her bladder decided it no longer needed to.

'Raise your skirt a little,' McGivern instructed. He teased at the hem with the tip of his crop. 'I want to see this when it happens.'

She did as he asked, snatching up the pleated folds to reveal the crotch of the unsoiled white cotton. Frowning with concentration, she tried to make herself release the hard ball of urine that pressed in to her abdomen.

'Thirty seconds,' he intoned, glancing up from his wristwatch. 'Should I pour you another glass of orange juice?'

She glared at him in silence, willing herself to release. 'I don't need another glass of orange juice, sir.'

'Wonderful,' he grinned. 'You really are adept at carrying out instructions, aren't you?'

Frankie didn't allow herself to grow angry with his words. She concentrated all her energy on her bladder, trying to force and relax in the same instant. The effort was more difficult than she would have believed but a tingling at the tip of her urethra told her she was close, making her aware of her simultaneous arousal as she willed her body to break its retentive impulse.

'Time's up for the first minute,' McGivern told her. 'Bend over.'

She glowered at him, unable to believe the time had passed so quickly. Unwilling to defy him, she pushed herself forward and waited for him to walk behind her. His hand stroked at the pantie-covered cheeks of her backside, and when she felt the gentle caress of the crop at the tops of her legs, she knew he was testing his stroke. The stark whistle and resounding sting were sudden and unexpected and left her gasping for breath.

'You might as well stay in that position,' he told her cheerfully. 'There's only fifty seconds to go until your next stripe.'

She barely heard the words, trying to ignore the burning line he had sliced across her buttocks. Her cheeks were now a blazing crimson and she wondered how she was meant to tolerate this much indignity for the remainder of the afternoon. Not wanting to give in to this desperate thought, she made a final gargantuan effort and was elated to feel her bladder relent.

The rush between her legs was sudden and surprisingly warm. In an instant, her pussy lips were soaked by the hot waters of her release. She could feel the wiry curls growing heavy with wetness and the panties struggling to contain her flow. Spatters of the harsh stream were flecking her anus, surprising her with their invasive intimacy. When the first droplets began to trickle down her inner thighs, Frankie shut her mind against the pleasurable sensations.

'Wonderful,' McGivern encouraged.

She could hear his excitement and felt repulsed that she had inspired it. The stream continued to pour from her and she was touched by a moment's panic that she might not be able to stop. Strong, hot and relentless, the flow weighed heavily against the gusset of the panties, filling her with a sense of shame that was infuriatingly exciting. This in turn stirred a spark of arousal in her pussy and she quickly tried to shut out the response. When the stream finally tapered to a trickle, she shivered with gratitude.

'Wonderful,' he said again.

She shut his voice out, thinking about the way the water now cooled her thighs and how it had soaked into the tops of her over-knee socks. There was no reprieve from her growing excitement. The wetness at her sex was darkly pleasurable and the shame that came with it obscenely exciting. Although she was loathe to admit it, she knew that the pressure of a well-placed finger would now send her into ecstasy.

'Stand up straight,' he told her. 'And turn to face me.'

She did as he asked, daring to meet his eyes. His smile shone like a beacon and in that expression she could see the hateful reflection of her own servility. He had wanted her submission and she could see he was already revelling in the little she had allowed him.

He straightened his expression, then feigned surprise. 'Good heavens, Frankie! Have you had an accident?'

His theatrical voice told her that she had to continue with the charade of being the schoolgirl to his teacher. Frankie tried not to let her tone reveal her contempt. 'I've pissed my pants, sir.'

He raised his eyebrows in mock horror. 'No! Let me see.'

For some reason, this felt worse. When she had released her bladder, he had been watching, and she had heard his appreciative sighs. But having to display the sodden crotch of her panties to him seemed totally intrusive. Reluctantly, she teased at the hem of her skirt and lifted it up for him. She dared to glance down and saw the stiff cotton had turned grey at the gusset. The fabric was now almost transparent and the dark curls of her pubic thatch were visible beneath it.

'It's true, Frankie. You have pissed your pants,' he exclaimed. 'Why did you do it, girl?'

She glared at him, wanting to say, 'Because you told me to,' but not daring to. 'I don't know, sir,' she told him grudgingly.

'What on earth possessed you to do something so disgusting?'

She blushed, hating his insidious way of teasing a dark arousal out of her misery. 'I don't know, sir,' she repeated.

He shook his head, his gaze still lingering over the sodden crotch. 'Don't you have anything to say for yourself?'

'Get down on you knees and lick me clean,' was the phrase she wanted to use, but he wouldn't allow such an outburst. He was going to make this punishment humiliating enough and she knew better than to try and make the situation worse for herself. She knew the words he really wanted to hear, and she forced each one out as though it pained her.

'I'm sorry, sir,' she growled.

He was still shaking his head, struggling to suppress his triumphant smile. 'Sorry just isn't good enough, Frankie. You need punishing for that sort of behaviour, just so you know it won't be tolerated again.'

She had expected as much but the idea still left her cold. 'Punishing how, sir?'

'Bend,' he growled. He raised the crop into the air and she saw exactly what he intended to do.

Lowering herself forward, Frankie pushed her backside out for him and prepared to suffer another punishing blow from the crop. The wet fabric of the knickers clung to her buttocks and she could feel the gusset clutching at her pussy lips. The water had already become chilled but that didn't make the sensation any less pleasurable.

McGivern brushed the skirt over her back and Frankie felt her flesh being treated to another cold draught. She stiffened in preparation for the blow and closed her eyes against the threat of shameful tears. As his fingers traversed her sodden cheeks, she tried valiantly to ignore the sparkle of excitement he evoked.

'Pull these up or take them down,' he told her. 'I don't care which.'

Given the choice, Frankie knew she had to select modesty. She reached for herself without straightening, making her posture momentarily ungainly. Tugging at the waistband of the panties, she pulled them until the gusset pressed hard against the lips of her sex. She could feel the wet cotton clinging to her arse-cheeks but even this shameful sensation had to be better than displaying herself to McGivern again.

He traced the shape of her sex through the crotch and she resisted the urge to shiver. As the finger moved idly against her, the sodden cotton made it feel as though there was nothing separating them at all. Repeatedly, she told herself that he wasn't exciting her and, by the time he had moved his hand away, she had almost started to believe it.

As the first punishing blow landed, Frankie drew a shocked breath. She didn't need to look to see that he had inflicted another line of red against her cheeks. The damp panties offered no respite from the punishment at all. His next blow landed with more ferocity and she uttered a small moan of protest.

'You've been a very good girl for me, Frankie,' he decided. 'Much more co-operative than I would have thought you could be.'

'I'm glad that you're happy, sir,' she replied dourly.

He sliced the crop through the air and she almost collapsed beneath the weight of the blow. She drew a deep breath and turned her thoughts away from the spreading warmth at her arse-cheeks. A fourth blow landed and she could feel it score on the same spot where the last had struck, the pain so intense that she was unable to resist the thrill it gave her. Blushing furiously, she felt the first tears of humiliation burn her cheeks.

'Because you've been so good for me, I have a penultimate request.'

'Penultimate?'

'Next to last.' He sliced the crop against her arse-cheeks again, almost knocking her from her feet with the force. 'I have a next to last request for you, Frankie,' he said carefully.

Speaking through gritted teeth, she said, 'Go on, sir.'

There was an evil smile filling his voice. 'I want you to call me master.'

Before she could reply, he had delivered the sixth blow of the crop. The pain was unexpected and blistering, adding to the despicable heat that warmed her cleft. She

202

sucked in lungfuls of air and half-turned to glare at him. 'I told you I wasn't going to call you master.' She could have added that he wasn't worthy of the title but that would only have antagonised him.

He shrugged indifferently. 'I'll beat your arse for every minute that passes when you don't say it. So, the choice is yours.' He glanced at his wristwatch. 'We'll make that effective from now, shall we?' Without waiting for her response, McGivern raised the crop and hurled it towards her arse-cheeks.

The agonising blow struck and Frankie could feel more tears streaking lines of mascara down her face. Miserable shivers racked her body and she half-turned to study him again. 'Master,' she growled, at last.

He beamed at her. 'It makes me so happy to hear you say that,' he said. 'Stand up straight and say it again.'

She did as he asked, glaring at him with as much malice as she could manage. 'Master,' she repeated.

McGivern clapped his hands together and moved forward to kiss her. The gesture was so sudden and unexpected that Frankie had no time to think. She half-expected him to make something sexual of the exchange, to feel his tongue exploring her or to endure his unwanted caresses on her breasts. Instead, he moved his lips away and graced her with a triumphant grin that seemed to mock her servile status.

'Call me master for a final time.'

Hating the sound of her own voice, and despising the way she was obeying him, Frankie said, 'Master.'

He clapped his hands together gleefully, unable to contain his own mirth.

Frankie watched him with guarded contempt, unsure of his response if he caught her sneering at him. She cleared her throat and said, 'Is that it? Are we finished, sir?'

He shook his head, regaining his composure quickly. 'No. That was the penultimate item on this afternoon's agenda. I want one final thing from you before you end your afternoon's submission to me.'

She contemplated him in silence, trying not to think

what his next degrading idea might be. In her time of knowing McGivern, she had seen him use enemas on his submissives and knew that he had tied more than one of them above a punishing device he called a wooden horse. Fears of both those humiliations had tortured her earlier this afternoon, and now resurfaced as she studied his flat gaze. 'What exactly do you want, sir?'

'I want you to take me back down to the banquet hall.' He checked his wristwatch and raised his eyebrows in mild surprise. 'The party should be in full swing by now and I want you to take me to it.'

She knew there was more to it than that and, if her need to end the embarrassment hadn't been so great, she would have waited for him to tell her but she couldn't stop herself from asking him to elaborate. 'You just want me to take you across to the banquet hall,' she repeated. 'Is that it, sir?'

'I want you to carry me,' he explained. 'I want you to get down on all fours. I'm going to sit on your back and you're going to carry me to the party.'

She shook her head and watched his hateful smile resurface.

Speaking as though he hadn't seen her defiance, McGivern said, 'I'll have your skirt up but you can retain your soiled panties for modesty. However, if I grow unhappy with the way that you're carrying me, I might use this crop on your arse-cheeks again.'

She was still shaking her head. 'With all due respect, sir, no fucking way.'

'Refuse and you'll have reneged on our deal,' he told her.

She glared at him. 'You promised this submission would be just you and me,' she reminded him. 'You promised that.'

'I said no one else would get the chance to abuse you,' he corrected. 'But you didn't think I could pass up an opportunity to humiliate you in front of all our mutual friends and acquaintances, did you?'

'Not that,' she muttered. She felt unnervingly close to

204

begging but she could live with that if got her out of this particular punishment. Her cheeks flushed crimson as she thought of the crippling indignity of his proposal. In her mind's eye she could imagine the lecherous stares of her peers and hear their taunting laughter. Not only would all her fellow dominatrices be present but she knew that Simon would be there too. The thought of having him see her in such a position left Frankie feeling sick. 'Not that,' she whispered. 'Anything but that, sir.'

'Get down on all fours, Frankie,' he told her, testing the crop through the air. 'Get down on all fours and get ready to take me to the party.'

Seeing the determination in his expression, Frankie understood that she had no choice left other than to obey. Hating her position of servility, she kneeled on the floor and bent forward so that he could climb on to her back.

Twelve

'Treasure hunt!'

Simon had no idea who shouted the words and he was beyond caring. Events were out of his hands now. He just wanted to return to his bedroom and drown his troubles with a bottle of Scotch. He could take out the humiliations of the day on a submissive's backside and try to console his flagging spirits by comforting her with cold cream afterwards. He hadn't decided which submissive: he had no preferences for any particular one at that moment. The important thing was to be alone first and then get his thoughts into order.

'You presented a marvellous auction, Simon.'

He glanced to his side and saw Babs standing there. Number seven and number eleven kneeled at her feet, holding hands as they waited for the next instruction from their new mistress. 'I hope you'll be happy with your acquisitions,' he told her.

'I'm sure I'll be more than happy with them,' she said, stroking an affectionate hand over number seven's hair.

The rest of the room had turned to chaos, Simon realised dumbly. It seemed as though everyone had been waiting for the last sale so that they could begin McGivern's facile treasure hunt. Not all of them were indulging in the search but there were enough people running around and barking instructions at their submissives to make the atmosphere riotous.

'If you'll excuse me,' Simon said, placing a farewell hand on Babs' arm, 'I have a couple of things to do.'

'You still have a final duty to perform as our auctioneer,' she said firmly.

'That's right.' Captain Wilde had joined them and his austere tone echoed Babs' sentiments.

Simon stopped himself glaring at the man and instead glanced from him to Babs with a suspicious frown. 'What am I missing here?' he asked.

Babs laughed. 'Auctioneer's privilege,' she reminded him, taking his hand. 'Come on, Simon. It's a tradition.'

He shook his head and eased his hand away from her grip. 'I think I'll pass on it this time, thanks.'

Captain Wilde stopped him, his hand on Simon's bicep. 'You can't pass on it. Some might construe that as being offensive.'

Simon knew there was no way out of the situation. It was the privilege of the auctioneer to make use of any submissive he chose. Simon didn't know when the idea had first come into practice and in the chaos of the afternoon, the habit had almost slipped his mind. Unhappy with the way the day had gone, the last thing he wanted to do was make explicit use of a slave in public.

'Maybe next time,' he told them.

'It's seen as a sign of trust,' Babs told Simon patiently.

Captain Wilde nodded. 'It shows that you are as satisfied with the stock you were selling as the buyer should be.'

Simon drew an impatient breath but he could see there was no escaping this final ceremony. Sullenly nodding his head, he said, 'If you insist.'

'Have one of mine,' Babs said. 'These two look like fine acquisitions. I can't wait to see how well they perform.'

Simon glanced down at the two kneeling slaves and contemplated them warily. They stared up at him, licking their lips and offering him smiles filled with lewd promise.

'You don't want one of hers,' Captain Wilde told Simon. 'She doesn't like her charges to be punished. Take one of mine, or a different one. One that you can use however you want.'

Simon blinked, surprised to hear that the captain had acquired a submissive at the auction. He couldn't recall closing a bid that the man had won, and he racked his brains, suddenly plagued by the doubt that he might have screwed up somewhere. It wasn't that he gave a damn about the complexities of administering McGivern's auction. He was simply fearful of having made some mistake that might make him liable to suffer the inevitable penalty.

'Why not take this one?' Captain Wilde suggested.

He pointed towards the banquet table and Simon tried to decide if the man was pointing at number three or Jane. He could see the platinum blonde was trying to do something with number three's gag and that worried him. Jane was a practised submissive and too obedient to go against the wishes of any master. To see her deliberately trying to release another slave from her bondage was a violation of all the rules she had learned so far.

'Don't tell me you've bought number three,' Simon said quietly. He glanced around the banquet hall and wondered if there was anyone else who could lay claim to her.

'I was pointing at the platinum blonde,' Captain Wilde explained. 'I believe her name is Jane. If I'd been granted the auctioneer's privilege, I would use her. Why don't you? I'm sure it will be pleasurable.'

Simon considered the suggestion, warming to the idea of having Jane in his arms. A thought nagged at the back of his mind but the raucous crowd around him blacked it out.

While he was still struggling to work out why this latest revelation troubled him, Captain Wilde escorted Simon to the banquet table and glared ferociously at Jane. 'You have been selected as the auctioneer's privilege.'

Jane glanced meekly from Simon to the captain. She moved her hands away from number three's gag to make it look as though she had been standing innocently beside the bound submissive.

'You will relish the honour of being chosen for this task,' Captain Wilde told her. 'And you will perform every task that he demands of you. Is that understood?'

'Simon hasn't said this is the one he wants,' Babs broke in. 'He could want to use one of mine.'

Smiling at Jane, Simon shook his head. 'I'll take my privilege from this one,' he told the pair. 'If you'll excuse us,' he added, climbing over the table and standing by Jane's side, 'I'm sure we'd both appreciate some privacy for this moment.'

Frankie wondered if it was possible for her back to break beneath McGivern's weight. She supposed that if it did, the trauma would give her some relief from the humiliation of his punishment. She had managed to scramble out of the bedroom door on all fours but she had already come close to toppling him twice. Both her shoes had already fallen off and she was near to losing her remaining over-knee sock.

McGivern was treating each ungainly lurch as a punishable offence and consequently she had already received two vicious stripes to her aching backside. As this thought passed through her mind, she stumbled to the left and only just managed to stop herself from collapsing on the floor. Before she could think of how close they had come to falling again, she received a third stinging blow and an intense shock sent a hateful thrill throughout her entire frame.

'Useless little bitch,' he growled.

Detesting herself for being so servile to him, Frankie felt a solitary tear trickle down her cheek. She hadn't known how high a price she would pay when she agreed to this submission. Dwelling on this punishment in the hours before McGivern had made her dress up and suffer his warped brand of humiliation, Frankie had wondered if she was losing her abilities as a dominatrix. Simon's love-making had made her forget her doubts briefly but now, as she remembered the tenderness of their shared passion, she thought that too signified a weakness on her part. A true dominatrix would never have given herself to anyone as an equal because a true dominatrix had no equals. She also knew that a true dominatrix would never have submitted herself to McGivern's humiliation and that brought another tear to the corner of her eye.

She was dressed up like a schoolgirl, wearing piss-sodden panties and carrying a dominatrix on her back who was striping her arse cheeks at every available opportunity. Even when he exhibited her degradation in front of all her peers, completing her humiliation, Frankie doubted she could feel worse than she felt at this moment.

And more than that – and this was probably the worst thing for her – she doubted she would ever feel like a dominatrix again.

Simon had only meant to give Jane a platonic kiss. His intention was to savour her lips for a moment, snatch her wrist and take her out of the banquet hall. Then, he could have left her to her own devices and gone to the blessed solitude of his bedroom. Admittedly, he wanted to know where Frankie was because the two of them had a lot to discuss. However, she had already told him that she was dealing with a private matter. While he felt sure it was something she would rather not be doing, he respected her need for privacy.

But then Jane kissed him and everything changed. He could taste an urgent need in her mouth and realised it matched his own. He had spent the last two hours exhibiting submissives and it had left him with a deep-seated arousal. When he had first entered the banquet hall, he had seen Jane rubbing herself, and the sight had excited him. As he relished her kiss, he could sense that she hadn't managed to satisfy her cravings entirely. He found himself responding eagerly when her tongue plunged into his mouth. She moved her hands to the front of his pants and he realised she was now reacting to his own demanding caresses.

'This is a very public place, Jane,' he warned her between kisses. 'Are you sure you want to do this?'

She shook her head and nodded at Captain Wilde. 'He's just told me to,' she explained. 'The man terrifies me and I'm scared to disobey him.' She paused, smiled shyly at Simon and added, 'Besides. I do really want to.'

It was as much encouragement as he needed. He pushed

her hands away from his fly and quickly released himself. Pushing her on to the banquet table, he admired her naked body for an instant before lowering his mouth to a breast.

Jane groaned loudly, her cry echoing in competition with the noises of the revellers and treasure hunters.

'I thought he would enjoy my submissive,' Captain Wilde told Babs.

Simon heard his voice from a distance but his attention was focused entirely on the slave beneath him.

'He would have preferred one of mine,' Babs replied. 'But it's difficult to explain that to some men.'

'Perhaps you and I should discuss our different methods of control some time?'

'Perhaps you should come to my boat and have dinner there tonight?'

Simon could hear a sly edge to Babs' voice as she said this. Remembering her promise to make all lovers live their lives in perpetual submission, he wondered if he should give the captain a word of warning. For some reason, he felt sure that Babs wouldn't tell the man until it was far too late, but he doubted the captain would be able to resist succumbing to such a fate.

Jane pushed her hands to the side of Simon's head. She moved his mouth to her other breast and he forgot all about the watching couple and their developing relationship. His attention was now devoted to the submissive beneath him and he could only think about the joy of relief that they could share with one another.

Simon nuzzled his shaft against her wetness and prepared to push himself forward.

Jane grinned up at him and bucked herself eagerly to accept him.

Savouring every exquisite moment of the penetration, Simon slid into her.

'This is absolutely bacchanal,' Grace exclaimed.

Elle couldn't decide if the woman was excited or appalled. She followed Grace's gaze, aware that the woman was taking in the sights of oral sex, rigorous

211

fucking and relentless domination. Although Grace sounded upset, Elle could see her eyes were shining with excitement.

'What's happening, mother?'

Elle glanced back in time to see the redhead's jaw drop. Her eyes were wide open, struggling to take in everything that was happening.

'Earlier today I wouldn't have let you see things like this, Chatelaine,' Grace told her daughter, speaking as though she was trying conceal her disgust. There was a damning edge to her voice. 'But considering the way I found you two on the boat, I doubt this will present you with anything new to think about.'

'You didn't really think we were up to anything, mother,' Chatelaine protested. She brushed stray red locks from her cheeks and glared unhappily at her.

'This girl's backside is peppered with hairbrush marks,' Grace exploded, waving a hand in Elle's direction. 'It couldn't be anything else, could it?'

Chatelaine looked set to make another protest then stopped herself. Elle sympathised with Grace's daughter, having heard her attempts at plausible excuses so far fail.

'I blame that Frankie woman for all this,' Grace said. This time, the distaste was evident in her tone. 'She's awoken certain appetites in you and I'm not at all happy. That woman has an awful lot to answer for and I'm going to make sure she pays.'

With a growing surge of unease, Elle saw Chatelaine's smile widen as she closed the door behind herself.

Jane was screaming with exhilaration and Simon realised his cries were close to matching hers. Although the pleasure wasn't as intense as it had been when he and Frankie made love, Jane came close to equalling the enjoyment with her responsiveness. She struggled to match his vigorous entry and embraced him with a passion that brought him ever closer to the point of climax. The world of revellers and voyeurs around them was forgotten as he lost himself in her welcoming warmth. As his shaft slid deeper, she reached forward and tugged his shirt open. Placing a passionate bite against his nipple, Jane sucked hard at his aching flesh, dragging him closer and closer to the moment of explosion.

He tried to force her back down on to the table but she resisted. He wanted to caress her breasts, then hold her legs and manipulate her thighs so he could penetrate more deeply. But Jane resisted and held herself against his chest, sucking harder at the nub of flesh.

Simon gasped. He hadn't anticipated having Jane in such a way and he hadn't expected the pleasure to be so swift and climactic. Unable to contain his orgasm for another instant, he thrust himself deep into the wetness of her sex and his shaft began to pulse with a glorious release.

It was enough to inspire Jane's orgasm and the blonde squealed as the pleasure coursed through her. She ground her teeth hard around his nipple then released him as she collapsed back on to the table.

He lowered himself over her, gasping and enjoying the pleasurable sensation of having her pussy tremble around his failing shaft. 'I think the word "privilege" is understating your abilities,' he laughed.

Without replying, she grabbed his face with both hands and pressed her mouth over his. The kiss was as intimate as their first one but Simon could sense desperation in her embrace. He studied her uncertainly and asked, 'What's wrong, Jane?'

'I want to know what's happening,' she told him.

She was whispering and he realised she was keeping her voice low so that Babs and Captain Wilde wouldn't overhear.

'We've just made love,' he told her. He tested a grin, knowing that wasn't the explanation she had wanted, but unsure of exactly what she was asking him. 'Normally when I make love to a woman, she doesn't need reminding that it's happened.'

Jane shook her head, casting a wary glance in the direction of the others. 'I don't know what's happening,' she explained. Her tone was etched with worry. 'Is that man really my master, or is it you? You've got my deeds of indenture, haven't you?'

Simon paused, not bothering to hide his puzzled frown. 'That's right,' he whispered. 'I have got your deeds.' He could feel something important in this discovery but felt unable to say exactly what it was. Ideas were beginning to collect in his mind when Jane broke into his thoughts again.

'And who owns number three? I heard you telling McGivern that you'd bought her, and then he offers her as a prize.' Speaking quickly, as though she had just remembered the fact, Jane said, 'And number three was desperate to tell me something before this auction nonsense began, but she never got the chance to. McGivern stopped her.'

Frankie felt the second sock slide from her leg as she approached the banquet hall door. It joined the boater and the tie somewhere on the trail behind her and she noted its passing with a disinterested eye.

For a while, as she had suffered the humiliation of the journey, she had hoped that the party hadn't happened. She had offered silent prayers that the dominatrices had given up after their auction. Those hopes were entirely dashed when she heard the noise coming from beyond the closed door.

McGivern striped her arse with the crop again. The pain was more severe and punishing than anything he had delivered previously but she accepted it with stoic resignation. Her backside had been ravaged beneath his blows. He had struck her repeatedly on the journey from her room until her knickers had been flayed from her backside. She could picture her arse-cheeks as a glowing, red furnace and it left her sick with giddy excitement.

'They should all be in there waiting for this moment,' McGivern told her. 'I offered a wonderful prize for a treasure hunt and told them the treasure was somewhere inside the banquet hall. No one will have left yet and everyone will be there to see how submissive you've been for me.'

She considered calling him a bastard, and then stopped herself. He had already told her what would happen if she showed any signs of disobedience and Frankie had invested too much in the afternoon to spoil things now. Her arse-cheeks were blazing and the lips of her sex burned with a need that she had never experienced before. The combination of shame and indignity was crippling but it brought with it an allure that she was finding more and more difficult to resist.

'Wait here,' McGivern demanded.

They had reached the doors and she stopped in front of them exactly as he had instructed. Her breathing was coming in laboured gasps and she told herself that it was solely due to the exertion and had nothing to do with any arousal he might have triggered.

'I want to savour this moment,' he told her, slapping a hand against her backside. 'I've often fantasised about having you as my submissive and this is going to be one of the crowning moments in my career as a dominatrix.'

Frankie bit back her retort.

'I could have done so much more to you this afternoon if I'd wanted, but I don't think I could have extracted much more satisfaction from the day.' His tone was wistful and she could hear a smile in his voice. 'I could have fucked you repeatedly or I could have had you swallow me again and again. I could have skewered your arsehole with my cock and then had you lick it clean, but none of that could have compared with the pleasure that you've given me.'

Frankie tried to shut his words out, hating the fact that he was speaking the truth. She knew she would have done whatever he asked, and the fact that she had gleaned some excitement from being used made her feel worse than she could have believed. Although the humiliation at the other side of the door was going to be as severe as all the indignities so far, that no longer troubled her. What now weighed heavily on her mind was her sense of failure. She no longer believed herself fit for the title of dominatrix. She wondered how life at the castle was going to change as she came to terms with her own submissive side.

'Do you know what gave me the greatest pleasure?'

She grunted, then remembering that she still had to show herself as being servile, whispered, 'No, sir.'

'The thing that gave me the greatest satisfaction was when you called me "master". You didn't want to, I could hear that, but when you said it, I got the impression that you considered yourself to be inferior to me. Perhaps I just have a lurid imagination but that was the way it sounded.'

Frankie didn't release her mortified sob. She was determined not to give him that much satisfaction.

McGivern pretended to ignore her distress. 'Call me that name again,' he urged her. 'Call me your master.'

'Do I have to, sir?'

He sliced the riding crop against her arse-cheeks using malicious force. As though he hadn't heard her reluctance, he said thoughtfully, 'One last time, before we go in and properly humiliate you, I want you to call me master.'

Despising herself and her servility, Frankie cleared her throat and prepared to say the hateful word. She swallowed twice and realised it was going to choke her when she did utter it.

The whistle of the crop suddenly seared the air and she gave a startled cry as the sting nestled against her buttocks. 'Master,' she called, spitting the word out as a sob. 'Master, master, master.'

'Perfect,' McGivern said cheerfully. 'Now, go into the party, and let's show everyone how tame you've become.'

'What are you trying to tell me, Simon?' Captain Wilde demanded.

He was studying the three of them with a wary eye and Simon could see he wasn't happy. Jane was busy fumbling with number three's gag, her fingers working against themselves as she tried to release the awkward straps. Babs was watching the scene with consternation. In a matter of moments, the mood had gone from playful to menacing.

'I bought her,' Captain Wilde insisted, pointing at Jane. 'I paid cash to McGivern, and that makes her mine.'

'These are Jane's deeds of indenture,' Simon told him,

thrusting the tube of vellum into the man's hands. 'I paid for them this morning, before the auction began. That makes her mine and it looks like McGivern has screwed you.' It was a harsh choice of words but he could see that they drove his point home.

'Where the hell is McGivern?' Captain Wilde demanded. 'At the very least, he owes me an explanation and if what you say is true –'

'McGivern is with Frankie.'

They all turned to stare at number three. The gag had been torn from her mouth and she studied each of their faces with a look of fearful panic at her outburst. She turned to Simon and beseeched him with her dark-brown eyes. 'I've heard everything that's been happening but I haven't been able to tell anyone. McGivern sold me to you, then told Frankie she could have me in exchange for ...' She paused, her voice faltering. 'In exchange for something he wanted.'

Simon forced himself to listen, already guessing what deal McGivern had suggested and quickly working out the lurid technicalities. He couldn't have felt more shocked if someone had delivered a blow to his stomach. 'Where are they?' he demanded.

Number three shrugged. Jane made the same gesture and Simon could see she was trying to empathise with his dilemma.

'Which one did you buy?' Captain Wilde growled. He pointed his finger at Jane then at number three. 'That one or that one?'

Simon chewed on his lip and glanced between the two submissives. The idea of leaving either of them in this man's charge unsettled him. 'I wanted to buy number three,' he explained. 'I thought I had bought number three, but McGivern duped me. He gave me Jane's deeds of indenture.'

Captain Wilde made an arrogant sound. 'Then the solution is simple. I will take Jane, and you can have number three, then we'll both be happy.'

Simon shook his head. 'I can't take number three

217

because she says that McGivern is trading her at this very moment. Not only that, but in case you'd forgotten, number three is supposed to be the prize in the treasure hunt.'

'McGivern's been toying with us all,' Captain Wilde bellowed. His voice was rising furiously and Simon could now understand why he had disliked the man on sight. With his temper showing, the captain's scowl revealed an ugly, vicious character and it was clear from the shine in his eyes that he didn't mind who he vented his fury on. 'I'm damned if I'm going to put up with being cheated. Where the hell is he? Where's McGivern?'

A sudden commotion made them all turn. There was a small crowd gathered in front of the doorway which obscured their view but, echoing throughout the banquet hall, they all heard McGivern's voice.

'Behold the master,' he proclaimed.

Frankie crawled into the room beneath him, her eyes closed against the shameful indignity of the moment. She had hoped that everyone would be looking away as they came in. If they had been, she could have foisted McGivern from her back and demanded that he conclude his part of the deal. Then, with that done, she could have taken number three back to her bedroom and found solace from the day's misery in the slave's arms.

But as he declared their entrance with a characteristic, theatrical display, Frankie knew that every head would be turned towards her. She steeled herself for the final humiliation.

'McGivern?'

The voice shouted above the rest of the rowdy throng and Frankie suspected it was Simon's. No one seemed to have noticed her yet and taking that, the only comfort left to her, Frankie attempted to push McGivern from her back.

He resisted and she felt his erection press between her shoulder blades. She struggled not to shiver against this brief reminder of his sexuality. His backside had trapped the hem of her pleated skirt and she felt the waistband break free beneath her rib cage. The garment fell away from her and, before he could reassert his position, Frankie stood up to watch him fall to the floor.

'McGivern? If that's McGivern, can somebody get hold of him?'

Now she was sure it was Simon's voice. McGivern made an attempt to stand up but Frankie stopped him by placing her foot on his back.

Simon, Jane, Babs and number three all rushed to gather around the fallen dominatrix. Frankie was touched to see a concerned expression on Simon's face and she was even more grateful when he put his arm around her in a comforting embrace.

'What the hell happened to you?' he asked.

She frowned, surprised that he hadn't made some acerbic comment about her schoolgirl uniform. Glancing down at herself, she saw the reason why. On the journey to the banquet hall most of the clothes had either fallen off or been torn from her body. The only items that remained were the blouse and the bra and, both being white, they looked nothing like the remnants of her humiliating uniform.

'There he is,' Captain Wilde declared as he joined the group. 'He's a cheat and a fraud and he needs punishing.'

Frankie glanced down at McGivern, grinning when she saw how flustered he was. 'What's happening?' she asked. She directed the question at Simon but she would have been happy if anyone could have answered her.

'McGivern sold Jane twice,' Simon explained.

'No,' McGivern broke in quickly. He was still squirming on the floor but Frankie held him firmly beneath her foot, determined not to release him from the servile position. 'There's been a misunderstanding,' McGivern said quickly. 'If you'd just allow me to explain things.'

'Penalty,' Babs shrieked. Her voice echoed around the banquet hall, slicing through the roar of excited squeals and groans. 'He's broken the auction house rules. He has to suffer the penalty.'

219

McGivern looked from one angry face to the other and Frankie waited patiently until he turned his pitiful expression on her. 'You can't let this happen to me,' he told her.

'Can't I?' She moved her foot and allowed a pair of burly dominatrices to drag him from the floor. As the crowd grew larger, hands began to snatch at his shirt, plucking it loose then tearing it away from him.

'This is your money,' McGivern said, turning to Captain Wilde. He started to pull banknotes from his pockets and thrust them towards his principal accuser.

'Damned right it's my money,' the captain told him. 'Have you got any other stock we can sequester?'

McGivern's panicked expression grew more fraught when he heard those words. 'You can't punish me,' he told them. 'I organised this auction.'

'No one is above auction house rules,' Babs reminded him. 'Sequestration of stock, punishment by peers, and what was that final one?'

'Exile or servitude,' Frankie told her. She stepped close to McGivern and grinned at him menacingly. 'And I don't think you'll get the option with that one, sir,' she whispered, keeping her tone so low that the exchange was only heard between the pair of them. 'This gives me the chance to have you as my slave now, and I'm going to enjoy every glorious moment of it.'

'Come on,' he whispered. Nervousness flitted in his expression as he tried to cajole her into showing some sympathy. 'You have to show me some leniency.'

She laughed and stepped back. 'You never know, one day I just might.'

'Wait,' Captain Wilde said sharply. 'Does he still own this submissive?' He had his fingers around number three's arm and Frankie saw that he was gripping the slave unnecessarily tightly. Tactfully, she moved his fingers away and placed an arm protectively around the slave's shoulders.

'This slave is mine,' she said firmly.

'She's meant to be the prize in a treasure hunt,' Babs

told her. 'McGivern said whoever finds the number three diamond gets to keep the number three slave. You'll have the rest of this hall to argue with if you try and go against that.'

Frankie could feel her moment of triumph escaping her. Everything she had gone through to get number three now seemed to have been in vain. She ground her teeth together with an anguished frown and glared unhappily at the slave.

Number three met her gaze with a knowing smile and took Frankie's hand in hers. Frankie watched as the slave brought her fingers to the lips of her sex and gasped in surprise when she saw the ring piercing the submissive's clitoris. In the centre of the ball closure, filling the space where the steel ball normally rested, was a sparkling diamond.

'You've found it, Frankie,' number three told her. 'That means that you've won the prize.'

Babs gave a wry smile. 'It looks like the submissive is yours after all,' she agreed. She turned to McGivern and glared at the two men holding him. 'Take him to the banquet table. It's time for his punishment.'

'I thought you were against punishments,' McGivern sneered.

Babs met his tone with a defiant grin. 'For you, I can make an exception.' She snapped her fingers and McGivern was led to the banquet table.

'This has been one hell of an eventful day,' Simon observed.

A woman's hand grabbed Frankie's shoulder and she whirled around to find herself face to face with an irate Grace. 'Unless I get an explanation, it's about to get a lot more eventful,' Grace hissed.

There was a look in Grace's eye that Frankie couldn't quite fathom. She could see that the woman was upset but she could also sense a spirit of arousal colouring the woman's cheeks. Trying not to think about it, she looked at Elle and Grace's redheaded daughter.

'You have a hell of a lot to answer for,' Grace said. 'And you can start by telling me why you had Chatelaine stripped naked and working in your field.'

Frankie allowed her smile to widen. She ignored Grace and snapped her fingers, summoning Chatelaine to her side. 'Follow me, young lady,' she said firmly. To Grace, she said, 'Your daughter and I are going to resolve this matter together. We will return in a moment and it will all be explained to you.'

Indignantly, Grace shook her head. 'I'm not allowing you to –'

Frankie ignored her, asking Simon, 'Please keep Grace company for a moment while Chatelaine and I talk.' Not waiting to see if he would, she led the redhead out of the banquet hall.

'My mother's livid with you,' Chatelaine whispered as soon as they were out of earshot. 'She'll have the best lawyers she can get working against you and they'll ruin you. Why don't you make it easy on yourself and just give me your half of this castle now?'

Frankie silenced her with a swift slap across the face.

The redhead stared at her in stunned silence. She held a hand against her cheek then studied the tips of her fingers as though she expected to see blood on them. 'You hit me,' she gasped incredulously.

'And I'll do it again if you give me reason to,' Frankie told her. 'Now listen to me because I'm only going to say this once. Your name is Chatelaine and you're the socialite daughter of a well-to-do family who would be publicly shamed if it was made known that you worked stark naked in a ploughing field.'

'You're bloody right they would,' Chatelaine agreed. 'And they'll have a team of lawyers –'

Frankie held up her hand and the threat of the palm made the redhead fall silent. 'What would they do if they heard about the cornfield?' Frankie asked.

Chatelaine blushed. 'What makes you think I haven't told my mother?'

Frankie laughed. 'If you'd told her about that, do you really think she'd be berating me for making you work naked and pull a plough? Get some perspective, girl.'

'What are you going to do?' Chatelaine whispered. 'Are you going to tell her?'

There was a meekness in her voice which Frankie knew was the sound of broken submission. Her triumphant grin broadened. 'Neither of us is going to tell her. You're going to go back in there afterwards and say that you're sorry for wasting your mother's time. You'll explain that it has all been a big misunderstanding.'

Chatelaine nodded, clearly unhappy with the situation but left with no other option. 'What did you mean by afterwards?' she asked slowly.

Frankie placed her fingers in the redhead's hair and dragged her down to her knees. 'You'll explain it all to your mother after you've done this for me,' she explained patiently. Pushing her pubic mound towards the girl's mouth, Frankie got ready to savour the moment. As Chatelaine's tongue teased at the nub of her clitoris, a shiver of pleasure coursed through her and she smiled fondly down at the submissive girl. 'Perhaps I should thank you for this,' she said quietly.

The redhead lapped harder, then shifted her face so she could glance warily upwards. 'Thank me for this?' she asked, tapping her tongue against Frankie's exposed nub.

'That as well,' Frankie agreed. With a reflective smile, she added, 'For a while back there, I thought I was losing my ability to dominate, but you've just reminded me that it never went away.'

The party was coming to an end. Music played from a stereo and, although most of the dominatrices had taken their acquisitions away, there were still enough left to watch as Frankie and Simon danced together.

'I imagine you looked quite good in that schoolgirl outfit,' he said earnestly. 'It would have brought out your demure side.'

He wasn't lying about his enjoyment: she could feel the pressure of his erection against her as they danced. 'Enjoy the image in your head for the rest of the night,' she encouraged him. 'You'll never get a chance to see it in reality.'

They continued to dance together, savouring each other's closeness.

'Did you get number three's deeds of indenture?' she asked suddenly.

He nodded and reached into his frock-coat. 'All present and accounted for,' he said, passing her the tube of vellum.

Frankie glanced at it and considered rolling it open. 'Did you check that this one was really hers?' she asked.

'Jane verified it for me,' Simon said. 'I couldn't make out her name – it was just some inarticulate squiggle beginning with the letter "C" – but after it, she'd written the number three.'

Frankie passed the tube of vellum back to him and told him to keep it safe.

'It's been quite an eventful day for the pair of us really, hasn't it?' Simon said, sliding the deeds back into his pocket. His hand went to her stomach and she saw that he was admiring her piercing, now that it was set with the diamond. The polished facets sparkled in the candlelight, sending out blinding shards of illumination.

'You can say that again,' she agreed. Holding up a silencing finger, Frankie added, 'But I'd rather that you didn't.' She placed a kiss on his pantomime frown and they smiled lovingly at one another. 'I suppose it has been quite an eventful day. We've got our IHS licence, I've acquired number three, and you've got Jane. More than that, we've got McGivern to share for our mutual entourage and I'm putting him to work on the plough first thing tomorrow morning.'

'Didn't you also say that Chatelaine would be revisiting us soon?'

Frankie nodded. 'I think she's looking forward to working under me in the cornfields again.'

As they danced together, she sensed he was going to speak before he actually did. It was warming to think that they were already so in tune with one another.

'It gives us a hell of a lot of submissives to do our work for us,' Simon told her. 'What are we going to do with all the free time we'll have on our hands?'

She laughed and planted a kiss on his lips. 'Maybe we could spend more time alone together, like we did this afternoon?'

Matching her smile with his own, Simon stopped dancing and led Frankie out of the banquet hall and towards the embattlements.

NEW BOOKS

Coming up from Nexus, Sapphire and Black Lace

Devon Cream by Aishling Morgan
March 2000   £5.99   ISBN: 0 352 33488 6

Devon Cream traces the history of the innocent but wilful Octavia Challacombe as she is corrupted by the wicked Maray family. Along with the bouncy Polly Endicott and a group of other buxom Devon girls, she is cajoled and teased, first into providing her own breast milk for the Squire and then into increasingly perverse services. Her unabashed pleasure in her own sexual enjoyment lasts through spankings, bondage and ever more peculiar uses for her milk, until finally she takes her revenge. By the author of *The Rake*.

Police Ladies by Yolanda Celbridge
March 2000   £5.99   ISBN: 0 352 33489 4

Deep in the Scottish highlands a curious training academy teaches young women how to pound a beat. Restrictive uniforms, strict training and the special use of truncheons characterise the Glenlassie approach to police training – but the recruits are slowly being siphoned off by a neraby pony-girl training establishment and a unique medical clinic. By the author of *The Discipline of Nurse Riding*.

Conduct Unbecoming by Arabella Knight
March 2000   £5.99   ISBN: 0 352 33490 8

Deep in the English countryside, a group of patriotic young Wrens are doing their bit for the war effort, interrogating women who may or may not have slept with senior enemy officials. Some are willing to talk; others are not so forthcoming. And that's where Captain Cordelia Quidenham comes in. Together with her small, efficient and perfectly formed team, Cordelia applies every method of persuasion to wring information out of her quivering subjects – especially methods that involve the smack of leather on flesh. A Nexus Classic.

Playthng by Penny Birch

April 2000   £5.99   ISBN: 0 352 33493 2

The latest book in the Penny Birch series continues with bad girl Penny's dirtiest antics yet. After going a whole month without doing anything naughty, she is desparate to be even more filthy, despite her imminent departure to Brittany where she is instructed to set up a university field course. Once there, her academic responsibilities get pushed aside for the more deliciously rude indulgences in knicker-wetting, anal play and her old favourite, pony-girl carting. This time, however, she will encounter a French voyeur called Tom, whose penchant for dirty fun will shock even Penny and her playmates. By the author of *Bad Penny* and *Brat*.

Slave Sentence by Lisette Ashton

April 2000   £5.99   ISBN: 0 352 33494 0

Chained in his own dungeon, former master McGivern is at the mercy of punishments far crueller than any he ever devised. The torture he receives is perverse, degrading and always sexually humiliating. Determined to overthrow his gaolers he forms an uneasy relationship with the most sadistic of his female tormentors and agrees to all her demands in his bid to regain control of the castle. But his greatest fear is that he will come to enjoy his bondage before he can return to his dominant position. By the author of *The Slave Auction*.

Candy in Captivity by Arabella Knight

April 2000   £5.99   ISBN: 0 352 33495 9

Candy Brompton is a smart ambitious girl working her way up in the world of real estate. When she journeys to a remote Hebridean island to investigate the sale of a castle her life is set to change irrevocably. She stumbles upon an all-female community who adhere to a lifestyle of strict discipline, and who intend to make her one of their bond-maidens. Delightfully painful consequences await those who are disobedient, and Candy's independent streak guarantees that judicious use of the cane will be employed before she knows what's happening to her. Very soon, a sore bottom and injured pride will be a prelude to the exquisite joys of submissive games. A Nexus Classic.

A new imprint of lesbian fiction

Getaway by Suzanne Blaylock
October 1999   Price £6.99   ISBN: 0 352 33443 6
Brilliantly talented Polly Sayers had made two big life shifts
concurrently. She's had her first affair with a woman, and she's also
stolen the code of an important new piece of software and made her
break, doing a runner all the way to a seemingly peaceful coastal
community. But things aren't as tranquil as they appear in the haven,
as Polly becomes immersed in an insular group of mysterious but
very attractive women.

No Angel by Marian Malone
November 1999   £6.99   ISBN 0 352 33462 2
Sally longs to test her limits and sample forbidden pleasures, yet she's
frightened by the depth of her yearnings. Her journey of self-
discovery begins in the fetish clubs of Brighton and ultimately leads
to an encounter with an enigmatic female stranger. And now that
she's tasted freedom, there's no way she's going back.

Fire and Ice by Laura Hamilton
March 2000   £5.99   ISBN: 0 352 33486 X

Nina, auditor extraordinaire, is known as the Ice Queen at work, where her frigid demeanour makes people think she's equally cold in bed. But what her colleagues don't know is that Nina spends her after-work hours locked into fiery games with her boyfriend Andrew, one in which she acts out her deepest fantasy – being a prostitute. Nina finds herself being drawn deeper and deeper into London's seedy underground, where everything is for sale and nothing is what it seems.

Wicked Words 2 ed. Kerri Sharp
March 2000   £5.99   ISBN: 0 352 33487 8

Black Lace anthologies have proved to be extremely popular. Following on from the success of the *Pandor's Box* and *Sugar and Spice* compilations, this second *Wicked Words* collection continues to push the erotic envelope. The accent is once again on contemporary settings with a transgressive feel – and the writing is fresh, upbeat in style and hot. This is an ideal introduction to the Black Lace series.

Gothic Blue by Portia Da Costa
March 2000   £5.99   ISBN: 0 352 33075 9

Stranded at a remote Gothic priory, Belinda Seward is suddenly prey to sexual forces she can neither understand nor control. She is drawn into a world of decadence and debauchery by the mysterious aristocrat André von Kastel. He has plans for Belinda which will take her into the realms of obsessive love and the erotic paranormal. This is a Black Lace special reprint.

Sauce for the Goose by Mary Rose Maxwell
April 2000   £5.99   ISBN: 0 352 33492 4

Sauce for the Goose is a collection of exceptionally filthy stories from the pen of a talented female author of erotic fiction. With fetishes and settings to suit all tastes, these lusty tales are guaranteed to amuse and arouse. From sleazy high jinx in the office to the dirty locker-room antics of the armed forces, a naughty sense of shame runs throughout.

Hard Corps by Claire Thompson

April 2000   £5.99   ISBN: 0 352 33491 6

The strong persona of army cadet Remy Harris belies a secret submissive, desperate to explore the realms of sadomasochism. Introduced to an elite secret society known as the Hard Corps, where slaves are bound and used for the pleasure of their masters and mistresses, Remy changes from virgin to slut, and learns to submit with grace and control. That is until one day a master goes too far and Remy fights back.

NEXUS BACKLIST

All books are priced £5.99 unless another price is given. If a date is supplied, the book in question will not be available until that month in 2000.

CONTEMPORARY EROTICA

THE ACADEMY	Arabella Knight		
BAD PENNY	Penny Birch		
THE BLACK MASQUE	Lisette Ashton		
THE BLACK WIDOW	Lisette Ashton		
THE BOND	Lindsay Gordon		
BRAT	Penny Birch		
DANCE OF SUBMISSION	Lisette Ashton		
DARK DESIRES	Maria del Rey		
DISCIPLES OF SHAME	Stephanie Calvin		
DISCIPLINE OF THE PRIVATE HOUSE	Esme Ombreux		
DISPLAYS OF EXPERIENCE	Lucy Golden		June
EMMA'S SECRET DOMINATION	Hilary James		
FAIRGROUND ATTRACTIONS	Lisette Ashton		
GISELLE	Jean Aveline		
HEART OF DESIRE	Maria del Rey		
HOUSE RULES	G.C. Scott		
IN FOR A PENNY	Penny Birch		
ONE WEEK IN THE PRIVATE HOUSE	Esme Ombreux		
THE BOND	Nadine Somers		
THE PALACE OF EROS	Delver Maddingley	£4.99	
PLAYTHING	Penny Birch		
THE PLEASURE CHAMBER	Brigitte Markham		
POLICE LADIES	Yolanda Celbridge		
THE RELUCTANT VIRGIN	Kendal Grahame		

RITES OF OBEDIENCE	Lindsay Gordon	
RUE MARQUIS DE SADE	Morgana Baron	
'S' – A JOURNEY INTO SERVITUDE	Philippa Masters	
SANDRA'S NEW SCHOOL	Yolanda Celbridge	
SKIN SLAVE	Yolanda Celbridge	June
THE SLAVE AUCTION	Lisette Ashton	
SLAVE GENESIS	Jennifer Jane Pope	May
SLAVE SENTENCE	Lisette Ashton	
THE SUBMISSION OF STELLA	Yolanda Celbridge	
THE SUBMISSION GALLERY	Lindsay Gordon	
TAKING PAINS TO PLEASE	Arabella Knight	
THE TEST	Nadine Somers	
THE TRAINING OF FALLEN ANGELS	Kendal Grahame	
THE YOUNG WIFE	Stephanie Calvin	May

ANCIENT & FANTASY SETTINGS

THE CASTLE OF MALDONA	Yolanda Celbridge	
NYMPHS OF DIONYSUS	Susan Tinoff	£4.99
MAIDEN	Aishling Morgan	
TIGER, TIGER	Aishling Morgan	
THE WARRIOR QUEEN	Kendal Grahame	

EDWARDIAN, VICTORIAN & OLDER EROTICA

BEATRICE	Anonymous
CONFESSION OF AN ENGLISH SLAVE	Yolanda Celbridge
DEVON CREAM	Aishling Morgan
THE GOVERNESS AT ST AGATHA'S	Yolanda Celbridge
THE RAKE	Aishling Morgan
THE TRAINING OF AN ENGLISH GENTLEMAN	Yolanda Celbridge

SAMPLERS & COLLECTIONS

NEW EROTICA 3	
A DOZEN STROKES	Various

NEXUS CLASSICS

A new imprint dedicated to putting the finest works of erotic fiction back in print

Please send me the books I have ticked above.

Name ....

Address ....

....

....

.... Post code........................

Send to: **Cash Sales, Nexus Books, Thames Wharf Studios, Rainville Road, London W6 9HT**

US customers: for prices and details of how to order books for delivery by mail, call 1-800-805-1083.

Please enclose a cheque or postal order, made payable to **Nexus Books**, to the value of the books you have ordered plus postage and packing costs as follows:

UK and BFPO – £1.00 for the first book, 50p for the second book and 30p for each subsequent book to a maximum of £3.00;

Overseas (including Republic of Ireland) – £2.00 for the first book, £1.00 for the second book and 50p for each subsequent book.

We accept all major credit cards, including VISA, ACCESS/ MASTERCARD, AMEX, DINERS CLUB, SWITCH, SOLO, and DELTA. Please write your card number and expiry date here:

....

Please allow up to 28 days for delivery.

Signature ....